Two Trees

ROBYN OAKES

Two Trees

Copyright © 2013 by Robyn Oakes

Published by
Bird Tree Publishing
Riverton, Utah
www.shimmertree.com

13 ISBN 978-1-941128-00-8

10 ISBN 1941128009

Cover and Interior Design: Robert A Jones
Cover Illustration: Nele Diel

This book was set in 12 pt Linotype Electra.

Printed in the U.S.A

1

Annor flopped beside the river to watch the daylight drain from the sky. Her back ached, and her arms trembled with fatigue. She'd spent the day clearing the overgrown garden. Her stomach rumbled, but she couldn't face her empty cottage. Not yet.

The opposite shore vanished slowly in the growing darkness. The rushing river soothed her lonely spirit, chattering to itself as it flowed past.

Annor sighed and let go of her tensions. A star appeared above the towering fir trees. And then another. Darkness enfolded her.

She'd never cleared the garden by herself before. Tears brimmed, but she clenched her teeth and held them back. She wouldn't give in to the memories.

Annor had only been two years old when her parents fled the great city of Betavar and journeyed to this island. Javan might have been overthrown by now. A lot could happen in fourteen years. She longed to travel back to Betavar and see the city for herself.

Her mind spun through the same argument it always did. She couldn't leave the king's gauntlets unguarded.

But no one else had stepped foot on this island in all those fourteen years. The gauntlets would be safe enough.

But the king and the Guardian entrusted the gauntlets to her father, and their stewardship had fallen on Annor when her father died. She couldn't leave the gauntlets unguarded.

She smelled burnt hair and peered through the darkness around her, puzzled and uneasy. The sounds of the river faded, and men chanted in deep, insistent tones. Annor's heart pounded and she held her breath. The acrid smell and the threatening voices sickened her. Staring into the night, she still saw nothing but dark trees and the black river. The chanting grew louder as more voices joined in and surrounded her. She heard the words clearly now.

"Prince of Darkness, hear thy servants! Slake thy thirst with our blood and help us find what we seek. We implore thee, destroy the veil of its hiding place."

The stink of death filled her nostrils. The trees and river faded and Annor saw white blots in the darkness, faces, menacing her on every side. She cried out. Unseen hands grabbed her right arm. Annor pried at them, but they held her fast.

One face loomed larger and larger, filling her vision. The man leered at her with bloodshot eyes and a bulbous nose. Spittle dripped from his chin. She shook with cold terror while he shrieked, "Name thyself!"

Annor glared into the man's dark eyes, her name trembling on her lips while she fought for control of her tongue. "Begone, Son of Darkness," she said at last. "My name is my own."

The man laughed. "Your words have no power over me, or any other Son of the Prince."

Exerting all her strength, Annor fought against the binding hands. It seemed impossible, but then she shouted, "In the name of Ben El, I rebuke you!" She lifted her right arm and inscribed a flaming spiral with her fingertip. It grew in the air before her, burning away the faces, until Annor sat alone in the darkness once more.

The river grumbled past and an owl hooted in the trees behind her. The stench had vanished along with the faces. Annor sobbed and gulped in clean air. She was drenched in a cold sweat. She shivered and hugged her arms to her chest.

The Sons of Darkness still reigned in Betavar, then. Papa had told her of their attacks on him over the years as they searched for pieces of the king's armor. But this was the first time they'd attacked her.

Annor had often wondered who the king chose for his other armor stewards. He wouldn't have chosen her. And if she'd surrendered her name, the Sons could have taken the sacred armor. The thought twisted her stomach. Annor leaned over and retched onto the dirt.

She rose unsteadily and limped down the path under the sheltering trees to the lone cottage hidden from the riverbank. She pushed open the door and fell beside her bed, too tired to kneel, trying to still her shivering limbs. "Thank you, Abba El," she prayed. "Thank you for the power of thy Son, and for his hallowed name."

Tomorrow she turned sixteen. Tomorrow marked a year and a day since Papa's death, and almost two years since Mama and the new baby's. Long enough to grieve alone. Tomorrow she would leave this island. She couldn't return to Betavar, but no matter. Anywhere was better than here.

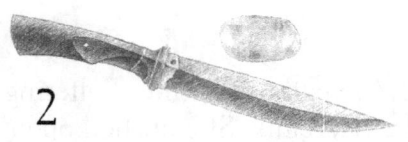

2

The sun hadn't risen more than a few handwidths above the horizon when Annor strode under the birch trees toward her parents' graves.

"Good morning, Mama," Annor said, placing a small sweetcake on the gravestone. "I'm sixteen today." She traced her mother's name, Dagny, where her father had carved it so carefully into the stone.

"Good morning, Papa," she said, setting a second sweetcake on his gravestone. She'd done her best, but "Gunnar" looked scratched into the stone rather than carved.

Annor swung her long, dark braid over her shoulder and sat between the graves. Her hair was almost as long as her mother's had been. She fingered it, remembering. Papa had loved to brush Mama's beautiful hair when she unbraided it each night before bed.

Annor ate her own sweetcake and wished herself a sweet year full of joy, though her voice sounded bitter to her ears. She brushed the crumbs from her lap. "I'm leaving today," she said. "I'm sorry Papa, but I can't stay on this island any longer. I'm not the hunter you were, or much of a gardener, either. I'm tired of going hungry and talking to gravestones. And after last night's attack, I don't feel safe here anymore. Don't worry. I'll make sure the gauntlets are well hidden before I go." Her voice caught. "I don't want to be alone anymore, Papa."

Annor rose to her feet and trekked back to the cottage. She had a vague notion some ceremony should take place now that she'd turned sixteen, some acknowledgment before Abba El. She didn't know what exactly, but she could at least present herself at the stone circle and pray at the altar before she left.

Annor crouched in front of the chest, dusting the top with her sleeve before lifting the lid. Wearing Mama's dress seemed a good way to mark this day. Though most of the clothes her family had brought when they escaped from Betavar had long since fallen into rags, Dagny had kept a dress as a reminder of their life before. Annor pushed the gauntlets aside and took the dress out of the chest, marveling as always how soft the blue fabric felt.

She stood and held the dress against herself, looking down to measure the length. Yes, she'd grown tall enough. Annor shucked off her skin pants and tunic, and pulled the soft fabric over her head. She caught a brief hint of her mother's scent and tried to breathe it all in before it vanished. The dress felt so light as it settled over her shoulders.

When Annor reached the stone circle, the sun shone high enough over the surrounding trees to bathe the altar in light. It wasn't a large circle. Her father had told her about stone circles big enough to hold a gathered village. But he'd built this one just large enough to hold the altar, the three of them, and the spirit of Abba El. That was all the Creator required. And besides, Papa said he'd grown tired of hauling stones.

Annor tugged off her shoes and left them outside the circle. She knelt before the stone altar, her dress billowing out, and took a handful of sand from the pouch that always rested beside it. She carefully dribbled sand through her fingers to form a spiral line on the rough stone that served as the altar top. Long ago they'd used powder made from golden flower petals. But when their supply ran out, her father had begun using the whitest sand he could find, saying Abba El would understand.

Annor closed her eyes and bowed her head before the altar. "Abba El," she said, "I kneel before thee today on my sixteenth birthday. I think there's something I'm supposed to do, but I don't know what. I'm sorry. Please accept the offering of my willing heart. I give it in the name of thy son, Ben El. Amen." Annor leaned forward and briefly touched her forehead to the sandy spiral.

"I accept your offering in the name of Ben El," a deep voice said. Kindness and warmth radiated from the voice, so different from the chilling tones of the Sons of Darkness.

Still, Annor trembled. A man in a pure white robe stood across the altar from her, shining so brightly her dazzled eyes blinked. She leapt to her feet. "You're the Guardian," she said. Annor had been too young to remember her father trying to give the Guardian the king's gauntlets, but she'd heard the story often enough.

"Yes. I'm sorry for your loss," he said. "Your parents served as worthy stewards and have gone on to a glorious future."

"About that," Annor said, awed and a little unnerved, but willing her voice to sound firm. "I can't watch over the gauntlets any longer. The Sons of Darkness attacked me last night, and I don't want to be here alone on this island if they try again. I'll go get the gauntlets for you, but I'm leaving today." A tear rolled down her cheek, spoiling the effect.

The shining Guardian stepped around the altar and gently wrapped his arms around her. "I know you were frightened, little one, but remember you are never truly alone. Abba El loves His children. He watches over you always and knows of your sorrows as well as your joys."

The Guardian's embrace reminded her of her father and her heart ached with loss. Annor drew back and wiped the tears from her face. "Thank you, but I still want to leave the gauntlets and get away from this island. Why do the Sons of Darkness want the armor anyway?"

"They hope to harness the power of the king's armor to increase their own," the Guardian said. "Attacking you drained their power, and it will take time for them to gather more before they attack again." He fell silent for a moment, giving her a considering look. "If you are determined to leave the island, you should read the message your father left for you first."

"Message?" she asked, confused. "You mean his writings?"

"No, I speak of the standing stone near the southern tip of the island."

"Oh yes, I helped him raise that stone when I was little. It had something carved on it, a picture or something."

"Your father began carving the stone soon after he brought you and your mother to the island. Open your eyes and the stone will show you your path."

"Open my eyes?" Annor blinked. "I don't understand."

"Believing is seeing," he said. "If you choose the wrong path, your blind steps may lead you into misery. The right path will lead you to the Gates of Horn and Ivory, and a life of happiness and wonder." The Guardian smiled. "I wish you a sweet year full of joy, Annor, daughter of Gunnar and Dagny." And he vanished.

The sunlight seemed diminished without his shining presence. If not for his footprints by the altar, Annor might have thought she'd imagined it all. She'd never heard of the Gates of Horn and Ivory. But at least she had the Guardian's blessing to leave the island as soon as she'd read her father's message.

It'd been ten years, at least, since she'd helped her father raise that stone. They'd hoisted it upright with a winch, it had been so tall and heavy. She smiled remembering how much fun she'd always had working beside her father. She'd change out of this dress, and go find that standing stone.

Vines had grown around the stone, concealing it in a blanket of green, so that at first Annor didn't see it there at the edge of the tree line. When she'd pulled back the vines, she studied the stone a long time. Her father had squared off four rectangular sides, each with its own unique carvings. She remembered her father being meticulous about which way the stone faced, orienting it once they'd hauled it upright so that one particular edge pointed south. He hadn't explained why.

On the southeast side he'd carved wavy lines and circles. She traced the marks with her finger. As a path it made no sense. And the other three sides made as little sense as the first, no matter how much she opened her eyes and tried to see.

Kneeling in the dirt beside the river, Annor re-drew the four pictures from the stone. On the southwest side her father had carved a spiral at the top, with lines radiating out like sunlight. She chewed her lip. A spiral sun? The northeast side had a little tree at the top. "Believing is seeing," she murmured to herself.

Annor spent the rest of the day staring at the carvings, but came no closer to deciphering her father's message. As the hours passed, her frustration built. She'd wanted to be gone by now, off this island and on her way somewhere else. Anywhere else. Her stomach grumbled. She'd had nothing to eat all day besides the sweetcake. Discouraged and annoyed at day's end, she trudged back through the trees to the cottage. Another night alone on this island.

Annor sat at the table and stabbed a bit of smoked fish with her knife. She glanced over at her father's empty chair.

"I don't get it," she said. "What does it mean? What message would you carve into a stone instead of just telling me about it when I grew old enough to understand? Why not just write it on a skin?"

The empty chair sat there, mocking her. She knocked it over and went to kneel beside her bed. "Thank you for the visit of the Guardian," she prayed. "Please help me open my eyes. I can't bear it here any longer."

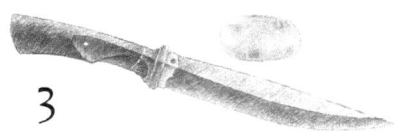

3

A young man strode quickly up a path on the slope below her. Annor focused on him and found herself beside him. "Hello," she said.

The young man didn't hear her, but kept walking with long strides that had Annor hurrying to keep up. "Hello," she repeated, louder this time. No response.

"He can't hear me." But in the way of dreams, that didn't matter. She continued walking beside him, glancing over at him frequently to memorize his face. If she didn't count the attack by the Sons of Darkness, this was only the fourth person she remembered seeing. His short, honey-colored hair framed his face, and his eyes shone blue with anticipation. He wore a dark blue tunic, with a pack slung over one shoulder, dark pants, and thick-soled shoes that ate away the distance as he hiked up the mountain path.

Annor reached over and touched his shoulder. He stopped abruptly and turned toward her, puzzled, his lips moving but making no sound. Annor dropped her hand and he began to fade, the path and the mountain with him, until Annor stood in her cottage doorway, looking out at the birch trees.

She gasped and sat up in bed. He had seemed so real. She remembered the texture of his tunic under her fingers, the eager light in his eyes. It had been such a vivid dream. Annor lay down and pictured his face. His blue eyes expanded so that she sank into them and back into sleep.

She dreamed of a lazy summer with her parents when she'd been nine years old. She was a strong enough swimmer to challenge her mother, but her father still swam circles around her.

It neared midsummer in her dream. To celebrate, Annor and her parents hiked several days upriver, as they had many times in the past. Here, falls plummeted down a cliff into a large, deep pool before the river flowed off toward their island. Annor loved to swim out to a sun-warmed rock and sit enveloped in the roar of the waterfall while it tried to spray her.

Annor dreamed that she swam with her father while her mother napped on the shore. Her father swam behind the waterfall, leaving her behind. He couldn't have done it outside of the dream. The falls raced down the very face of the cliff. But when her father vanished behind the cascading water, Annor swam over and found a cave behind the falls. Her parents sat inside, drying off in front of a large, burning tree. She sat between them and watched the tree blossom and grow a crop of white fruit.

Annor woke a second time, surrounded by the sweet smell of the fruit. Her mouth watered. She bolted upright and the last lingering scent of the fruit faded away.

She rubbed sleep from her eyes and swiped at a rivulet of water running down her cheek. Her hair was dripping wet. She checked her pillow only to find it bone dry. A sign?

She dressed quickly in the pre-dawn darkness and hurried along the path under the trees to where the stone waited, a tall, dark blot against the star-filled sky. She sat beside a tree and waited impatiently for dawn.

The river glimmered faintly in the starlight, chattering to itself as it passed her. She dug her fingers into the leaf litter and closed her eyes, wondering what the Guardian had meant when he said believing is seeing. Annor believed she would understand her father's message. He wouldn't have spent all that time carving nonsense into the stone. But she still couldn't grasp what the carvings meant, nor what path they could show her.

"Believing is seeing. Believing is seeing," she murmured, staring at the stone. She couldn't see the carvings yet in the emerging dawn, but she knew this side of the stone had the carving of the spiral sun. Would Abba El allow her to see forward to a time when she would understand the message?

"When I've figured it out," Annor prayed aloud, "what will I see? In the future, when this day is an old woman's memory, what will the message look like? What will it mean to me?"

She opened her eyes and gazed at the stone once more. The sun peered above the treetops across the river, illuminating her father's carvings. Surprisingly, Annor recognized the tree as the highest carving, instead of the spiral sun. But then she saw the spiral sun as well, superimposed over the tree. She gawked at the suddenly translucent stone, transfixed by the carvings glowing with the light of the real sun, so that the tree appeared to blaze. She blinked, and the sight vanished.

Annor leapt to her feet and knocked on the solid stone with her fist. It wasn't hollow as she'd half expected. But then, how had she seen two opposite sides of the stone at the same time?

She found a stick and started a new drawing that incorporated all four sides. She drew a blazing tree at the top, and a triangle beneath it with a crying eye in the center. Then came a circle and one long wavy line. Below that she drew a spiral on a square in a circle.

She pondered the combined drawing for several minutes. The blazing tree was the burning tree from her dream. The Guardian's Tree. The Shimmertree. But the Guardian had said to find those Gates, not the Shimmertree.

She traced the spiral on the square with her finger. The altar. And the crying eye was the waterfall pouring into the pool at the base of the mountain, just as it had in her dream. But the falls began at the top of the cliff, not partway down.

Her father's message told her to travel to the falls and somehow find the Shimmertree behind the crying eye. But she'd be as much alone on that path as if she stayed on her island. Annor didn't want to be alone any more. She didn't want to dream about strangers. She wanted to meet them, talk to them, make friends, live amongst them.

She contemplated the heavens and opened her heart. "Please, Abba El, can't there be an end? Haven't I done enough? How long does this burden have to last?"

The shining Guardian appeared beside her, and Annor rose from the dirt to look him in the eye. "I did it," she said. "Figured out my father's message. But I don't want to follow that path, even if it does lead to those Gates, whatever they are."

"The Gates of Horn and Ivory."

"Yes. I just want to be with people."

"You can leave the gauntlets, Annor. But you'll still be their steward, and the Sons of Darkness will still seek to control you."

"Can't you take them?"

"As I told your father, I can't." He paused, thoughtful. "I could send you forward a hundred years to a time when the Sons won't think to look for you. You must confront them, though, if you're ever to be truly free of them. If you refuse the path your father carved for you," he said, nodding toward the standing stone, "then maybe it's best if you go to Asseldam, the city once named Betavar."

Annor grinned. The Guardian could send her out of Javan's reach in spite of his Sons of Darkness. And back to Betavar. It was everything she could have wanted.

"I must warn you, though," the Guardian said. "The Sons of Darkness have changed more of the city than just its name. You'll need to guard against their influence while you learn to combat their power over you, but you'll be with other people as you desire."

"Let's do it," Annor said. For the first time in a long time, she felt hope. Hope that she wouldn't always be mourning her parents, miserable and alone.

"Let me arm you with a little knowledge first," the Guardian said. He plucked a small bowl out of nowhere and handed it to her with a spoon. "This is chocolate pudding. The Sons of Darkness have perverted chocolate to their own uses. You need to know the true taste to fortify you against their corruption."

Annor took a cautious spoonful. The brown pudding didn't look particularly appetizing. Her eyes opened wide, though, when the exquisite flavor touched her tongue. She savored every mouthful and licked the spoon clean when she'd emptied the dish. "That tasted amazing."

The Guardian chuckled. "Yes, I noticed you liked it."

"Where did you get it?" Annor asked, licking her teeth and relishing the taste left in her mouth.

"It's made from the seeds of cacao trees grown on another world, though now cacao trees grow on this world, too. Abba El has many worlds," the Guardian said, "and all are connected by a Shimmertree."

"That dream I had," Annor said, "about the Shimmertree in the cave behind the waterfall, I understand what that means, I guess. But what about the dream before it? The one with the young man walking up the mountain path? I've never had a dream that seemed so real."

The Guardian considered her for a moment, his eyes boring through her. "Well," he said at last. "That was not truly a dream." He held up a hand. "Before you ask, I can tell you no more. You will understand it when the time is right."

"Fine," Annor said. As long as she got off this island, nothing else mattered. "Just send me to Betavar, or whatever it is."

"Asseldam, the city of the Sons of Darkness."

When the Guardian said it like that, Annor caught her breath. Was she being foolish? But the path carved into the standing stone only led to more loneliness and misery. It's what her father had wanted, but he hadn't spent a year talking to gravestones.

She checked that her knife was securely strapped to her leg, and said, "Yes. Send me to Asseldam, the city of the Sons of Darkness."

"As you wish." The Guardian stepped forward and placed his warm hands on her head.

The warmth spread until Annor felt cocooned in warmth and peace, like a moment stolen from heaven. And then the warmth vanished. The standing stone and the Guardian had vanished as well, along with her green island. Annor stood on a stone-paved path running along the edge of a barren, dusty hill.

4

Bald Erik sat fishing on the splintery dock, leaning against a post and half dozing in the afternoon sun. Last night had been another torture session with Olaf, the Sons' High Priest. Erik's old bones still ached from the pain of it, not to mention his wounded right thigh that never did heal. He shifted his weight against the post, trying to find a more comfortable position, but it didn't help.

Maybe today he'd catch something. Fresh fish would bring some small bit of pleasure into the agony of his life, but few fish escaped the appetite of the monstrous water dragon that guarded this island prison. Bald Erik shifted his weight again. When would the Sons of Darkness have their fill of tormenting him? He had nothing new to tell them, and hadn't for years.

Last night when the priests prodded him into the desecrated temple's once Holy Place, Bald Erik had shivered at the large green stone waiting for him on the torture table. As always. He craved its healing power, ached for it most days, and despised himself for that yearning. He couldn't use it to heal himself, or even reach out to touch it. The priests used the stone to prolong the torture. It had torn him from death into life, but could never heal him completely.

Bald Erik had been prodded across the domed room and onto the stained table while the Sons of Darkness readied their usual array of barbed implements. Then Olaf had hefted the stone and touched it to Erik's lips with a wide grin plastered on his pasty face. The High Priest loved a good torture session, and if he needed to heal Erik before the torture even began, he planned to have the agony last for hours.

Erik couldn't help sighing now as he thought about how marvelous it felt to be healed, though it didn't last. The stone would touch his lips, and the pain in his thigh would vanish from body and soul as though it had never been. If he hadn't been surrounded by the hideous priests in their black robes, Erik could have run from the desecrated temple. Not that he'd be able to run farther than the shore and the dragon.

But shortly after the healing, his wound would throb. Then it would ache, and then pierce him with the peculiar agony that never diminished, no matter how many years passed.

More than the dragon trapped Bald Erik on the island. The green stone's healing power kept him here, as well. He craved that brief moment when he felt free from pain, that brief glorious moment, during all the other moments of his mournful existence.

Erik studied the city of Asseldam sprawling on the opposite shore. Boats darted along the riverbank. The ramshackle wooden dwellings on the south gradually gave way to sturdier stone structures on the north. In the city center, the Black Citadel towered above all the other buildings. The Sons' nest, swarming with young acolytes who grew into murderous men.

Bald Erik wished he didn't have to watch while the abased city decayed across the expanse of the river. But the pain of his wound kept him hobbled within sight of it as securely as a chain around his ankle. And he'd been starving after last night's torture.

The dock shifted on its pilings, the dry wood creaking. The dragon must be swimming nearby. No, Erik had no chance of catching a fish today. He pulled in his line, set the pole beside him, and closed his weary eyes.

The Sons of Darkness stole his freedom, tortured him relentlessly, and cut him off from everyone he loved. They took a peculiar delight in leaving him alone on this island with nothing but a dragon for company. If only Erik had some small way of striking back, just so they didn't have it all their way. But he sat powerless, a broken, hopeless old man. Only the dregs of his faith remained. He'd long since given up pleading to the heavens for relief. But maybe Abba El could find a way for him to avenge himself upon the Sons, even if he must be left in torment.

He considered the clear, blue sky. "Is there a way, Father?" he asked.

When the heavens didn't answer, Erik closed his eyes once more. Mercifully, he dozed.

5

The dried-out island looked nothing like Annor's tree-covered island. Neither did the wider and faster river. A mass of buildings crowded the far shore. Betavar. Or Asseldam, as she must learn to call it.

A building loomed behind her. Annor could feel it there even before she turned to look. It rose above her in tier upon tier until six towers capped it like sentinels, guarding a central dome. The stone path beneath her feet curved to meet a set of steps that climbed to a gaping entrance halfway up the building's side.

Annor recognized the building from a drawing in one of her mother's books. The temple of Abba El. The sheer overwhelming size of it, rearing above her, awed her. The door hung open on one hinge, and broken windows yawned wide, their remaining shards catching the afternoon light. Strange, since it had been morning on her island.

Someone had painted Blessed be our Prince Heyl El in broad, black strokes above the temple's doorway. The paint had run, so that the "P" stretched downwards toward the landing at the top of the steps.

Annor turned her back on the temple and looked across the surging river to the city opposite. She sank to the ground, absorbing all she could see. Excitement quickened her pulse.

Asseldam's myriad of buildings filled a vast swath of land. Smoke streamed from chimneys, and a haze hung over the city from the river to the hills rising at the city's back. Boats lined the riverbank, some with cargo, some empty.

But Annor feasted her eyes on the people. They swarmed Asseldam like ants on an anthill, looking almost as small at this distance. She smiled. She need never be alone again.

She dragged her gaze away from the city and noticed a dock below her, jutting out into the river. A lone man sat leaning against a post. Annor flattened herself to the ground, hoping he hadn't seen her appear out of nowhere. She loosened the knife in her sheath. The old man looked harmless enough, bald and thin. Maybe he could tell her about the city before she ventured across the river.

Annor rose and stalked slowly along the path and down the hill. She paused at the edge of the dock, listening to the river lap against the posts. The old man had rolled up his pant legs and his bare feet dangled in the water. His fishing pole and an empty bucket lay near him.

Annor cleared her throat and stepped onto the dock. The dry wood creaked and shifted under her weight, uneasy on its pilings, but the old man didn't stir. "Hello?" No response. She raised her voice. "Hello?"

The old man jumped and turned toward her, eyes wide.

"Sorry to startle you," she said, settling down next to him on the dock.

The old man smiled. "That's all right. It's just I don't get many visitors." His movement had caused a dribble of blood to seep through his pants over his right thigh.

"You're hurt."

"Not fatally." This was no new injury. Lines of pain had been graven on his face.

Annor shrugged. "Can you tell me of the city?" She nodded toward the other side of the river.

"You didn't come from there?"

"I did long ago, but I was a baby when my parents left to work the land." The man frowned at her leather tunic and pants. Maybe farmers didn't wear skins, but it was too late to change her story now.

"You've run away to the city? The land didn't hold your heart, then."

"My parents are dead," Annor said flatly.

"I see." He frowned again. "I'm sorry for your loss. I'm called Bald Erik." A fitting name. The gaunt man didn't have any eyebrows, or even eyelashes. Erik's blue eyes flicked up to her hair, with her long thick braid hanging over one shoulder.

"I'm Annor," she said.

"The city may be dangerous if you're unaccustomed to its ways, Annor, and I'm not the best informant. I've been away a long time, held on this island."

"Held?"

"I'm a prisoner of the Sons of Darkness."

Annor frowned. "You're not shackled. Why not swim for freedom?"

"The Sons don't need shackles. They have more creative solutions."

Annor glanced toward his right thigh, but the bloodstain had faded into the cloth and vanished. "I could help you, if you're too injured to swim on your own."

"Thank you child, but a beast of the deepness patrols the river, circling the island and holding me captive." He smiled. "Don't worry, the dragon won't concern himself with you. You may swim for freedom whenever you wish."

Annor eyed the river skeptically. "I could build you a raft if you don't want to swim."

"Heh. You don't believe my water dragon is real." He pushed himself painfully to his feet and tottered to the end of the dock where he raised his arms and bent his knees, as if he planned to dive in.

An oily sheen spread across the water in front of Bald Erik, and a horrific black beast reared suddenly out of the river. Annor jerked her knife from its sheath, her mouth hanging wide in horror. Inky darkness roiled around the enormous creature, obscuring its shape. Eyes gleamed red and furious below the wavy horns on its many heads. One head had a luminous pearl imbedded in its neck. The head coughed, and mucus spewed from its wide throat and hung dripping from rows of large, black teeth. The stink of rotting flesh made Annor gag.

Erik took several steps back and dropped his arms to his sides. The beast snorted through its many nostrils and sank slowly under the surface of the river, eyeing him suspiciously all the while. Erik made his way back toward Annor and sat heavily on the dock, a bloodstain spreading once more across his right thigh.

Annor re-sheathed her knife and tried to bring her breathing back to normal.

"Thank you for your kind offer," Bald Erik said, "but I'll be staying here a while yet. As I said, the dragon won't disturb you. It guards only me. My own personal nightmare."

"I'm sorry for doubting you," Annor said. She nodded toward his thigh. "Your wound, let me wrap it for you."

Erik flinched and shook his head. "No need." He glanced up at her hair again. "Hide your hair in the city, Annor. You'll stand out with a mane like that. And your clothes will also mark you as a stranger. If you want to survive the rigors of Asseldam, try to blend in a little. On the surface, at least."

Annor shrugged and tucked her long braid down the back of her tunic.

Erik smiled gently. "Are you sure you wouldn't rather go south or west and find a smaller town to explore before you venture into Asseldam? It'll chew on you and spit you out crippled unless you're lucky."

Annor glanced back at the decayed temple on the hill. "Or blessed."

"If you're a follower of Abba El, have you asked for guidance? You know he can always make more of your life than you can on your own, and bring you more joy in the process. Running from the life he's given you is the worst mistake any of us make."

Guilt tugged at Annor as she remembered the standing stone her father had so laboriously carved, but she shook off her regrets. "My life is no business of yours," she said.

"True." Erik took up his fishing pole and sent the line flying out into the water. "Swim from the northern tip of the island. If you swim strongly you may miss being swept through the sludge flowing out from the leat," he said, gesturing across the river.

Annor could just make out a black line in a gap between buildings on the opposite shore. Her parents had spoken of the large ditch that carried river water through the city. "Why is the leat water black?"

"The Sons' corruption pollutes everything they touch. I think the water dragon relishes the sludge pouring into the river," he said, "but you won't."

"Thank you for the advice. I'm sorry for your imprisonment and I wish you well," she said.

Annor stepped off the dock and turned toward the north end of the island where the weedy shoreline was dotted with rubble. The temple on the hill drew her eye, though, and she decided to explore it before swimming for the city. She wouldn't admit the water dragon terrified her, but it seemed a good idea to wait before braving the river.

She turned back the way she'd come and took the path to the top of the hill. Annor watched Bald Erik fishing on the dock below her. He could be wrong. He was just some old man the Sons of Darkness hated. She wasn't running away from her life. She was running to embrace a new life.

She walked on, following the curving path. Annor tried to imagine her parents here. She knew they'd come to the temple often before the usurper forced them to flee Betavar.

She hesitated at the base of the broad steps. Maybe this was a bad idea. She shrugged off the thought and started to climb. Her footsteps grated on the dirty stone.

When she reached the landing at the top, she turned. She had a spectacular view of the city from this vantage point. Blue leat water flowed through the northern part of the city, vanished under a black stone building, and emerged dark as pitch before curving to bisect Asseldam and rejoin the river.

The enormous black building straddling the leat had no windows, just a wide door, black in the blackness. A path ran from that door to a bridge which spanned the river north of the island.

A large ruin lay in the midst of the city beside the blue leat. That must have been the castle where her mother served the queen and her father had been captain of King Beraqel's guard. Nothing but the foundation and part of a staircase remained now. The stones had probably gone to build some of the smaller buildings scattered around it on the north end of the city. A large tree grew out of the center of the ruin, evidence that the Guardian had truly sent her forward in time. It had taken decades for the tree to grow so wide.

Holes pockmarked the hills behind the city. Annor couldn't tell if they were natural or man-made. She remembered her parents talking about kings being buried at the base of the hill, so some of the holes might be burial chambers. She wondered if the usurper had buried King Beraqel in one of those caves after the Sons sacrificed him on the temple altar. Strange to think that was ancient history now.

Annor turned from the view and approached the doorway of the temple. She lingered on the doorstep. An eerie feeling swept over her. But she took her courage in hand and strode inside. It must have been beautiful once. Strips of paper hung from the walls. Annor rubbed the dirt off one patch to reveal a sparkling ivory sheen. Hanging crystal lights had been smashed. They crunched under her feet, mixed in with the dirt.

Past the entrance hall, she came upon a branching passageway. She could turn left, right, or continue forward. The left passage had light at the end, so Annor walked toward it.

The light grew brighter as she crept forward, until Annor came to the heart of the temple beneath the large central dome. She paused in the entranceway, awed to see the roof soaring so high above her. The apex of the dome was a circle open to the sky. The sunlight illuminated the cream-colored stone of the dome and walls. The base of the room was square, and the only furniture a scarred wooden table. No sign of the stone altar. Most likely the Sons of Darkness destroyed it after slaughtering the king.

A large green stone sat on one end of the table. The stone, rough and uneven like a chunk of thick glass, was the size of a small melon. Annor stepped closer and reached out one finger. The stone was slick and cold to her touch. Unclean. She shivered with distaste, but also yearning.

She backed away from the table, wiping her finger on her pants, longing to touch the green stone again, but repelled by it at the same time. She turned and ran from the room, back toward the square of light that marked the entrance to the temple. She didn't pause on the outside landing, but rushed down the stairs, two at a time.

Annor slowed once she reached the path and skulked past Bald Erik slumbering on the dock. Overgrown weeds hid rubble. She skirted it carefully on her way to the northern tip of the island.

The river rushed past the shore. Erik had said the dragon wouldn't trouble her, but her stomach still clenched at the thought of swimming through its terrain. She touched the knife strapped securely to her leg for reassurance. It wouldn't be much use against all those heads and teeth, but it'd been her father's. She dove into the water, swimming with sure, strong strokes toward the city. The water dragged at her skins, and the swift current carried her downriver faster than she'd expected.

Something brushed past her leg. She panicked, swam faster, kicked harder, and swallowed a mouthful of bitter river water. Relief flooded through Annor when she reached the reeds lining the far shore. Weak and shaking, she crawled onto the mushy bank.

6

Annor sat on the grassy riverbank, dripping and exhausted. Beside her, the leat flowed black and rank into the river. She shuddered. She'd come so close to being enveloped in that muck. But even though the city had its flaws, she'd rather be here than alone.

The Guardian could have set her down in the city, instead of on that island. Meeting Bald Erik hadn't changed her mind about coming to the city.

Annor watched the parade of people on the broad path beside the riverbank. She checked her braid. It still hung hidden down the back of her tunic. No one in Asseldam had long hair. Male or female, they'd clipped it short. Like Erik, a few had even shaved their heads. Though they still had their eyebrows and eyelashes.

The soos lumbering down the path made her jaw drop. Her parents had described them, and Annor had seen a drawing in one of her father's books, but that hadn't prepared her for the massive size of the creature. It was as wide as three deer, or maybe four, so that the man on its back didn't straddle it so much as perch up there. Hard to believe female soos were even wider. The horns looked amazing, too. Spiraling lengths as long as Annor's arm grew straight back from the creature's head so the rider could use them to steer.

The best part of coming to the city was the variety of people. Annor drank in the sight of them from her patch of grass. Some of them wore skimpy, little costumes, while other people strolled past draped in layers of rich fabrics.

Annor was excited to get to know her new home. She weighed
her options. She could follow the river path northward toward the
stone buildings, or cross a bridge over the leat into the southern side
of Asseldam. It looked shabbier over there, but more people were
wandering around so she'd be less noticeable.

Annor joined the crowd crossing the bridge. The sun had crept
behind the hills and the twilight disguised her well enough for now.
Tomorrow she'd find herself some new clothes.

People chattering made a steady noise like the river. The layout of
the city confused Annor. The streets wandered randomly every which
way. Tall, rickety buildings squeezed in beside squat houses. The
buildings had been painted in bright colors, mimicking the people
shuffling through the streets and alleyways. A cheerful place. Her
heart lightened the more she saw of it, though she kept a hand on her
knife hilt just in case.

Smells assaulted Annor's nose, some as noxious as the leat, while
other tantalizing smells set her empty stomach to rumbling. It'd been
a long time since she'd eaten. She chuckled. More than a hundred
years. No wonder her mouth watered when she passed the food stalls.

Darkness stole slowly over the city. Annor's steps faltered as fatigue
caught up to her. She'd seen so much, but Asseldam was enormous.
Her whole island could have fit smack in the middle of it, and the city
would still have stretched past it in every direction.

The streets had begun to empty. She came to a small square lined
with booths and stalls, though the sellers had packed up their wares
and gone home. The smell of fried meat lingered in the air. Annor
licked her dry lips and squelched down her hunger. A few rough-
looking people, all with shaved heads, lingered in the square. They
settled themselves in as if, like Annor, they had nowhere else to go.
She felt their eyes assessing her.

She sat on her heels next to a booth. She wouldn't feel safe
sleeping here. Any one of these strangers might attack her while
she slept. Annor's eyes flicked to the hill west of the city. Maybe she
should sleep in one of the caves. In the morning she could help a food
seller in exchange for a meal. And find work. Life on her island hadn't
given her the skills to thrive in a city, but she'd learn.

A girl walked through the square, black with soot from her short hair to her sturdy shoes. A brush on a long pole, thick with more soot, hung over one shoulder. Annor watched the girl from where she crouched. She looked different from most of the people Annor had seen. Dirtier, obviously, but more peaceful. More approachable.

Annor rose from her crouch and smiled. She and the girl were about the same height. "Hello," Annor said. She swallowed.

The girl paused and looked her up and down in the dimness. "You're not from Asseldam."

"No."

The girl caught the watching eyes around the square. "Are you hungry?" she asked.

"Yes. If you'll help me, I can work for you."

The girl snorted. "You're a bit old to apprentice as a sweep. I'll have to quit soon myself. But come along, then. If you stay here you'll lose your virtue, and maybe your life."

The eyes followed Annor out of the square. She felt them on her back as she chased the girl down a cramped alley.

"My name's Gunilla," the girl said over her shoulder.

"Thank you for your help, Gunilla. I'm Annor."

The alley dead-ended at a two-story building. A large man leaned against the wall near the doorway, guarding the entrance. He toyed with his knife and gave Annor an appraising glance.

"She's with me," Gunilla said.

The man grunted. "Picked up a stray?"

Gunilla ignored him and entered the building. Annor followed her through the doorway and up a set of rickety stairs that creaked under their weight.

At the top of the stairs, Gunilla led her down a central hallway past doors thick with paint. Annor saw a sunset door, a black door, and a striped door. One door had HERE painted on in large, red letters. Gunilla opened a green door on the left side of the hallway. Inside, only the starlight filtering through a small window illuminated the darkness.

"Wait here," Gunilla said. She entered the dark room, dropped her brush with a clatter, and fumbled in a drawer for a lightstone. She set it in a holder screwed to the wall. Two narrow beds filled most of the small room, one on each side wall. The window's small, square panes were gray with soot. A dresser stood beneath the window, wads of clothing bulging from the open drawers.

"My brother's not here, so you can use his bed," Gunilla said, waving to the bed on the left.

"Thank you." Annor sat on the bed and soot puffed into the air.

Gunilla chuckled. "Sorry about that. So where are you from?" She eyed Annor's clothes, lingering on the knife strapped to her leg. "You're not from the city, but you don't look like a farmer."

"No, I hunted game with my father, but he's dead now." True enough, though the bald statement left out so much it felt like a lie.

"And you thought you'd give the city a try?"

Annor shrugged. "I've always wanted to see it."

"The city can be cruel to girls who're alone." Gunilla dug in a cupboard behind the door. "I don't have much food here. No way to cook it. Tomorrow I can show you the best food stands. Hopefully this'll hold you till then." She handed Annor some jerky and a handful of carrots.

"Thank you." Annor bit into a carrot.

Gunilla sat on her own bed and coughed hoarsely into her arm. "Do you have any money?"

"No, but like I said, I can help you in your work, and maybe learn your trade." A dirty job, but as a chimney sweep she'd earn an honest wage.

Gunilla frowned. "I can take you along tomorrow, and help you earn enough to feed yourself, but sweeping's not a trade you'll want to follow long. Not unless you want sweep's cough like me."

Annor chewed doggedly on the jerky, wondering what kind of meat it was.

Gunilla nodded toward the braid that had slipped out of Annor's tunic. "I don't think I've ever seen so much hair on one person."

Annor swallowed. "Why does everyone have short hair here?"

"To pay for fudge, of course." Gunilla smiled. "Don't worry, I won't cut your hair when you're not looking. I don't eat fudge myself. Or go to the parties. I only sell my hair when I'm short on money."

"What's fudge?"

Gunilla's eyebrows shot up a notch. "Wow, you are from somewhere else. The Sons of the Prince make fudge from the seeds of cacao trees. I'd stay away from it until you have a sure source of money. Otherwise you'll be bald and craving it, with no good way to get more."

"Cacao trees. So fudge is like chocolate." Annor licked her teeth, remembering the chocolate pudding.

Gunilla shrugged. "Never had it. You can't get chocolate any more. Just fudge. The Sons control all the fudge farms where the cacao trees grow. Anyway," she said, yawning, "I'm beat."

Annor crawled beneath her dusty covers while Gunilla stuffed the lightstone back in the drawer. "Thanks for taking me in, Gunilla."

"Well, I'd hate to see your corpse lying in the square tomorrow. Glad I could help." Gunilla sighed happily when her head hit her pillow. "Best part of the day is when it's over."

Annor smiled in the darkness. Her new life had begun.

7

Yevleh leaned back in his chair and stroked his bare chin, wishing he could grow a sleek beard like the Prince Heyl El. But even if the priests allowed beards, Yevleh's few hairs would look pitiful. Girls might give him a second look, though, if he had a beard. Especially in Asseldam. But the Prince must stand above his priesthood always, in all ways.

Yevleh couldn't complain. He'd made his share of conquests. Some girls would lie with anyone in a black robe for a square of fudge. It'd be more satisfying though, if they wanted him for himself.

Yevleh rubbed his tired eyes and stretched. His back ached from hunching over the manuscript of the long-dead High Priest. He'd been trying to decipher Halvard's handwriting ever since he'd come back from dinner, and the mold and spider droppings speckling the fragile manuscript hadn't helped. Halvard had been Javan's scribe when he ascended the king's throne to become the first High Priest, before Halvard killed Javan and became his successor. Or so it was said.

The manuscript told of Halvard using brute force to try to recover the rest of the king's armor. Stupid man. He might have been successful if he'd used a little subtlety. He probably did kill Javan, not that Yevleh would ever say so to any of his teachers. Not unless he wanted to get sent home in disgrace with almost six years wastedóthree as a laerling, two as an under-priest, and this last year as a journeyman. Almost eighteen years old now, and in the fall he'd be ordained a full priest to the Prince.

Approaching footsteps froze Yevleh in place. A priest. No apprentice would dare wander the Black Citadel at night. The shoe jammed in front of his door would give Yevleh time to hide the manuscript, but it might get his room searched, too.

He held his breath and eased open his desk drawer, willing the footsteps to walk past his room and down the corridor. Getting caught with the manuscript would get him sent home for sure. But first they'd whip him until he passed out, and then snip off his fingers.

The footsteps passed his door and continued down the corridor. Yevleh let out his breath. That'd been enough excitement for one night. He slipped the manuscript into the drawer between some of his essays on New Kingdom history, and straightened the papers on top of his desk. Thankfully, as a journeyman, he no longer shared a room, or he'd never have had a chance to read Halvard's account of the search for the armor.

A half-written letter home poked out from under a stack of books. Yevleh stroked it. He promised himself he'd finish the letter tomorrow before he started in again on the manuscript. He was too tired right now.

The even glow of his lightstone gave no hint of the time, but Yevleh's gritty eyes meant the night must be half gone. He covered the lightstone, shucked off his black robe, and slipped into bed in just his underclothes.

Before his mother sent the quilt, he used to sleep in his robe. Yevleh couldn't have faced a sixth winter shivering under a thin blanket, and his mother had been happy to send it. Even in spring, the Black Citadel chilled him to the bone.

He lay in bed and stared into the dark while he fingered the stitching on the quilt. In half a year he'd be ordained a priest and allowed to go home and visit. He might not recognize his little brother and sister after so many years. Would they recognize him?

Even though he'd been homesick his whole time as a laerling, Yevleh had been glad to escape the farm. His longing had faded to a dull ache, but sometimes he couldn't help wishing he still sat there bumping elbows while they ate at the small table. He'd like to gather around the blazing hearth again and listen to his father's stories. Yevleh had a few stories of his own now. He smiled and rolled over, stroking the quilt once more before he dropped off to sleep.

8

Gunilla dug into the overstuffed dresser and found an old shirt for Annor. The shirt fit snugly, the high collar right under her chin, while the sleeves had been torn off. In a different drawer she dredged up a thick pair of pants. Soot streaked the clothes gray and black so that Annor couldn't tell what color they'd been originally.

Annor fingered the shirt, the fabric reminding her of her mother's blue dress. "What's this made out of?"

"Cotton."

"Cotton?"

"It's a plant," Gunilla said. "Haven't you ever worn anything besides animal skins?"

Annor shrugged. "Not that I remember."

"The shirt should hide most of your hair, and a cap will do the rest." Gunilla dug in the drawer where she'd found the pants and pulled out a soft cap. "I used to wear this to keep the soot out of my hair. But after awhile, I didn't bother." Gunilla pulled the cap snugly over Annor's head. "And here's a scarf to cover your face when we're sweeping."

Copying Gunilla, Annor tied the sooty square of fabric loosely around her neck. She eyed her leather clothes lying on the dusty bed. Spending one day up a chimney couldn't be enough to give her sweep's cough. Hopefully. Gunilla had coughed off and on all night.

"Perfect," Gunilla said. "Before you know it you'll be black from head to toe." She chuckled at the look on Annor's face. "Don't worry, there's a washroom downstairs where you can clean up if you want." Gunilla handed Annor a chimney brush. "Let's go find some breakfast."

They walked downstairs, past the guard fingering his knife, and into a morning that reeked of rotting food and unwashed bodies. Annor wrinkled her nose. Gunilla bought them a quick breakfast of boiled eggs, and then threaded her way westward through Asseldam with Annor close beside her.

"First we'll stop by the Guild and find out what jobs Sven has lined up for today." She frowned. "Don't tell Sven your real name. You don't want the Sons finding out."

"Why?"

Gunilla shrugged. "Names have power."

The Sweeps' Guild owned a stone building near the base of a cliff. "This used to be the Quarry workers' Guild," Gunilla said as they drew near, "but they're around the backside of the hill nowadays."

The cliff behind the Guild rose in tiers above a large flat area marked off with a fence. Gunilla noticed Annor's gaze. "We can take a look at the theater first if you want. All the country folk come and stare at it. The Quarry workers' Guild cut the steps and the stone benches right into the cliff face. That was maybe a hundred years ago now, back during the days of the kings."

Back in King Beraqel's day. The cliff formed a semi-circle and the flat space in front of it was a stage. Her parents had climbed those steps and sat on those benches when they'd been freshly-cut stone. Part of Annor's desire to come to the city had been to feel closer to her parents, so it unsettled her to hear their day described as ancient history, even though she knew it was true.

Her parents had told her bedtime stories of theater events. There'd been concerts, plays, sword fights with blunted weapons, award ceremonies, and so on. Her father had once stood on that stage and been crowned Betavar's best swordsman. Annor had always longed to attend the theater and be part of a crowd. "What sort of events do they have here?" she asked Gunilla.

"Sabbath worship, mostly. You can go to a fudge party in the city any time," Gunilla said, waving her hand at the mass of buildings behind them. "But during Sabbath worship, the fudge is free, no hair needed for admission. So they're huge things, with people jammed in so tightly an ant could walk from thigh to thigh to thigh, without ever touching the bench."

"That's it? There aren't any concerts or plays?"

"Well, the Sons have music machines dug in below the stage, and they pipe the music up into the seats during the worship service. So, that's kind of a concert, I suppose. Though the music at a regular fudge party is more intense. It's more compelling in a closed room with incense burning and all that."

Annor frowned. She didn't want to sound stupid and ask what incense was. Gunilla already thought she was a bumpkin.

"And the stuff they do on stage is entertaining," Gunilla said. "They don't just stand there in their black robes praying to the Prince Heyl El the whole time. I mean, they do at first, and the audience stands and sways along with them, but after that they do healings."

Gunilla coughed into her sleeve. "Then they have champions on fudge highs do some incredible feats to show how strong they are, or how brave. Anyone who wants to challenge them can come down and compete for the right to wear the gold circlets on their brows and eat all the fudge they want." Gunilla sighed and looked away.

"What's wrong?"

Gunilla shook her head. "That's what happened to my brother," she said. "Challengers get an extra piece of fudge, so Isak thought it'd be worth it. But if you're no good, you get booed by the crowd and whipped by the Sons until you're bloody and unconscious." She grimaced. "That's part of the entertainment, with the crowd cheering and counting every stroke. And then they ship you off to one of the fudge farms."

Gunilla looked up at the benches. "Yeah, so I don't go to Sabbath worship any more, or eat fudge, either. Isak craved it so badly he couldn't work anymore. He thought if he was a champion he'd have it made, all the fudge he could eat.

"But they whipped him until the blood ran down the front and back of his shredded shirt," Gunilla said, her voice flat and expressionless. "That's the last time I saw him."

Annor put a hand on Gunilla's shoulder, wanting to comfort her but afraid of being rebuffed.

A faint smile touched Gunilla's lips. "I'm glad I found you. My brother was the only family I had left." She turned away from the theater. "Let's go get a job."

Annor followed her back toward the Sweeps' Guild. "So, that's all they ever do in the theater?" she asked. "Just these fudge services every Sabbath?"

Gunilla shrugged. "Sometimes there'll be a public execution. That sort of thing. I don't go to those either."

Annor stooped through the Guild's low doorway. A mass of chimney brushes leaned against the walls. Soot clouded the air and grit rasped under her shoes.

A thin, stooped man looked up from the heap of papers covering his desk. His greasy hair stuck up from his scalp. "Who's this then, Nil?"

"Hey Sven," Gunilla said. "Nor's helping me for a day or two."

"Whatever," Sven said. "I've got you down for the glass factory first thing."

"Again? Don't you ever send anyone else there?"

"Why should I when they like you so much?"

Gunilla shrugged. "I don't think it's my sweeping they find so appealing."

Sven chuckled. "Maybe not. But in that case, they'll like you even more when you show up with her." He leered up at Annor's chest.

Annor flinched.

Gunilla snorted. "Stuff your nasty eyes back in your skull. Let's go, Nor."

The glass factory stood tall and imposing, with clouds of smoke billowing out of a long row of chimneys down the center of its roof. Gunilla pounded on the thick door.

A man's sweaty, red face poked out. "Yeah? Oh, it's you." He noticed Annor standing behind Gunilla and his eyes widened. Grinning, he swung open the door. "Welcome, ladies."

Gunilla stepped past him and Annor followed.

The factory bustled like a burning hive. The ceiling soared three bodylengths above their heads, with a myriad of open windows near the ceiling. Even so, the room sweltered. Annor shuddered to think what it'd be like at midday in the heat of summer.

Furnaces ran back-to-back down the center of the room, glowing orange, red, or blue. Workers sweated in front of them turning long metal pipes in the flames, or labored at nearby workbenches, blowing into their pipes to turn molten orange blobs into expanding bubbles of glass. One worker carefully settled his glass bubble into a metal mold, then snipped the hot glass off his pipe with large shears.

Long tables, heaped high with finished product, lined the side walls. This left an aisle on each side of the room between the tables and the workbenches. Gunilla led Annor toward the far end of the room where three furnaces sat cold and dark.

Glass workers grinned and whistled as they passed. Gunilla glared and marched on by. Annor held her head high, but a blush stained her cheeks.

When they reached the cold furnaces, Gunilla covered her mouth and nose with her scarf, then swung her brush off her shoulder and got to work. Annor climbed up beside her and watched for a few minutes. It looked simple enough.

She took the next furnace over and tried to copy Gunilla's quick, sure movements while shoving her long-handled brush up the chimney and scrubbing at the interior. Annor couldn't see what she was doing, and it wouldn't have helped to stick her head up the chimney to look. Charcoal rained down in clumps amidst a continual storm of fine ash.

Annor worked hard, but Gunilla had finished one chimney and started on the next while Annor's still rained soot. Her muscles ached, and sweat soaked through her cap and shirt. Even her arms glistened so that ash clung to them like a gray second skin. Breathing through the scarf didn't keep the finer ash particles out of her lungs. She coughed nearly as much as Gunilla.

When the three chimneys had been brushed clean, Gunilla brought over a couple of brooms, a dust pan, and a large trash bin from a storeroom. Their ash cloud had spread out beyond the furnaces in a large, gritty semi-circle on the factory floor.

"You're doing great," Gunilla said in a low voice.

She handed Annor a broom and together they slowly swept the ash into piles, trying to keep it from billowing back into the air.

While Gunilla swept the piles of ash into the dust pan, Annor pulled the scarf away from her sweaty face and looked around the factory. The tables along the side walls held a variety of glass bowls in graduated sizes, from smaller than her fist to the size of large mixing bowls. Strangely, none of the bowls had bottoms.

"What's with the bottomless bowls?" Annor asked Gunilla, nodding toward the heaping tables.

"Sh." Gunilla looked over at the nearest workers, but they hadn't heard. "They're for the Sons' music machines," she murmured. "Only the priests know how they work, and they don't tolerate questions."

Someone banged on the door and one of the workers went to answer it. A breeze tickled Annor's face when the door swung open. A young Son of Darkness strode in, his long black robe flowing behind him. He glanced her way, looking past the long row of busy glassblowers to meet her gaze.

Annor dropped her eyes and helped Gunilla finish sweeping, her heart pounding. This was the first Son she'd seen since the frightful ring of faces that night on her island.

He walked over to one of the tables of bottomless bowls, the worker following. "Are these ready to ship?" he asked.

"Of course."

"Then pack them into crates. The High Priest is anxious to expand our reach." The Son's hair had been clipped short, except for a sleek braid tightly plaited against his scalp from his forehead to his neck, where a handwidth hung free. He turned on his heel, his black robe flaring around his legs. The workman hurried to open the door.

Annor whispered to Gunilla, "What's with the braid?"

"That shows his rank. Since it's on the left side of his head, halfway between his ear and the top of his head, he's a journeyman priest."

"Which means?"

"That he's not a full priest yet, but almost. Watch out for him, Annor. His name is Yevleh. All the girls know him, if you know what I mean."

Annor didn't.

Gunilla snorted and shook her head. "Hard to believe you're still that innocent." She put away the brooms and the dustpan and they started back to the Guild.

Annor's arms ached from holding them over her head while she swept. "Are all your jobs like that?"

Gunilla coughed and shook her head. "No, the Light Guild is the only place with furnaces like the glass factory, and they don't have nearly as many. Most chimneys have a few bricks inside that jut out a bit. That way you can climb all the way to the top, and brush your way down. It's a lot easier on your arms.

"And some of the bigger buildings have connecting chimneys to heat more than one room. The Guild has to send a whole crew to sweep the Black Citadel just because there are so many chimneys and the priests want them done all at once while they watch over the sweeps."

"What's it like inside the Black Citadel?"

Gunilla shuddered. "Creepy."

Annor believed it. Just looking at the blank walls of the building had given her the shivers on her walk through Asseldam. Seeing it loom over the other buildings was one of the reasons her footsteps had taken her south across the bridge.

After the first sweeping job, Annor followed along with Gunilla on two more before their day ended. Her whole body hurt, her eyes were red and weepy from all the ash, and she'd coughed half the day trying to clear the gunk out of her lungs. Maybe she wasn't cut out for life as a sweep. But until she learned more about Asseldam, Annor didn't know how else to make a living. At least talking to Gunilla made sweeping bearable.

9

Days went by, and then weeks, and Annor's muscles ached less the more time passed. She used her chimney brush like a trained sweep now, so it took less effort to knock out the chunks of charcoal and sweep the bricks clean. She'd swept chimneys in large stone houses on the north end of Asseldam, chimneys in rickety apartment buildings south of the leat, and even a tanner's chimney on the edge of town. Spring was a busy time for sweeps.

She'd thought many times about finding a different job, but she'd never had a friend before. Talking and laughing with Gunilla made the longest days fly by. And so far Annor only coughed when she was on a job.

The Black Citadel always seemed to be looking over her shoulder, though Sven never assigned them to sweep it. Annor got used to seeing Sons of Darkness in her travels around the city, though she hadn't seen Yevleh again.

On a rare day off, Annor wandered around the ruins of the king's castle. The tree growing in the center had cracked and heaved up the paving stones around its roots. She picked a flat spot between them and lay under the tree's spreading canopy. Green leaves against a blue sky felt like home.

She missed the shaded paths, and the wildflowers growing in the clearings. But she didn't want to go back to her quiet cottage. After a year of missing her parents, hardly able to think of much else, Annor was now too busy to think. Her grief had dwindled and settled into a dull ache. It was better this way.

Still, the ruined castle hurt her heart. Her parents had loved the festivals in the great hall, her father had trained daily in the courtyard, and her mother had attended the queen in the long-vanished rooms. Annor walked north of the ruin and found a wizened apple tree between two stone houses, all that was left of the orchard that used to flank the castle. Small green apples covered it in abundance. Annor promised herself she'd come back in the fall to taste them.

She followed an alley to the riverbank and looked toward the sprawling temple of the Sons of Darkness, so different from the Black Citadel. It reminded her of a spider, with legs radiating out from a central tower. The Guardian had been right. The Sons hadn't found her in this time, even though she lived amongst them. The king's gauntlets were safe on her island, and she was safe in the city. Life was perfect.

Her weeks as a chimney sweep turned into months, and Annor learned to love Gunilla like a sister. Working together every day was just the beginning. They'd spent many a night talking until their throats were sore. They'd laughed about Sven until their sides ached. Sometimes they even craved the same foods. And they looked out for each other. It gnawed at Annor that she'd never told Gunilla about her island. Sometimes the words hovered on her tongue, but she bit them back. She'd abandoned the path her father carved into the standing stone, but she couldn't betray her stewardship of the king's gauntlets.

One Sabbath Annor talked Gunilla into watching the Sons' worship service. Gunilla refused to crowd into the theater seats with the rest of the city, so the two of them climbed the Guild's chimney and watched from the rooftop.

The praying Sons filled the stage with their black robes. They gave off a palpable sense of power that sent chills down Annor's back. The music, at least, was thin and feeble at this distance. The champions impressed her with their incredible strength, but they were creepy, too. Unnatural. Thankfully no challengers braved the stage, though Gunilla tensed up until that part of the service ended.

The spectacle had been nothing like the Sabbaths Annor shared with her parents. Those had been days of quiet joy, not this frenetic fervor. The people who'd packed into the theater shrieked ecstatically during most of the service. Annor was glad to be on the roof.

Eventually Annor got to know the city almost as well as Gunilla. On one day off while Gunilla rested, Annor headed west through the streets and alleys of Asseldam toward the pock-marked hill behind the city. She ignored the beggars and the lewd looks. The hand resting on her knife kept anyone from accosting her. She side-stepped a soos cart in the clothing district. The driver gave her an evil look, flicking his whip between the soos' horns to urge it past.

She walked on, ignoring the fudge addicts lying in their vomit or crouching wild-eyed in the gutters. Maybe it'd been different in Betavar-that-was. Her parents never spoke of paid or stolen couplings. Didn't mention violence erupting over empty stomachs and stolen goods. Of course, fudge cravings hadn't been a problem in the city they'd known.

Asseldam had its troubles, but Annor didn't regret her choice. She had a friend. She had a job and made money she could spend on goods she hadn't made. She could eat food she hadn't caught, killed, and cooked.

Annor passed the Sweeps' Guild and stopped at the theater. Maybe she'd never see a play here, but she'd seen for herself what marvels people could achieve with time and determination. The city itself was a marvel. King Avar would be amazed to see the city he founded grown large enough to fill the entire plain between the hill and the river.

Annor followed the edge of the stage north. Here the burial chambers of the kings had been dug into the base of the hill. Gunilla had shown her the small stone huts shielding the entrance holes, little houses with three upright stones for walls, and a slab resting on top. The kings lay in underground tombs below them, waiting for the resurrection.

Her greatest regret was leaving her parents' graves behind on her island. Her father had been a guardsman when King Hoozeh was laid to rest. He'd described the pomp and ceremony for her in such vivid detail that Annor could hear the horns even now, see the royal blue banners flapping in the breeze. The young King Beraqel, barely twenty and newly crowned, had supported his weeping mother.

Just beyond the stage, the first tomb Annor came to was Beraqel's own. Surprising that the Sons of Darkness would bury him here after slaying him on the altar of Abba El's temple. But his name was carved into the low lintel, and his chamber stood in line with his forefathers'.

Annor traced the name with her finger: Beraq Ben Hoozeh. Maybe one of her uncles had carved that. Her father's father had been a master stonecarver. His eldest son chose the king's guard over his family's heritage, but he'd had other sons.

Annor might still have relatives in Asseldam, if they hadn't all fled. But she didn't know how to find them without the Sons finding her. Her father would be disappointed knowing she hadn't taken the path he carved, but he would be horrified if she lost the king's gauntlets.

She passed King Hoozeh, and his father and grandfather. Natural limestone caves dotted the hillside above the tombs, entrances to a bewildering array of tunnels. Gunilla said people got lost in them all the time. Before the castle had been built, in the early days of Betavar, people escaped to the tunnels in times of war. That was one reason King Avar moved his city across the river.

Annor continued past the long line of dead kings until she reached King Avar's tomb. She stood north of the Black Citadel, north of the castle ruins, and even north of where the old apple orchard had been. She'd reached the beginning of the city in more ways than one.

Her stomach rumbled. She jingled the coins in her pocket and smiled. Today she'd splurge and get some of that spicy roasted meat wrapped in flat bread.

10

Some weeks later, Annor walked beside Gunilla along the
Ceremonial Road leading from the Black Citadel to the bridge.
Gunilla walked stiffly, full of pent-up anger. Sven had been more
irritating than usual this morning, assigning just the two of them to
sweep the Sons of Darkness' temple, even though he knew it
to be a huge job.

Gunilla had tried to argue. "I was part of the group who swept it
last summer, so I shouldn't have to do it this year," she said.

"Then it's only fitting you go back," Sven said. "The Sons have
been sending complaints all winter about smoking vents. I'll bet your
group only swept the outside furnace."

"That's all you told us to do, for the amount they were paying."

"Well this time you'll sweep the furnace, the chamber, the flue
channel, and the chimney." He smirked and scratched his greasy head.

"Just the two of us? We'll be there all day."

"Won't hurt you. In my day…."

"Yeah, yeah," Gunilla cut in. "I know. You worked harder in a day
than I do in a week." She sighed. "Fine, but we want two days pay for
this job, up front."

"Prince below! I'd never pay you that."

"Alright. Half now, half later."

The two of them argued for another five minutes while Annor
stood beside Gunilla, twirling the brush handle on her shoulder.

She'd get to see inside the Sons' temple. She'd wanted to ever since
she looked across the river one night and saw the temple windows
glowing red in the darkness, as if a fiendish fire burned in every room.

The temple had no windows on the first floor. So even if Annor snuck over there, she wouldn't be able to peek inside. She wanted to see their altar, and watch them worship Heyl El. But only Sons were allowed past the guards and through the door.

The cobblestones of the Ceremonial Road had been arranged in a serpentine pattern, red cobbles oscillating amidst the usual gray, so that the road rippled under their feet. It gave Annor the creeps.

"They must like snakes," she said to Gunilla.

"Huh? Oh, those are Heyl El's sacred four-legged serpents."

"Serpents with legs? You mean lizards."

"No, they're serpents. I've never seen one, but they bring them out for executions sometimes. There's a room in the temple swarming with the creatures. At least, that's what everyone says."

They reached the end of the Ceremonial Road and started across the bridge. It didn't have much traffic this early in the day. The bridge was wide enough that four men could walk abreast, and she and Gunilla only squeezed against the rail once when a whole group of Sons paraded past, solemn and silent.

Annor looked downriver toward Bald Erik's island and wondered again why the Sons condemned him to stay there, wounded and guarded by a monster. "What's that island called?" she asked Gunilla.

"Torment Island. It's a prison or something."

Torment sounded about right. The bridge rose to an apex in the center of the river before sloping down toward the temple. When they strode from the wooden bridge to another cobblestone path, complete with twining red serpents, Annor's footsteps faltered. It felt like they'd stepped into darkness, even though the sun shone in her eyes. She ached to run back across the bridge.

"I hate this place," Gunilla said.

The temple of the Sons of Darkness crouched alone on the east bank. Its blackened limestone was pitted and corroded. The windows along the two nearest wings stared down at them with dead eyes. Gunilla led Annor along the cobbled path to where the only door stood at the end of one of the wings.

The temple entrance resembled a gaping serpent's mouth with ivory fangs, so that anyone entering had to duck beneath the glittering tips. Red cobbles formed a long serpent's tongue that flickered under Annor's dragging steps, pulling her within range. Two guards in black cloaks stood behind the fangs, to either side of the gray stone door. The guards drew their swords when she and Gunilla approached.

"Hail to the Prince," Gunilla said, stopping in the center of the red cobblestone tongue, just beyond reach of the swords. "We're here to sweep the furnace." She flourished her sooty brush.

The two guards didn't shift aside or lower their swords.

"Don't fret yourselves," Gunilla said. "We're not trying to get inside. I just wanted you to warn the outside patrol. I don't think we need another incident like last year."

The guard on their right sheathed his sword. "I'll do that." He ducked out from under the ivory fangs and strode off toward the south. The other guard centered himself in front of the door, sword still at the ready.

"Right. We'll be off then. Come on, Nor." Gunilla stepped off the cobbled path and turned her back on the temple entrance, leading Annor northward along the plain. They passed the ends of several more wings before she turned between two of them and headed toward the central tower.

The two wings closed in upon them, swallowing them as they walked. The blank windows mocked Annor for wanting to see inside their secret corridors. Her back itched from the dread bearing down on them. She tried to shrug it off, following Gunilla down stone stairs leading to a paved space in front of the furnace at the base of the tower. She breathed easier when the overhanging roof blocked the windows from view.

Stacked wood filled the wall to their right. A shed stood against the wall on their left, while the furnace had been built into the wall directly in front of them, its large metal door shut and latched. Gunilla tossed her brush on the ground and wrenched the shed open, revealing two wheelbarrows, a stack of shovels, and a few brooms.

Annor unlatched the furnace door and swung it open, hinges screeching. "How fast can we clean this furnace and get out of here?"

"I told you, we're going to be here forever. The furnace is just the beginning." She stooped down and pointed through the furnace door. "It opens on the back side into a low pillared chamber as wide as the whole center of the temple. Before we can see to clean it, we'll have to find the lightstones on the walls and wipe the soot off them. A flue channel leads from the chamber to a chimney on the far wall. There aren't any lightstones in the chimney, so once we shut the grates on each floor it'll be pretty dark in there."

Annor bit her lip. "Sounds like loads of fun. Why wouldn't you bring a lightstone to a job like this?"

"I've told you, I don't want to lose my one and only lightstone. And yes, I could buy another one, but that's not where I want my pay going."

"Whatever. So what do we sweep first?"

"Let's shovel most of the muck out of the furnace. We'll give it a good sweep once we've got everything else done. After that you might as well climb up and sweep the chimney while I sweep out the chamber."

They set the wheelbarrows side by side at the base of the stairs. The furnace was heaped high with ash, so it didn't take long to fill them. When they'd helped each other haul both wheelbarrows up the stairs, they rattled their loads of piled ash and bits of charred wood past the blank temple windows and out onto the bare ground northeast of the temple.

"Why here?" Annor asked as they dumped the ashes in a heap.

Gunilla shrugged. "Because I'm tired of pushing the wheelbarrow. Anyway, this should be far enough away that they won't complain to Sven."

Further east a solitary stone towered above the empty plain. "What's with the standing stone?" Annor asked.

"That's the Sons' gravestone. They pour the ashes of dead Sons over the top and offer them to the winds."

"A gravestone with no graves. That's sad."

"Maybe. What's creepy is that before they burn the bodies, they cut off the heads and hands. Then when the flesh has rotted off, they mount the skulls along the hallways in the temple, with every skull cradled in its own skeletal hands." Gunilla shuddered. "Or at least that's what they say. Since only Sons of the Prince ever go inside the temple, who knows if any of the stories are true."

Annor wrinkled her nose. "Nasty."

They swiveled the wheelbarrows around and rattled back toward the steps. South of the temple, random stone walls lay scattered across the barren plain, humped and uneven. "What's all that?" Annor asked. "One of the Sons' failed building projects?"

Gunilla laughed and stopped her wheelbarrow. "That, my country cousin, is the ruins of the old city, before King Avar moved across the river, hundreds of years before the Sons of the Prince reared their hooded heads." She rattled off again.

Annor hurried to catch up, the temple wings soon hiding her view of the ruined city. They filled and emptied the wheelbarrows several more times before their shovels scraped down to the floor of the furnace. With the furnace cleared, Gunilla crawled into the chamber beyond it and searched the walls for lightstones.

Annor crouched down and looked through the furnace. "Are you sure there are lightstones in there?"

"Yes," Gunilla said, grunting as she crawled around in the dark. "They're from when the Sons built this place. Though, that was a long time ago. What do you bet the stones are dead?"

"If they are," Annor said, "you get to go back to the entrance and ask the guards to fetch some new ones." She looked back up the stairs to where the temple wings crowded out the sunlight. "Please find a lightstone. I just want to get out of here."

Gunilla grunted. "Well, since you asked so nicely." A moment later a ray of light shone out through the furnace door. "Stupid walls are so rough and unfinished I couldn't tell what was a lightstone and what was just a bump. Time for you to get off your tail and shimmy up the chimney."

The one lightstone Gunilla had cleaned sent striped shadows across the chamber from all the pillars holding up the floor above their heads. Crawling through the chamber, brush in hand, set Annor's teeth on edge. Something about knowing a whole tower stood above them, and only these scattered pillars kept it from smashing down on their heads.

She found the flue channel and crawled down it toward the chimney. Her body blocked the light from the lightstone, so Annor felt her way through the gritty darkness. She wished she'd thought to take at least one of the lightstones from her cottage when she left, since her pay didn't add up to much after food and rent.

Relief swept over her when she got to the chimney and could stand. Maybe she wasn't any safer here than out in the chamber, but Annor felt protected in the chimney. Sweeping chimneys every day had made them familiar places.

The base of the chimney was heaped with ashes shoveled in from above. She felt around the walls, found the usual jutting bricks, and started climbing. It was dim, but not pitch dark, since the grates on each floor let in a small amount of light from the rooms beyond them, plus a vent at the top let in a little more.

Annor paused when she reached the grate on the ground floor of the tower, breathing softly while she peeked through the slats. Something smelled acrid and awful.

The room on the other side of the grate was empty except for a large, rectangular box sitting in the center of the tiered floor, made from blackened wood. The box intrigued her. She felt drawn to it. Staring at the box, puzzled, she leaned a little too hard on the grate. It swung open and Annor half fell into the room. She ducked back out into the chimney, quickly pulled the grate closed, and slid the cover shut. She clung to the grate for a moment, willing her heart to stop pounding.

When she could breathe again, she climbed up to the next level. It would be dark once she had all the grates shut, but she couldn't let soot billow into the rooms while she swept. Sven would get an earful from the priests, and then she and Gunilla wouldn't get paid.

The grate on the next floor opened into a roomful of chairs, as did the grate above that. Annor thanked Abba El no Sons sat in the chairs to see her eyes peering through the grates.

The last grate let in less light than the other three, and when Annor peeked through the slats, the room beyond it gave her chills. The gray walls, the gray floor, the high gray ceiling, all looked like they were moving. It smelled strange, too, like dried snails. An inverted spire pointed down from the ceiling toward an elaborate throne on a platform. The throne was built of polished bones decorated with patterns of teeth. Clear goo from the spire above dribbled onto the throne, so that it glistened in the grayness. Dried puddles encircled its base. Nearby, a half-full basket sat on a small table.

Malignance radiated from the room. Annor wanted to scurry down the chimney, through the flue and the chamber, and out into the sunlight. Yet she couldn't drag her eyes away from the grate. The feeling repulsed her and attracted her in equal measures. She crouched inside the chimney for the longest time, staring into the room, careful not to lean on the grate.

She realized why the walls and floor moved. Four-legged serpents swarmed everywhere except the platform with the throne and table. They were gray like everything else. Four-legged serpents, indeed. These were not lizards.

Power throbbed in the room so that Annor's head ached with it. Like the green stone she'd seen in Abba El's desecrated temple, it was vile but enticing. She'd never felt power this strong while kneeling at the altar in the stone circle on her island, even when the Guardian appeared. She tried to remember the peaceful feeling the Guardian had given her, but the throbbing power from the throne room drowned everything else out. Maybe Heyl El had more power than Abba El.

Annor closed her eyes and slid the grate cover shut. She crouched there for a moment longer, her forehead pressed against a chimney brick, before she could rally enough strength to climb to the top of the chimney. Once there she breathed in the fresh air coming through the vent, letting the trickle of sunlight warm the chill from her face.

Refreshed, Annor swept her way down the chimney, floor by floor. She breathed as shallowly as she could while she scrubbed at the bricks, but she still choked on the ash filtering through her scarf. Her eyes watered and stung and her arms ached by the time she reached the base of the chimney. She crawled back out of the flue to get a shovel.

Gunilla had found five more lightstones, so the pillared chamber felt less menacing. Either that, or the gray throne room had made the chimney less appealing. Gunilla helped her shovel the piled ash from out of the base of the chimney. They took turns crawling back through the chamber with their shovels full of ash and dumping them into one of the wheelbarrows.

Annor stood beside Gunilla at the base of the stairs, rolling her shoulders and stretching her back. "I don't understand why they swept ash into the chimney, instead of cleaning it up."

Gunilla inspected a scrape on her elbow. "Maybe the higher ups don't want to let a cleaning crew into their secret rooms."

Annor thought about the room with the wooden box. That acrid smell reminded her of the horrible night on her island when she'd been surrounded by the ring of white faces. "Makes sense."

Gunilla leaned over the wheelbarrow and poked around in the chimney ash with one finger. "Whatever they were burning, I don't think it was wood. It doesn't look the same as the ash from the furnace."

"Yuck." Annor shuddered. "I don't want to know what it was. Let's just dump it and get out of here before the sun vanishes completely."

11

Pink-tinted fog swirled over the river in the early morning air as the sun edged over the horizon. Annor stood on the empty bridge and looked downriver. Today was one of their rare days off, and while Gunilla spent it sleeping, Annor wanted to visit Bald Erik on his island. Torment Island. She had some questions for him.

The passing months had warmed the air, but the river still ran cold and strong from the continual snow melt in the mountains. The island lay downstream from the bridge, so getting there would be easy. She'd still have a hard swim back to the city, but she was stronger than she used to be.

Best to get on with it. Annor ducked under the wooden railing and launched herself into the river. The chilly waters embraced her, and the current pulled her south.

It nearly pulled her past the island, but Annor fought it and grinned when her feet touched bottom. She'd made it. It felt good to be away from the city. Some days she missed the peacefulness of her own island, and though Erik's island lacked shady trees and green undergrowth, it also lacked the city's pungent odors and restless inhabitants.

She squeezed the water from her hair and tucked her braid back down her shirt. It might be too early to find Bald Erik on the dock. He probably slept in the desecrated temple on the hill. Annor cringed from the thought of searching the temple. That green stone had shown up in her dreams more than once, pulsing with a polluted glow that left her shuddering and sleepless.

The dock was empty. Annor picked up the fishing pole leaning against the first post, and walked out onto the splintered boards. Erik might be more welcoming if she caught his breakfast.

12

Bald Erik stood at the top of the path and watched Annor fishing off his dock. Conversation with someone besides a Son of Darkness would be a pleasant beginning to another endless day. Still, he hesitated. Why had she come to the island? He eyed the heavens. "I suppose You brought her here?"

He made his way slowly down the path. No torture last night, but Erik didn't want to aggravate his everlasting wound any more than necessary. Annor looked up, smiling, when he stepped onto the dock. It lifted his heart. It'd been years since someone had been happy to see him.

"Good morning," he said.

Annor set down the borrowed fishing pole and got to her feet. "I caught you some breakfast. I'll light a fire and we can talk while it cooks."

She busied herself cleaning and gutting the fish while the cooking stone heated. "Do the Sons give you any food supplies?" Annor asked, laying the strips of fish on the stone.

"Now and then. Some of it's even fit to eat." He leaned carefully against the hill behind him, and nodded toward Asseldam. "How do you like the city? I see you still have all your hair."

"I didn't believe you when you warned me about that." She chuckled. "It's strange to see so many cropped heads, but even the shaved ones have more hair than you do."

"There must be a few desperate souls who pluck out their eyebrows," he said, touching his own hairless brow.

"Maybe, but not their eyelashes, too. Why do you do it?"

"Me?" Erik grimaced and shook his head. "It's the Sons who keep me hairless. They use my hair for all kinds of little experiments. So, why did you decide to come cheer up a lonely, old man?"

Annor leaned forward and flipped over the fish slices. Not meeting his gaze, she said, "I'm a chimney sweep now, and the other day I swept the furnace at the Sons' temple." She swallowed. "I peeked through the chimney grate into Heyl El's throne room. I felt so much power in that room, I almost emptied my stomach."

She shivered and rubbed her arms. "And Gunilla, my friend, took me to a roof outside the theater once, where we could hear the Sons' music at the Sabbath service. And the crowd of Sons praying together, swaying there on the stage in all those black robes, gave me the same feeling."

She bit her lip. "I've never felt power like that before, even when I met one of Abba El's servants. And I don't understand. I thought Heyl El was weaker than Abba El, or at least that's what my parents taught me. But look around," she said, gesturing toward the desecrated temple above them and the bustling city across the river. "How can I believe Abba El has more power?"

Bald Erik rubbed his chin, still bare from the plucking on the Sons' last visit. "Abba El loves His children too much to compel them to follow Him," he said. "Heyl El loves only power. With music, potions, or whatever else comes to hand, he tricks people into handing him their free will, and then he uses it to compel their devotion."

Annor frowned. "So, what does Abba El do?"

"Besides creating worlds where He hopes His children will grow to become like Him?" Erik pondered what to say.

"Maybe a story will help," he said. "It's been over a hundred years since Javan overthrew his nephew, the king. Those were dark days, when the streets of Betavar ran with the blood of neighbors and brothers. Monarchists remained loyal to the dead king. Others supported Javan's theocratic government and his cadre of priests."

Bald Erik stretched out his legs to soothe his aching thigh. Even such a small movement re-opened the wound so that a few drops of blood soaked through his pants. He hid the spot with his hand until it could dissipate.

He continued. "With the king dead, and the members of
parliament fled or killed, the monarchists had no leader. Eventually
all opposition to the Sons of the Prince had been stamped out, except
for a few Puerán who hadn't fled the city."

"The Puerán," Annor said. "My parents told me of the priests
of Abba El. So why didn't they overcome the Sons of Darkness? If
Abba El's more powerful, then his priests should be stronger than
Heyl El's."

"The Puerán are only as strong as the people's faith in Abba El." He
cleared his throat. "So yes, seven Puerán remained. They could have
kept silent or changed their loyalties. Many monarchists did when
faced with death. But these Puerán walked the streets proclaiming the
wickedness of Javan and the Sons. They urged the people to repent
and return to Abba El. But Javan sent vaettir to take them and throw
them into prison."

"Vaettir?"

"You haven't seen them in the city? I suppose the Sons don't need
them much anymore. They're ghastly creations."

"Ghastly how?" Annor asked.

Erik frowned. "The Sons don't burn all the bodies of those they
execute. Some they reanimate with a splinter from the Hollow
Altar inserted into their heart, brain, or hand. Depending on where
the Sons insert the splinter, it produces a different type of servant,
obedient to their will in every way."

Annor shuddered. "The Hollow Altar. That's the altar in their temple."

"Yes, Javan discovered the withered Knowing Tree up in the
mountains, and used the wood from the Tree to build the Hollow
Altar." Erik raised his plucked eyebrows. "Any more questions?"

Annor smiled and shook her head. "Not right now."

"So, seven Puerán priests sat bound in Javan's cells awaiting
execution. The Sons smote them, spit on them, and starved them, but
the seven remained strong in spirit. Javan wanted to make a public
display of their deaths, to take the heart out of any who might have
believed in their words. He also wanted to show his power over them.
So he gathered the people to the theater and paraded the weakened
Puerán onto the stage, clad only in rags and bruises.

"Javan fed the Puerán fudge to cloud their minds, the only thing they'd eaten in days. Then he commanded the seven, 'Tell the people how you've been deluded. Heyl El is stronger than Abba El. That's why I'm the one sitting on the throne.'

"The fudge had no affect on the Puerán, though Javan had made it extra potent. Their minds clear, their hearts undaunted, they called to the people to repent and throw off Javan's yoke. 'Humble yourselves before Abba El,' they cried, 'and call on His name. He will fight your battles and give you the victory.'

"But the people remembered their dead friends and family. The vaettir and Javan's army stood gathered just beyond the edge of the stage. So the people wouldn't listen.

"Since the fudge had no affect on the Puerán, Javan used the power of Heyl El to create an illusion. The Sons of Darkness caused the people to see the Puerán kneeling and worshiping the black-robed liars.

"But the Puerán called on Abba El and the illusion disintegrated. The people gasped when they saw the seven Puerán standing steadfast and honorable, in the midst of their enemies.

"So the Sons brought out gray wolves, caught and caged on the plains far to the west. The Sons had tormented and starved the wolves to make a marvelous spectacle for the people to enjoy.

"When the stage had been cleared of all but the seven Puerán, the Sons loosed the beasts to tear the seven to pieces. But the Puerán frolicked with the wolves, playing with them like well-beloved pets. When two puzzled Sons stepped onto the stage, the wolves tore them limb from bloody limb."

Erik cleared his dry throat. "So the Sons brought in great cartloads of wood and called down fire from the skies, one of their favorite tricks. When they had a roaring bonfire, they cast the bound Puerán into the flames one by one. The heat from the flames could be felt even in the top theater seats. But the Puerán stepped forth from the midst of the flames, unbound and unharmed, their rags intact.

"The Sons raged and called down curses upon their heads. The leader of the seven hushed the Sons with a gesture and raised his hand high. Drawing a sacred spiral in the air, he commanded the fire to die and sent a whirlwind to clear the stage of all the props and trickery the Sons had used to fool the people.

"Once more the seven Puerán stood alone on the empty stage. The Puerán leader commanded Javan, the usurper, to come forth and kneel before the crowd.

"'Is this man worthy to be your king?' the Puerán brother called to the people. 'He sits on yonder throne in a castle built by the loving hands of your ancestors, plotting in his wickedness to strip you of your divine inheritance. But no more.'

"The Citadel hadn't been built yet, so the people could see the castle rising above the rest of the city. The Puerán leader raised his hand and commanded the castle stones to obey. While the people watched, astounded, the castle crumbled. Stones toppled and smashed to the ground, leaving it as you see now, struck by the power of Abba El. The leader turned back to the people. 'Choose whom you will serve,' he said, 'this puppet without a throne, or Abba El above.'

"The seven closed their eyes and vanished, one by one, before the wondering gaze of the entire city. The people rose to their feet, amazed by the power of Abba El. But Javan got off his knees and called his army. He gathered his vaettir, and the people fell into his grip once more. Generations have passed, and Heyl El's power has only grown stronger because of the devotion the people render to him."

Erik relaxed back against the hill. "And that, my dear, is the story of the seven Puerán and how they used the power of Abba El to proclaim truth and stand against evil."

Annor sat silent for several minutes, staring down at the flickering fire between them. She raised her eyes to search Erik's face. "Is the story true?"

"That you must decide for yourself. We all choose who or what is worthy of our worship. If we make no choice, the choice is made in spite of us. No one can be neutral in the battle for souls."

Annor handed Bald Erik a strip of fish and sat back on her heels. "I don't know, taming wild beasts, surviving fire, commanding stone. It sounds like just a story. And even if it's not, I'd still like to see for myself. Go to one of their fudge parties and see what all the fuss is about. I need to see it, just to know what I'm rejecting."

Bald Erik opened his mouth and let Abba El fill it with words. "So is this your path?"

"You mean, do I choose Heyl El over Abba El? Of course not. And even," she hesitated, "even if I've made stupid choices before, taking an easy path instead of a hard one, I can change my mind, right? My parents told me that change is always possible, no matter what I've done in the past."

"Of course." Erik said. "You can't change the outcomes of your choices, but you can always begin again."

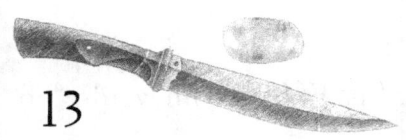

13

Gunilla frowned. "Why do you want to go to a fudge party? Haven't you seen the bald, miserable people puking in the gutters?"

"I want to see for myself what it's all about."

"I'll tell you what it's all about. My brother shaved his head, his legs, and everything else to pay for fudge parties. When he ran out of his own hair, he'd talk me into giving him some of mine. And when he was desperate, he'd cut my hair while I slept. I'd wake up bald on one side.

"He started smoking the fudge because it took less to get his head flying. That's when he started puking out his insides. He stopped working, stopped eating, stopped coming home. He'd go to fudge parties and stay until they kicked him out. Then he'd sleep outside the door until he could find a way back in."

Gunilla rubbed her face. "So it was probably for the best when the Sons whipped him half to death and sent him to a fudge farm. At least he's himself now, even if I'll never see him again."

"They don't give him fudge on the fudge farm?"

"One square a week. Not enough to burn out his head, but enough to keep him working. The addicts cultivate the cacao trees, harvest the beans, and make the fudge. A kind of torture, if you think about it. And they never get to leave. They're slaves. Annor, you don't want to start down that path."

"Trying fudge one time won't send me to a fudge farm." Annor said. "But fine, I'll go to a fudge party, but I won't eat any fudge."

Gunilla shrugged. "Whatever. Don't forget you need some hair to pay the entrance fee."

Annor tugged her long braid out of the back of her shirt and grabbed her knife. "I think I can spare some." She sawed off a fingerwidth and wrapped the cut hair in a square of cloth.

Asseldam had fudge parties all over town, day or night. Annor left the apartment and walked north through the dark streets, then crossed the bridge over the leat. A party on the nicer side of town might have fewer addicts camping out, waiting to attack anyone with hair.

The music hooked her when she turned down the alley. Annor didn't hear it as much as felt it in the cobblestones under her feet. The vibrations compelled her, and drew her farther down the alley.

The stone building squatted in the moonlight, dark and windowless. A feeble lightstone illuminated a carving in the center of the wooden door, just at eye level. Annor traced it with her finger. A four-legged serpent swallowing its own tail. The beat of the music was louder here, insistent. She pushed and the door swung open.

A dingy hallway sloped down into darkness. Annor stepped forward and the door swung shut behind her. The music tugged at her, and she grinned. A little fun couldn't hurt. Work, work, work. Why live in the city and not enjoy herself? She strode down the dim hallway until she came to a doorman sitting on a stool beside a closed door.

The man yawned. "Payment?"

Annor unrolled the square of cloth and brushed her clipped hair onto the small tray he held out.

"Here you go," he said, handing her a square of fudge in return. He opened the door, and the music pulsed all around them.

"Thank you," Annor said. She stepped through the doorway, wrapping the fudge in her bit of cloth and tucking it back in her pocket. The fudge smelled divine, just like chocolate, and it took all her resolve not to take a bite. She patted her pocket. Maybe she'd nibble it after she looked around.

People swarmed throughout the chamber, sweat dripping down their skin and staining their clothes. The blaring music drowned out all thought. Light pulsed in time with the music, red and orange and yellow, while aromatic smoke swirled through the colored air and embraced the whirling crowd.

Two bloodied men battered each other on a stage. The crowd
cheered when one flattened the other. The victor dove onto
the loser and pummeled his face. The loser kicked him off and
staggered to his feet. They were equally bloody now, and Annor
couldn't tell them apart.

The smoke wafted from the stage, from a brazier set on a short
black pillar. A black-robed priest stood behind it in a wide stance with
outstretched arms, hooded and motionless.

Annor shook her head to clear it, and pushed her way toward the
center of the room. The music blared from all directions, insistent
and otherworldly. Even the music during the Sabbath service hadn't
sounded quite like this. She couldn't see who was making it, or how.

One of the fighters flattened his opponent with an uppercut,
knocking him unconscious. A Son rewarded him with a square of
fudge, before dragging the loser to the edge of the stage and pushing
him off. Several dancers took the fighters' place. They danced
savagely, howling to the beat of the music. The hooded priest with his
outstretched arms was the center of their storm.

Annor smelled fudge all around her, intoxicating and enlivening,
as other patrons nibbled at their squares. Some people crammed the
whole square in their mouths at once, chewing frantically, licking
their hands to get every morsel. Annor shivered and looked away,
suddenly glad she hadn't nibbled on hers.

The smoke, the music, the throbbing light, and the crowded dance
floor all conspired to overwhelm her. She closed her eyes to breathe
in the sweet smoke and focus on the music, ignoring the sweaty
people who pressed against her on every side.

Annor swayed to the music, feeling lighter and lighter. She peeked
just to be sure she hadn't floated above the floor. Her emotions swung
between exhilaration and brief tastes of ecstasy. If only the ecstasy
would last. She longed for it as she'd never longed for anything before.
For the first time in over a year, she felt something like joy.

The Sons of Darkness weren't that bad. They offered a different
choice. Not bad. Just different. Her mind spun on that thought for
a long time, repeating the word different over and over. It sounded
more desirable with each repetition.

Then her mind flicked to the night on her island, that night before her birthday, with the ring of chanting faces white in the darkness. The image startled her with its clarity, cutting through the cloud in her mind and silencing the repetitions.

Annor snapped her eyes open and stumbled to the wall. She retched onto the floor, heaving until nothing but bile remained. Her puddle of vomit joined others already there. Mesmerized by the smoke and the music and the stage show, no one noticed her shivering by the wall.

She staggered to the door, pushed past the doorman, up the hallway, and out into the night. She leaned against the wall outside the door and gulped in deep lungfuls of air until her stomach stopped twisting.

When Annor stumbled into the apartment, Gunilla coughed and waved her hand in front of her face. "You reek."

"Sorry. You didn't tell me about the smoke." Annor sank down on her bed and pulled off her cap. She turned it in her hands. "You were right. I shouldn't have gone." She pulled the cloth-wrapped piece of fudge from her pocket and set it on the bed. The smell percolated throughout the room.

"Ugh." Gunilla picked up the fudge and stuffed it in the back of a drawer, under a wad of clothing. "We'll sell it tomorrow and buy you a new shirt or something."

Annor smiled. "Deal, though this shirt is awfully flattering," she said, tugging at the torn edge where a sleeve used to be. Her smile faded. "You've gone before, right?"

Gunilla shrugged and crawled into her bed. "Yes, I went with my brother sometimes."

"Did you feel the ecstasy? Nothing ever felt so good before."

"That's why I told you not to go. It would have been more compelling if you'd eaten your fudge. And you'd have an awful time trying to stop yourself from going back. People shave off all their hair trying to get the ecstasy back. It strips the joy out of everything else."

"I noticed." Annor crept under her covers. A tear trickled down her cheek.

14

In the basement below the fudge party, a multitude of lightstones lit the chamber bright as day. The priests wanted the apprentices awake and focused. As Olaf, the High Priest, said at every gathering, "Concentrate on the work, or go home."

Yevleh had been assigned grinding duty, the worst job possible. Grinding hair wasn't difficult, but the finely ground hair filtered through his mask, clogged his nose, coated his mouth, and penetrated his black robe so that he itched all over.

He scraped his tongue along his teeth. Body hair tasted worse than head hair, just because he never knew where it'd come from. Laerlings or under-priests should have this job, not a journeyman. Yevleh couldn't wait to be a full priest so he'd never have to grind hair again.

Tomas had been assigned mixing duty. He gave Yevleh a sympathetic glance when he collected the ground hair for his next batch of powder. Since everyone in the basement wore ear plugs, talking was pointless. Yevleh shrugged in reply.

Tomas set the ground hair briefly on a square metal plate at his workbench before brushing it into the mixing bowl. The plate could detect the hair of an armor steward, or at least someone who'd touched the king's armor. But the armor stewards had vanished into the wilds a century ago. Even if one were in the city, he wouldn't be stupid enough to attend a fudge party.

Yevleh longed to go back to the priorities of Halvard's day, when Sons of the Prince actively sought for the armor stewards. That would serve the Prince better than checking the hair of every idiot who craved a square of fudge. But Yevleh couldn't reach Olaf's ear until he'd been ordained a full priest.

One of the priests working the music machines wiped his forehead with a black sleeve. A corridor had been glassed in along the entire perimeter of the basement. Music machines filled the corridor, manned by priest after priest. The area got stuffy quickly, and the priests played for hours, spinning the glass bowls to produce the music piped to the dance floor above all their heads.

Yevleh could hear the uncanny harmonies even through his ear plugs. His dreams were always haunted after a work shift at a fudge party. He didn't know how the priests imbued the music with power, but it clearly worked.

Yevleh finished grinding a batch of thick, brown hair, and sat back to wait for another batch to be delivered. Idly, he watched Tomas finish mixing the previous batch with an array of potent powders. When he had the proportions balanced, Tomas delivered the mixture to the journeyman in charge of topping off the powder on the stage.

The journeyman climbed onto the hoist and flipped the lever that opened the trapdoor above his head. A laerling pulled on the rope to send the journeyman up to stage height to pour the powder into the burning brazier.

Yevleh loved filling the brazier. Those quick glimpses of the fudge party were always amusing. He held his breath so he wouldn't inhale the smoke himself. The powders Tomas stirred into the concoction masked the scent of burning hair and gave a kick to the fudge effect. Patrons inhaling their own burnt hair were affected the most. But the mixture was heady stuff and Yevleh preferred to keep his mind clear.

Tomas came back to Yevleh's workbench and scooped up the brown batch of hair. When he set the hair on the square plate, the plate visibly vibrated. Tomas just stared at first. Then he jumped and covered the vibrating plate with a square piece of glass. This sealed in the ground hair and stopped the vibration. He stared at Yevleh, eyes wide.

Yevleh swallowed and shrugged with his hands up, just as astonished.

Tomas carried the covered plate to the priest in charge day-dreaming by the door. When the priest saw what Tomas carried so carefully in his trembling hands, he put his ear plugs back in and leapt to his feet. He rushed over to the laerling manning the rope and sent him off to seal the front door of the fudge party and find the general of the vaettir troops.

The priests on music duty continued to play, oblivious to the excitement in the room behind them. Everyone else stopped what they were doing and waited for the vaettir to arrive. The priest in charge took the plate of ground hair from Tomas' hands. Freed, Tomas dragged his stool over by Yevleh so they could watch the commotion together.

Tomas grinned at Yevleh when he sat down, still amazed the armor steward detector had gone off.

Yevleh grinned back. He'd always wanted to see how the vaettir worked.

The laerling must have run all the way to the Citadel. They'd only waited a few minutes when the basement door crashed open and the vaettir general strode into the room. Three vaettir crowded in behind him, awkward and glassy-eyed.

One priest on music duty saw the vaettir enter. He looked over at Yevleh and raised his eyebrows.

Yevleh pointed to the armor steward monitor.

The priest's eyes grew wide and his hands faltered on the spinning bowls of his machine.

The priest in charge waved his arms to catch the music priest's eye, then dragged the edge of his hand over his throat. "Cut the music."

The music priest lifted his hands from his machine and threaded his way along the glassed-in corridor, tapping the other priests on the shoulder and shouting in their ears. The music thinned and tapered out until a welcome silence permeated the basement.

Yevleh pulled the earplugs out of his ears and pocketed them. He'd never been down here without music endlessly playing. It changed the quality of the air and cleared the tired fog from his head.

The music priests filed out of their glass enclosure, bringing with them the smell of stale sweat. Their braids of office hung bedraggled from their sweaty scalps. They stood in a clump, smiling and wiping their foreheads with damp sleeves.

Yevleh wondered if he could escape music duty when he became a full priest. Even grinding hair would be better than being trapped in that corridor choking on the smell of sweat.

He wanted to be the priest on the stage. He'd stand there with his arms outstretched, supported by hidden threads, channeling the power of Heyl El to rewrite the minds of the patrons. He'd imagined that power so many times, coursing through his body and flowing out of his fingertips to fill the room.

Either that or command the vaettir troops. The vaettir general's braid of office hung thick and long, with a red cord running through it to mark his position.

Power. Yevleh craved it, ached for it. If he had that much power, he could change the world. He'd purify the worship of Heyl El, and have all the populace bend their knees to the Prince. He'd find the missing armor and use it to augment the power of the Hollow Altar. He'd even learn to use the power of the Ivory Gates and conquer the Puerán.

Yevleh licked his lips. That old man on Torment Island, for example. The High Priest had been torturing him for years, and still hadn't uncovered all his secrets. Yevleh wouldn't waste more time. If he had the power of the green stone in his hands, he'd use it to its full capacity.

The general took the glass-covered dish of hair and set it on the mixing table. Gently, he lifted the cover and scooped a little up with a mixing spoon. He tapped that into one of the smaller bowls and re-covered the remaining hair. Holding out the bowl, he motioned a vaettir closer.

"Inhale it," the general said.

Yevleh leaned forward to watch.

The brain vaettir held the mixing bowl up to his face, and inhaled deeply through his nose, over and over. Yevleh cringed. That was nasty. When the bowl was empty, the vaettir slid to the floor, dizzy and weak.

"Whose hair is it?" the general asked.

The brain vaettir opened his mouth several times, exposing brown, rotting teeth, but no words emerged.

The general tried again. "Is it a male or a female?"

"Female." The vaettir's voice rasped down Yevleh's spine, harsh and cold.

"All right then," said the general, nodding his head with satisfaction, "a female with brown hair. What else can you tell us?"

"I see trees and a little house."

"Where is this?"

The vaettir shook his head. "Don't know."

"Are there any other people?"

The vaettir hesitated. "Yes," he said. "Maybe." He shrugged.

"How tall is the female?"

The vaettir struggled to his feet and held his hand under his chin. "This tall."

"What color are her eyes?"

"Green. Like trees."

The general mumbled to himself, pacing. "Trees. And a little house. So, not from Asseldam. Though," he tugged on his braid of office, "maybe she moved to the city after she'd grown that bit of hair." He turned back to the brain vaettir. "How long since that hair grew?"

"Uh." The vaettir drooled while he thought. "Four years."

Yevleh's jaw dropped. Who went four years without cutting their hair? Definitely not someone from Asseldam.

The general cursed. "Prince below," he said. "Four years ago this female lived in a little house near some trees. After so much time, that could be anywhere in the world. At least we have her description, and if she still has four years of hair she should be easy to find. If she's not sealed in upstairs, we'll put up notices, offer a reward, and see what happens."

15

Annor sat on her bed in her shirt and underwear, stitching a rip in her pants. "Leather is more durable," she said. "It wouldn't have torn like this."

Gunilla stretched under her bed covers and smiled. "Yes, but would you rather be sweating in your leather clothes up a chimney?"

Annor chuckled. "No. Some days I want to chop my hair off just so I can stop wearing that sweaty cap."

A jumble of footsteps tramped down the hallway outside their room, and someone pounded on their door. They both jumped.

Gunilla called, "Just a minute!"

She hopped out of bed and smoothed her covers while Annor yanked her pants on and shoved her dirty cap back on her head. Just as Gunilla reached for the handle the door burst open, smacking her on the brow bone.

Two men stood there, filling the door frame.

"Vaettir," Gunilla said, her voice bleak. She stepped aside.

Annor glared at the men. "What do you want?"

The vaettir stepped back to reveal the priest smirking behind them. "Good evening," he said. His black robe strained to cover his large belly, and his braid of office was short and narrow. He strolled into the room. "Which one of you ladies is Nil?"

Gunilla raised her hand halfway.

"Well, Nil, as soon as I report to the High Priest, a messenger will be sent to the fudge farm and your brother will be on his way back to Asseldam. Here's this in the meantime." He handed Gunilla a fat, jingling bag.

Annor frowned. Before she could ask Gunilla what was going on, the priest stepped back and one of the vaettir grabbed Annor by the arm and pulled her into the hallway. The second vaettir grabbed her other arm.

The priest tore off Annor's cap and tugged her braid out of the back of her shirt. He smiled. "Thank you for your assistance, Nil."

Gunilla looked stricken, a welt above one eye and the bag of coins in her hands. "I'm sorry," she whispered.

The vaettir dragged Annor down the hallway while her mind whirled. Gunilla didn't know she was steward of the king's gauntlets, and Annor had never mentioned the Guardian. What had Gunilla told the Sons?

Annor could try to escape. The vaettir were slow and awkward. They'd be easy to ditch. She glanced back at the Son. He smiled, his eyes crinkling, and feinted with a throwing knife. She bit her lip.

Their little procession marched down the rickety stairs and through the apartment doorway. The guard outside chuckled when he saw her in the vaettir's grip.

They filed through the alley and into the empty square. The vagrants had fled. A few people wandered the dark streets, but they ducked into doorways when the vaettir appeared with her in tow.

Annor had never seen the streets so empty. Even the night district was silent. She and her escort came to the bridge and clomped across. The leat stunk as much as ever, but Annor hardly noticed. When they turned onto the Ceremonial Road, her heart sank into her stomach. The Black Citadel loomed in front of them, blacker than the night.

Annor choked down a sob. Of course a brother mattered more than a friend. She tried to be happy for Gunilla, but she couldn't. Annor felt sick just thinking about it, like she'd lost her parents all over again. She stumbled.

The Ceremonial Road ended at a flight of steps. They'd arrived. Annor's heart pounded in her chest and fear dried her mouth. She counted sixteen steps, and then they were at the doors. The solitary guard snapped to attention and motioned for them to pass.

Menace radiated through the entrance hall and beat against her. Annor staggered. Clumps of black-robed Sons turned away from their conversations.

One called out, "Is that the one the High Priest seeks?"

The portly priest pulled Annor's braid above her head, and chuckled. "What do you think?"

"Prince below! Good catch, Filip."

Sons of Darkness filled the hallways. They dodged out of the way of Annor and the vaettir, but clapped Filip on the back, congratulating him over and over. The vaettir plodded on.

The corridors throbbed with the power of Heyl El. But the seven Puerán had been more powerful than the Sons of Darkness. Hadn't they? Malice clamped onto Annor's aching temples and squeezed.

Her knife was strapped to her leg, under her pants. Did Filip still have a knife aimed at her back? Her spine tingled.

They paraded down hallway after hallway, randomly turning corners until they reached the stairs to the basement. The steps had been polished by the passage of many feet. Annor slipped on the way down, but the vaettir held her up by her arms.

The basement was dim, the lightstones weak. She gagged on the stench. The vaettir tromped past cell after cell, dragging her along between them. Filthy prisoners huddled on cots or slumped on the floor near piles of excrement, oblivious or uncaring.

Filip led her to an empty cell, swinging the door wide and stepping out of the way while she and the vaettir shuffled inside. A cot with a thin, shredded blanket hugged the left-hand wall, while a wooden armchair stood centered in the remaining space. Annor shuddered.

The vaettir sat her in the chair and stood impassively while Filip busied himself with a rope, grunting and squatting to tie her wrists and ankles to the chair. A loop around her waist pressed Annor against the back.

One vaettir had a trail of saliva dripping unnoticed onto his shirt, and both had gray skin. Their eyes were glassy, without pupils. Their expressions never changed. They exuded death, like her first deer lying glassy eyed at her feet. Her father had been proud, but Annor had felt almost as sick then as she did now.

The vaettir left as soon as Filip finished tying her up. A second Son entered her cell, a younger one, with his black robe hanging loosely from his shoulders. His braid of office marked him as a journeyman. Annor dredged up a memory of her first day as a sweep in the glass factory. This was the one Gunilla had warned her about. Yevleh.

Yevleh produced a pair of scissors and held up Annor's braid. "That brain vaettir had the right of it. Four years growth, at least. Should I take all of it?" he asked.

"Every last bit." Filip tugged on his narrow braid hanging limply from his balding scalp.

Annor closed her eyes while Yevleh snipped away her braid. Then he made shingled cuts up the back of her head. She gritted her teeth against the tears as he yanked her head this way and that. She could regrow the hair. He hadn't snipped off a finger or anything.

Still, her past life lay severed and vulnerable on the floor. Her life on the island, her time with her parents, chopped off and discarded. Now she was Nor of Asseldam.

It didn't have to be that way. She'd get away from this dirty city and regrow her hair. Get her life back.

When Yevleh had finished, he gathered up the hair and left, scissors glinting. Annor's head felt light, and cooler. Unprotected. She wished she could put her cap back on.

16

Filip left right after Yevleh did, locking Annor's cell. She sat shorn and alone. How long did they plan to keep her tied up? She'd had a long day sweeping chimneys, and she wanted to curl up on that cot and sleep away the horror of her day. Time trickled past. Her ear itched but she couldn't scratch it. Her head drooped and she slipped off into slumber.

As if that had been a signal, a crowd of Sons tramped down the corridor, jerking her awake. Filip unlocked her cell and they filed inside, one by one. There were nine priests, all hooded, plus Filip, who pulled up his own hood once he'd relocked the cell. They gathered around her, encircling her with black robes, like that night on her island with the ring of white faces.

But this was no apparition. This was her reality, and even if she could raise her right hand and inscribe a sacred spiral in the air, it wouldn't banish them. Annor swallowed down bile. At least the nasty one with the bulbous nose wasn't here. Since the Guardian had sent her forward in time, he must be long dead. The Guardian. What an idiot she'd been, asking him to send her to Asseldam.

Filip pulled an enormous lightstone out of the pocket of his robe. He needed both hands to affix it to the low ceiling. It shone like the sun just in front of where she sat bound in the chair. The Sons adjusted their hoods to shield their eyes while Annor sat bare-headed in a blaze of light, blinded. She blinked repeatedly and tears sprang to her eyes.

The Son directly in front of her was the High Priest, no less. Annor glimpsed his gold-laced braid of office centered on top of his head before he adjusted his hood to shield his eyes. A leather strap bound a green amulet to his forehead, and he wore a necklace of finger bones. A twig hung from the center like a talisman.

"Now then," the High Priest said, "open your hand."

He held a triangular, blood-red stone above her left hand, but Annor clenched her fist. "Why have you brought me here?" she asked.

Smiling, the High Priest stamped hard on her foot with his big boot. Annor yelped. Her whole body jerked and her hand opened. He grabbed her hand and set the stone in her palm, wrapping her unwilling fingers over it. Another priest swathed her entire left hand in fine cord, around and around, tight enough to dig into her flesh, leaving white bloodless skin patches between the lines of cord. A corner of the stone dug into her palm, and soon her hand turned numb. Apprehension chilled her spine.

The High Priest turned to Filip and held out his hand. "How strong did you make the fudge?"

Filip fumbled in his pocket and brought out a wrapped square. "The strongest grade possible, Olaf."

"Good."

When the High Priest unwrapped the square and held it out to her, the rich scent tickled Annor's nose and her mouth watered. Her mind darted to the heavenly taste of the chocolate the Guardian had given her. But this wasn't chocolate. Annor clenched her teeth together. She hadn't eaten any at the fudge party, and she wouldn't eat it now either.

Olaf chuckled. "Not hungry? Too bad. Maybe I can whet your appetite. You can do without one of your fingers, can't you?" He handed the square of fudge to the Son on his right and drew a knife out of his sleeve.

When he picked up her right hand she clenched it into a fist, wishing she could drive it into his stomach.

"Such a little fireball. Do you think that'll stop me?" He dug the tip of the knife into Annor's wrist until a spot of blood appeared.

It stung, but Annor had endured worse.

Olaf frowned. "Would you rather lose your whole hand? Come

now, I'm sure you can spare one finger."

He dug the knife in deeper so that the blood ran on the blade and Annor flinched in spite of herself. Choking back a cry, she opened her hand.

The priest deftly grabbed her fourth finger before she could close her fist again. "This finger doesn't do much for you." He held the knife at the base of her finger and sliced it just enough to start it bleeding, too.

Annor trembled, though she tried not to.

"So what will it be? Open your mouth? Or lose your fingers one by one." Olaf's hooded eyes shone with anticipation.

Annor opened her mouth.

"Good girl."

The other priest crammed the entire piece of fudge in Annor's mouth before she could change her mind, then tied her mouth shut with a band of cloth under her chin and around the top of her head.

Olaf grinned. "Wouldn't want you spitting it out."

The Sons stared at her, avid and intent, waiting for her to swallow. Annor almost didn't want to spit it out. It tasted so good. Better than the chocolate. Better than anything she could have imagined. It sat there melting on her tongue like a piece of angelic nectar.

Annor, tied to the chair, left hand numb, right hand bleeding, foot aching, mouth bound tightly shut, glared up at the circle of black robes. But inside she reveled in the taste, the glorious taste. If her mouth hadn't been stuffed so full, she would have groaned from the pleasure of it.

She swallowed. The Sons waited patiently while the fudge melted a little more, and she swallowed again. Her head spun and she breathed rapidly through her nose, spiraling out of control. She chewed and chewed and savored and swallowed. Her saliva came thick and fast so that she almost couldn't swallow it quickly enough, until her mouth was empty and she licked her teeth, searching for one last taste of it. Just a little more. She smiled hopefully at Olaf. Maybe one small piece?

He laughed. "Blindfold her," he said to the Son on his left.

This priest tugged the cloth away from her jaw and wrapped it around her eyes instead.

"Tell us about the armor," Olaf said.

They knew she was steward of the king's gauntlets, even though the Guardian had said they wouldn't be able to find her. Annor chuckled, remembering hiding from her parents as a small child, then popping up from behind her bed when they got close. "Found me!" she squealed.

"The armor," the High Priest repeated, less patient. "What piece have you touched?"

"Armor?" Annor's mind flicked to her father opening the chest and showing her the king's white gauntlets. The chest spun at their feet. No, Annor and her father were spinning in a circle around the chest. Her father held the gauntlets high above Annor's head and they shone like a star, with a piercing white light that blinded her even under the blindfold. She shook her head. "Too bright. Can't see."

Olaf sounded irritated now. "What piece did you touch? Filthy little slut."

Filthy, yes. Annor was on a sweep job, climbing up an endless chimney, dragging her brush, soot swirling in the air in front of her. She inhaled it and coughed. Olaf slapped her hard so that her head smacked back against the top of the chair and the light shining through the blindfold glowed red.

"The armor. Tell us about the armor."

Annor shook her head. "No, too bright."

The High Priest growled.

Filip said, "Let me try, Olaf."

"So be it."

Footsteps shuffled around her and the world began spinning again. A beautiful day on her island spun past, green trees growing straight and tall, reaching for the blue of the sky. Her island! She missed it so much. She noticed the stone altar where she knelt, then gazed up at the shimmering Guardian. "So bright."

"Nor," Filip said, "where is the armor now?"

Did she give the gauntlets to the Guardian? She'd wanted to. The Guardian shook his head. That's right, Annor had tried to give him the gauntlets, but he didn't want them. She'd left them in the chest on her beautiful, green island instead. "So green."

"This is ridiculous," the High Priest said. "Did you make the fudge too strong, Filip?"

Fudge. Yummy, yummy fudge. Annor licked her lips. So much better than plain chocolate. "More, please."

"I measured it carefully, Olaf. She's unusually susceptible. Maybe she didn't eat enough at the fudge party to build up a threshold."

"Well, I have more productive things to do than this. Keep at it and give me a report in the morning."

"Of course," Filip said.

Walking feet. Clanging door. Silence. Annor sat in a white bubble under the blindfold, alone and free.

Filip grabbed what was left of her hair and yanked upwards. "Now it's just you and me, Nor. Isn't that nice? A private party."

Party. Why did it hurt to cut off a few fingerwidths of hair? But what a great fudge party. Her bubble was red, not white. The smoke swirled around Annor's head and the music filled her mind. She danced in circles around the stone her father had carved. It stretched above her. Tall, so tall. A mountain, not a stone, crowned by blue sky. And there was the mountain path. She just needed to climb out of reach of the smoke and music and she'd be free.

Someone spoke. A man very far away. She listened hard, but she couldn't hear him above the wind whistling past her bare head. The wind felt so good, blowing her clean as she hiked. Annor turned to Bald Erik hiking beside her on the arrow-straight path, and laughed. "Look, I'm clean!"

Erik had gotten off his island. That couldn't be right. Was this real? Annor stopped and looked around. She stood alone on the smooth, stone path, wind blowing her shorn hair into a chaotic halo. She wore her leathers, and happily fingered one sleeve. She'd missed them. Her nails were black crescents of soot, but otherwise her hands were clean. Her knife was securely strapped to her leg.

The sound of rushing water reminded her of her thirst. Annor continued up the path, reveling in the deep blue sky, the sun shining clearly with no haze tainting the air. She breathed in deeply, savoring the freshness of it. She was getting closer to the water, and a breeze blew cool and damp across her forehead. She crested a hill and saw a waterfall pouring down a cliff face into a deep, round pool. Her stone path dead-ended at its edge.

Annor fell to her knees. The sparkling water smelled so refreshing she felt light-headed. Her lips parted, anticipating the taste of the pure water.

The blindfold was ripped away. She stared into Filip's angry eyes. Annor licked her lips.

"Where's the armor?" Filip screamed. Spittle flew from his lips and spattered Annor's cheek.

As if she would tell him. "What armor?" she asked. Annor blinked, trying to dispel the haze that surrounded Filip's face. He stepped back and she realized his whole body had a hazy shell. So did the cot and the bars of her cell. When Filip moved, a trail of hazy light followed, mimicking his motions. She blinked again. His black robe had faded to a dirty brown. Or maybe it was black. Now she wasn't sure. She shook her head to clear it.

Filip lifted his hand to slap her. Annor watched his hand come nearer and nearer, trailing a mimicking line of haze. The blow rocked her head to the side and she cut her lip on a tooth. She licked the trickle of blood.

"Having fun yet?" Filip's gray eyes gleamed bloodshot and strained in the harsh glare of the lightstone above them. A tic under his left eye caught Annor's attention. She watched it throb, fascinated. Time ebbed and flowed around her.

Annor looked down at her left hand where the edges of the red stone peeked out between the encircling cord. Her hand was purple now. She'd never seen a purple hand before. It looked pretty next to the red stone. Another slap rocked her head back against the top of the chair so that she faced Filip. His face was purple, just like her hand. And there was the tic again. She watched it beat in time with his voice.

Minutes flew by. Hours maybe. Was it morning yet? Gunilla would miss her help sweeping chimneys today. But maybe Gunilla didn't need to sweep chimneys any more. Filip had given her a lot of money. Money, money, money. A funny word. She let the sound of it drown out Filip's angry voice.

An eternity later, Filip's voice changed to chagrin, piercing through the haze in her mind. "Did you even know you touched a piece of armor?" Filip asked.

Did she know? Her parents had been outside when Annor rummaged through the chest, looking at their treasures. She hadn't known what the strange white gloves were. Her father hadn't shown them to her yet. She shook her head. "No, I didn't know. I'm sorry." She shouldn't have looked in the chest without permission.

Filip sighed and started untying the ropes that bound Annor to the chair. He untied her arms, her legs, and the last rope around her chest. Then he slid his knife under the cords around her hand, slicing through them and prying the red stone out of her dead grasp. "Go to sleep," he said as he exited her cell, clanging the door shut behind him.

17

The cot, so far away. Annor willed her limbs to move, but she still sat slumped in the chair. She wiggled the bloody fingers on her right hand until she could lift her arm. She tugged on her pant legs, trying to shift her feet. She bit back a cry when she lifted her purple left hand with her bloody right, then stumbled the few steps to the cot. She fell on top of it.

She lay in a stupor a long time, her head foggy, but slowly clearing. The taste of fudge lingered in her mouth, delicious and horrible. Annor hugged her left hand to her body. Her head throbbed from the pummeling, and her foot smarted from when the High Priest tromped on it, but nothing had ever hurt as badly as her hand.

Gunilla would get her brother back. She wouldn't be alone any more. Annor wondered what it would have been like if her own baby brother had lived, even though her mother died birthing him. If he'd lived, Annor wouldn't be alone now, either. She wiped a tear from her eye.

Her mind skated away from the building heavy above her. She thought about the Guardian. "Stupid," she whispered to herself. She should have taken the path her father carved into the standing stone, not asked the Guardian to send her to Asseldam. She'd chosen the easy way, or at least it'd seemed easy at the time. Lying alone in her cell, it didn't seem so easy any more.

Annor pulled the shredded blanket around herself and gave into exhaustion, letting herself drift off into sleep where she wouldn't have to think or regret. She slept deeply until the dream began.

On a riverbank, a city spread before her. The cliff face in the distance and the river at her back marked it as Asseldam, but not the Asseldam she knew. The leat flowed blue and clear instead of scummy and black. The city smelled cleaner, too.

The buildings were different, and the people. Annor couldn't quite identify what had changed. This wasn't her parents' Betavar. The Black Citadel loomed ahead of her, though plain cobblestones had replaced the Ceremonial Road.

She walked through the city in her dream, the streets familiar, yet strange, until she stood before the entrance to the Citadel. The doors stood wide, and no guard kept watch. Annor hesitated. People passed her on the street, oblivious. One man rushed by her and up the stairs.

Annor followed him inside the Citadel. She climbed up stairs, plodded down hallways, and climbed down other stairs. She didn't see a single black robe, just men and women going happily about their business.

She let her feet take her where they willed until she found herself in front of her cell in the basement. And yet, it had an open doorway, not bars. Annor entered the room, half expecting to see herself lying asleep. But a young man sat at a desk, writing. The same young man she'd seen in her other dream, back on her island. The one who'd been hiking the mountain path.

Annor stepped to his side, gazing at his profile while he wrote on, absorbed in his task. He was older than before, but not much. His frame had filled out, and he might have been taller than she remembered.

The paper he labored over began, "Dear Father."

No matter how tempting, she wouldn't read his private correspondence. Annor scanned the room instead. A small table stood along the back wall, opposite the door, and a large bookcase, crammed full of books, filled the wall to the right.

The young man signed his name with a flourish and leaned back in his chair, running ink-stained hands through his thick, honey-colored hair. Annor leaned forward and read his name. Thaeri. She tried it out silently on her tongue a few times, and then said it aloud, "Thaeri."

The young man looked up, startled, and swiftly covered his letter. "Who are you? I didn't hear you come in."

She blushed. "Annor. My name is Annor."

"Wait." Thaeri rose to his feet, his blue eyes shining. "You're the girl I saw on the path up Mount Nevo, but then you vanished. You look different though," he said, eyeing her cropped hair and soot-streaked clothes. "I asked the Puerán, when I came to their city, but they had no knowledge of you."

"I'm surprised you recognize me," Annor said, folding her arms to hide her chimney-sweep clothes. "So, this isn't a dream? You're real?"

Thaeri cocked his head to one side. "If you think you're dreaming, then anything I say could be part of your dream. But yes, I'm real."

He smiled, an infectious, friendly smile. "Pardon my saying so, but you look a little worse for wear. Can I get you something to drink? Would you like to sit?" He gestured toward his chair.

The taste of fudge still lingered in Annor's mouth. "A drink would be nice."

"Of course." Thaeri hurried to the table and poured her a glass of water from a pitcher.

He handed her the glass. Their fingers touched and their eyes met. A thrilling shock rushed through Annor, a feeling so divine, she couldn't quite catch her breath. It erased the false ecstasy from the fudge.

And then she found herself sitting bolt upright on her cot. Thaeri had vanished. But Annor still held the glass of water.

18

Yevleh knelt on the hard floor between his narrow bed and his cluttered desk. Fists raised high and wide to embrace the magnificence of Heyl El, he prayed to the Prince. His room faded from his sight as he poured out his heart.

"Help me endure the months until I'm a full priest with a say in thy worship. Help me bite back the angry words and be patient with the incompetence of thy leaders. Help me rise above the lesser journeymen to the status I deserve. Hear me, oh Prince of this world. Let my words travel from my mouth to thy glorious ear."

Yevleh bowed low and pounded his fists on the floor. Before he could rise from his devotions and get off his aching knees, a rich, cultured voice addressed him, stunning him into immobility.

"My glorious ear has heard your petition, child of my heart. Rise, proud one, and greet your master."

"I accept your obeisance. Rise now, and sit. I wish to instruct you."

"My Prince," Yevleh said scrambling to his feet, "my life is yours, heart and soul."

Heyl El settled himself on top of Yevleh's desk, and rested his boots on Yevleh's chair. The Prince adjusted his cuffs and sat as graciously as if Yevleh's chambers were the throne room in his temple. Books poked through Heyl El's intangible body.

Yevleh sank onto the edge of his bed. His eyes darted to where his black robe hung on the back of his door. He felt ridiculous in his underclothes. "How may I serve thee, my Prince?" he said. "Command me that I might obey."

Heyl El stroked his beard, the rings on his fingers glinting with jewels. "My High Priest Olaf drifts off course. His fears outweigh his imagination, and I'm tired of his failures."

Heyl El leaned forward, his gaze drilling into Yevleh's eyes. "You, on the other hand, have enormous potential and vast ingenuity. Your abilities transcend those of ordinary, lesser men. I am promoting you that you may be of more use to me." He looked Yevleh up and down approvingly, his eyes lingering on Yevleh's bare torso. "Yes, an injection of your youthful enthusiasm is just what my priesthood needs. But it would be wasteful if you languished as the newest priest in my temple. My child, I claim you as my new High Priest."

Heyl El rose and approached Yevleh.

"Forgive my pride, glorious Prince," Yevleh whispered. "But I thought you said High Priest."

"I celebrate your pride, young one," Heyl El said. "You will be my one true acolyte." He reached out and stroked the top of Yevleh's head.

The Prince's touch felt like the icy wind of mid-winter, blowing through Yevleh's hair and rustling his thoughts. The sweet scent of toffee enveloped him.

"Yes, that looks much better," Heyl El said.

The wind traveled down Yevleh's back, raising goose bumps on his flesh, and up his chest as Heyl El's index finger traced a line from Yevleh's navel to his chin.

"Mortals are so delightful." Heyl El stepped back and spread his hands. "Behold, my new High Priest."

Yevleh touched his head. His braid of office had shifted to the center of his scalp. His fingers traveled the length of it, four handwidths beyond the base of his scalp. He stroked the end of his braid where dark brown hairs mingled with those of purest gold. Eyes wide, he gazed up at the Prince.

"Of course, no one else will be able to see it until you've earned it. To help you, I have one more gift." Heyl El flourished his empty hand and placed a wizened fruit on Yevleh's desk.

The fruit was a dark, purplish-black, round and wrinkled. It nestled on top of Yevleh's scattered papers like a jewel. "That's…" Yevleh's voice caught in his throat. "That's fruit from the Knowing Tree."

"Indeed. Olaf hoards a basket of them next to my throne and never thinks to put one to use. He thinks he must save them for some future need." Heyl El flicked an invisible speck from his sleeve. "What future? Today is all there is, for tomorrow he might be dead." Heyl El smiled, his blood-red lips parting to reveal large, white teeth. His tongue flicked out like a serpent's, tasting the air. "Yes, even now, he might be gasping his last, stale breath. Eat, my son, and open your mind to greater thoughts."

Yevleh hesitated. "Eat the fruit?"

Heyl El studied him from under his dark brows. "Are you afraid?"

"No," Yevleh said, swallowing and sitting tall.

"I'm giving you my kingdom, and the world. Just eat the fruit."

Yevleh picked up the piece of fruit, its weight heavy in his hand. Solid. He took a bite, a nibble, and the enticing taste filled his mouth. Sweet, achingly sweet. He took another bite, and then another.

Heyl El watched closely, his eyes greedy and his lips parted. "Yes. Yes, now you will gain the knowledge to rise high in my service."

Yevleh swallowed the last morsel, shuddering. The bitter aftertaste brought tears to his eyes. He wiped them away with a shaking hand. "Master, I want nothing more than to serve you all my days."

"Go talk to the girl who touched the armor." Heyl El licked his lips. "She'll find you irresistible. After that you must restore the Ivory Gates. Your reign will be a triumphant time for my kingdom." Heyl El stepped back and vanished in a clap of thunder.

Yevleh flinched. His lightstone flickered and went out.

Tentatively, he reached up and stroked his new braid of office. High Priest. He smiled. Rumor said the girl hadn't talked, but she'd talk to him. Yevleh would find her piece of armor, and all the rest of the armor, as well. He'd make the Hollow Altar and the Ivory Gates so powerful, no one would deny him the role of High Priest. He'd be a worthy servant to his god. And powerful, so very powerful.

Yevleh sat in the darkness long into the night, stroking the end of his braid. Thinking. Plotting.

19

Annor huddled on her cot. The shredded rags of blanket couldn't ward off the chill of the Citadel basement, but her shivering had a rhythm to it that kept her thoughts from spinning. Sometimes, though, a shudder would rock her whole frame and throw off the rhythm.

She shuddered when her mind flicked to Filip's face and the long night of torture. Annor tried to keep her thoughts away. But then her left hand would throb and she'd be back in the chair, looking up into Filip's angry eyes, his face livid as he towered over her.

The glass of water had been a gift from Abba El as much as from Thaeri. It had washed the taste of fudge into memory. But she'd been left with a clarity of all the things her eyes had witnessed that night, the horrid along with the good.

She'd seen Thaeri again. Touched him, learned his name. She turned his face around in her thoughts in time with her shivering. He was real, and kind, and yes, pleasing to the eye. Annor smiled.

Her first dream of Thaeri had come before she'd seen any other young men, and after a time she'd dismissed him as just an odd dream. But now she knew Thaeri was real.

He had a full head of hair that hadn't been cropped to buy fudge. He'd been confident and at ease like her father had been. He'd be comfortable leading men, but he didn't crave their adulation. His eyes had radiated kindness and concern. And he'd remembered Annor. He'd even asked the Puerán on the mountain, Mount Nevo he'd called it, about her. If she ever escaped the Sons, she could join the Puerán on their mountain.

But Thaeri didn't live in this time. He'd been working at his desk in the Citadel with nary a sign of the Sons of Darkness. He was out of Annor's reach, except in dreams.

She rubbed her fingers, remembering when Thaeri handed her the water. The thrill of that contact had trembled through her, body and soul. Somehow Annor had been in Thaeri's time, and she had the water glass to prove it. She replayed the sensation over and over, when their fingers had brushed. It took her mind off her aches.

But except for her dreams, Annor was stuck in the days of the Sons. Stuck because she'd turned her back on the path her father carved into the standing stone. She'd asked the Guardian to send her to Heyl El's stronghold. Too bad she hadn't known then about the Puerán on their mountain.

The Guardian had offered her a choice, and Annor had walked away from whatever she might have learned on the hard path to end up in a cell in the Citadel. Maybe she would have learned how to find Thaeri. Bald Erik had said she could begin again. Maybe she could go back to the path her father carved.

Annor gathered strength, and rolled off the cot and onto her knees beside it. Her prayers had been infrequent of late. She'd been so tired at the end of a day sweeping chimneys. No, that was an excuse. She'd gotten lazy in her devotions. She'd let the city distract her from what was important.

The lightstones in the corridor shone dimly through the bars. Annor stroked the empty glass, then let her eyes fall shut. Aching and shivering, Annor poured her heart out to Abba El.

"I'm sorry, so sorry," she whispered through her chattering teeth. "I know when I chose Asseldam, I chose this, too. Please forgive me. Thank you for letting me make a choice, though, and for the people I've met. Thank you for letting me be with people." A tear trickled down her cheek and landed warm and wet on her sore left hand.

"Annor, is that you?"

Annor heard the whisper, or thought she did, but maybe it wasn't real. She turned her head and saw someone peering through the bars of her cell. Her vision still wasn't quite right. Hazy streaks framed the person all around the edges.

"It's Gunilla. Are you…are you all right? I mean, I'm so sorry." She choked back a sob. "I didn't know why they wanted you, but I didn't know how else to get my brother back. Every day I wondered if he even lived."

"How did you get in here?" Annor tried to stand, but her knees had locked while she knelt on the hard floor.

"I brought an answer from Sven to the High Priest's message. It's time to clean the Citadel chimneys again." Gunilla crouched and tinkered with the lock on the cell, metal scraping on metal.

Annor slid off her knees and onto her bottom, then straightened her legs. She hadn't forgiven Gunilla yet, but her brother had been a prisoner of the Sons longer than Annor had.

"I truly am sorry," Gunilla said, her voice low. "Please, I want to help you."

Annor blinked, trying again to dispel the haziness of Gunilla's outline.

"Do you still have your knife, or did they search you?"

Annor dropped the glass into her lap and rested her bloody hand on her right leg. "Still here." Filip must have been too busy knocking her around to search her.

There was a metallic click, and then the door to her cell swung open.

"My brother taught me that trick when he wanted me to steal to feed his fudge addiction." Gunilla stepped into the cell and pulled Annor's arm around her neck. "Let's get you out of here."

"But." Annor swallowed down nausea while Gunilla got her up on her feet and half dragged her into the hallway. "I can't just walk out the front door."

"This way," Gunilla said, guiding Annor away from the stairs. "Why are you holding a glass?"

Annor clutched it tighter. "It's mine."

"Well, you won't need it where we're going." Gunilla wrenched it out of Annor's grip and tossed it back into the cell where it rolled into a corner.

"Hey." She tried to turn back, but Gunilla dragged her further down the hallway.

"Are you all right?"

"I have no idea. Maybe?"

Gunilla chuckled softly. "I've missed you." She reached around to hold Annor up by her waist. "We need to walk faster."

They passed cell after cell, some occupied, some not. A few inmates were too far gone to notice them, but others pressed up against the bars, filthy and battered. "Please, let me out," a man called. "Help me," an old woman cried, wearing nothing but bloody rags. Annor's heart went out to them.

"Later," Gunilla said. "Be quiet and I'll help you later."

Annor raised one shaky hand to her head and discovered several tender bumps. Filip had smacked her more times than she could count.

Gunilla steered Annor down another gloomy corridor. Their shadows stretched long and thin in front of them before blending into the darkness ahead. "This should be it," Gunilla said. She leaned Annor against the left wall and ran her hands along the right.

"What are you doing?"

"Have a little patience." Gunilla tugged at the wall and a small metal door swung open with a shriek of hinges. "The Sons don't heat the prison block, so I think they've forgotten about this access hatch. In you go."

"You want me to climb a chimney? I can barely stand."

"Your muscles will loosen up once you get going. Come on. Get in there or you're fired."

Annor chuckled. "Fine, I'll go. But just so you know, after this I quit."

They climbed into the shaft and up the jutting bricks. Gunilla steadied Annor when her left hand refused to obey. They climbed up one floor level to a horizontal vent. Gunilla helped Annor into it. The vent was too constricted for her to crawl. Annor tried to wriggle along under her own power, but Gunilla pushed on Annor's feet to speed up their progress. They didn't dare talk.

It was pitch dark inside the vent system. Annor almost fell down the next shaft. Luckily Gunilla caught her by the ankle while she hung upside down with just her legs still in the vent. The blood rushed to her sore head, and Annor choked back a giggle. It came out as a snort.

"Don't fall apart on me now," Gunilla whispered.

She tugged Annor back into the vent just enough for her to grab hold of one of the shaft's projecting bricks and swing herself out into the vertical space.

"Down," Gunilla whispered, her face close to Annor's.

"Down?" Annor breathed. "I thought we were trying to get out of here."

"I'll leave by the front door, but you're going to have to swim for it."

"Swim?" The river was nowhere near the Citadel.

"Don't play dumb. You've come back to the apartment dripping once or twice, so you must know how. Now, down you go."

Annor made it down the chimney shaft without falling, though her left hand cramped and throbbed. Gunilla waited above her while she eased open the hatch and peeked out. It opened into darkness, and soon the two of them stood in another corridor.

Annor took a cautious sniff. "Mildew?"

"Among other things."

"You know, this would be a good time for you to whip a lightstone out of your pocket," Annor said. "It's not like you can't afford a few extra stones now."

"Heh, yeah. Well, I haven't had time to go shopping yet. Too busy rescuing people."

They started off down the dark corridor. Gunilla went first, feeling her way along the wall. Annor held onto her waistband. Before long, murmuring water reached their ears, like a stream over rocks.

"We've arrived," Gunilla said softly, her voice echoing in the vast space around them. "There aren't any lightstones, so the Sons probably don't come here much."

"This is the leat," Annor said, understanding at last.

"The leat, and the Sons' sewage system. Swim upstream if you don't want to bathe in their waste."

"It's as simple as that?"

"Not exactly," Gunilla said. "You'll need your knife to cut through the net tied across the entrance."

"Underwater?"

"Yes, my brother found it when he tried to sneak into the Citadel once. Not one of his brighter plans. Once you've cut through the net, you'll have to swim out from under the building, still underwater. Hold your breath and you'll be fine."

"What about you, Gunilla? Won't the Sons notice I vanished just when you happened to be in the Citadel on an errand?"

"Don't worry about me. I have a few ideas." Gunilla gave Annor a fierce hug. "Just get out of here and go some place the Sons can't find you." She patted Annor's arm in the darkness. "Gotta go."

"Wait. Come with me. You can't be a sweep much longer anyway."

"But my brother will be back soon, and he needs me. Take care of yourself, Annor."

Annor swallowed. "I'll try."

20

Gunilla's footsteps faded back down the corridor. Annor dropped to her knees and crawled forward, hands running along the floor in front of her, until she came to the edge where floor met rushing water.

"All right then," she whispered to herself. "Let's see what's upstream."

Annor crept along the edge of the leat, trailing her left hand just along the drop off. Gunilla had been right about the glass. Still, she regretted losing her proof that Thaeri was real. But maybe the Sons gave her the water and she imagined the rest. Thaeri might have been a hallucination like the others the fudge gave her. She shook her head, not wanting to believe it.

Annor's aches had faded to the back of her mind while Gunilla dragged her through the Citadel, but now everything hurt worse than ever. She dipped her left hand into the leat when it stung more than she could bear. The cold water helped a little.

Annor bumped into several pipes during her crawl through the dark. She scrambled over them and kept going.

By the sound of the rushing water, she had a hard swim ahead of her. The narrower the channel, the less chance she had of fighting the current.

Annor ran into a wall and relief washed over her. She'd begun to wonder if escaping her cell had been a hallucination, too. She leaned against the wall, her aching legs stretched out before her.

"This is real," she told herself, rubbing her sore knees. "This is real."

Annor pulled her knife out from under her pants, and strapped it back on the outside. She should have asked Gunilla the time of day. A dark city would give her a better chance to escape.

No point in delaying any longer. The Sons might place a guard on the leat as soon as they discovered her missing. Annor bowed her head and sent a plea to Abba El. "Please, help me. Help me be strong enough. Let it be dark enough. I know I've fallen short in so many ways. Forgive my past mistakes, Father. I'll try to do better."

She closed her prayer and slid into the chill of the rushing water. Holding onto the edge of the leat, she took one last gulp of air and plunged beneath the surface, kicking frantically while she reached for the net Gunilla had promised would be there.

Her fingers found it, and Annor grabbed and held on. She slipped her knife out of its sheath and sawed at the rope with her free hand. It frayed quickly under her blade. Annor blessed her father for teaching her to always keep it sharp.

She'd made a large opening in the net by the time her air supply gave out. Gasping and coughing, Annor hung onto the edge of the leat and breathed in glorious lungfuls of air. She secured her knife in its sheath and rested her forehead against the edge. The current tugged at her, powerful and compelling, trying to drag her downstream. She still felt weak and shaky, and she didn't know how thick the Citadel wall was. If her strength and energy weren't enough to fight the current and escape, she'd be trapped under the building and drown.

Gunilla might have gotten it wrong. Her brother was a hyped-up fudge addict. There might be another net blocking her way on the outside of the building.

One final breath, and Annor plunged back beneath the water. She found the net and felt along it for the opening she'd slashed with her knife. There.

She wriggled through the net, careful not to snag her knife on the ropes. A mass of sticks and leaves were caught against the back of the net. She pushed them aside and kicked off against the net behind her. Annor swam with all her strength against the battering current. She was hungry, hurt, and exhausted, but fear lent her vigor. Before her breath ran out, she swam out from under the Citadel and into a star-studded night.

Annor forced herself to breathe small, quiet breaths. She thanked Abba El for the darkness. Huddling in the scraggly reeds on the embankment, she grinned like an idiot. She'd made it.

Gunilla had said to get out of the Sons' reach, but how? Annor wanted more than anything to make it back to her island and take another look at her father's standing stone. But that couldn't happen without the Guardian's help. And she'd been so stupid, he might not want to help her.

The desecrated temple on Bald Erik's island was the only remnant of Abba El Annor knew of near Asseldam. She'd go there and pledge her heart to Abba El once more. Afterward, she could float downstream and away from the city.

Annor listened hard for a guard or anyone else nearby. But the noisy water, compressing itself into the channel beneath the Citadel, drowned out any other sounds. Crawling ever so slowly up onto the bank, Annor paused barely out of the water's flow to peer around.

This side of the Citadel had few buildings, and most of them were older stone houses from the time before Javan's overthrow. Annor had cleaned a few chimneys near here. The residents were wealthier and quieter than the population further south where the night life would be in full swing. Only an occasional lightstone gleamed through the curtained windows.

Annor crept along the path beside the leat, toward the ruins of the king's castle and the apple tree. If she were blessed, she might find enough ripe apples to make a meal before she tiptoed to the river and swam for the island.

21

Sometimes they came in the light of day, climbing out of the rowboat like dark-robed vultures come to tear at his bleeding carcass. Sometimes they came at night and rousted him from sleep. Bald Erik liked the night torture better because he didn't see their arrival. Watching them tie up at the dock only prolonged the torture with expectations of what would come.

This was a night session. Bald Erik woke from his pile of straw to see them gathered around him, rubbing their hands in anticipation. Erik closed his eyes a brief moment to thank Abba El that the Sons waited for the darkness.

They yanked him to his feet, cracking open his wound so that the blood ran freely down his leg, and herded him through the dark temple hallways to the room once called Haelig. The Holy Place. Desecrated and defiled, it'd lost its name and its identity. The Sons pushed him onto the table in its center.

Now the part Erik dreaded and craved. The green stone. He didn't know where the Sons found it. He only knew they couldn't have created it. The stone was both holier and unholier, and more powerful than anything they could have devised.

The High Priest picked up the large stone and hefted it in his hands. From this angle Erik couldn't make out the man's expression. A small reprieve. The desire he occasionally glimpsed in the priest's eyes chilled his heart and sickened him almost as much as the Sons' more physical torture methods.

Olaf leaned over him, holding the glowing green stone above Erik's head, tantalizingly, repellently close. Erik often wished the man would use it to bash in his head and leave him dead on the table. Tonight was one of those times.

This ritual had been going on so long that all the players knew their parts. No one needed stage direction. But the blessed silence couldn't last. The High Priest caught Erik's eye and licked his lips. "Beg for it, slave," Olaf said.

Erik longed to laugh in the man's face and reject the stone, but its proximity had increased his craving more than his repulsion. "Please," he croaked.

The High Priest chuckled and looked around at his audience, the other Sons hooded and anonymous while they readied their infernal tools. Olaf's necklace of finger bones glinted in the moonlight shining through the dome above. "Listen to how polite the slave is," Olaf said. He turned back to Erik. "Again, but even nicer."

Might as well get it over with. "Please, kind sir," Erik whispered.

"What? I didn't hear you." The High Priest leaned closer, gloating, his eyes reflecting the green light of the stone, his naked desire revealed.

Abba El, will this never end? "Please, most kind sir." Erik's words were firm and strong. He recognized his voice for the first time in years. That thought strengthened him enough to look into the priest's cackling face as the Son brought the stone to touch Erik's lips.

Usually Erik closed his eyes, the healing power of the stone enveloping him in such bliss that he could think of nothing else. This time, he kept his gaze fixed upon the priest's face. And so, for the first time, he saw that the amulet strapped to the priest's forehead shone with the same green light as the stone in his hands. Not a reflection. It glowed in its own right, like a miniature healing stone, a small piece of the larger. Strange.

Erik plunged into the bliss and lost control of his conscious thoughts, a groan of pleasure escaping his throat. But not joy. Never joy. The sensation ended too soon.

Now that he'd been revitalized to withstand the torture, it began. Bald Erik gazed through the perfect circle in the dome above him and contemplated the stars, the work of Abba El. He tried not to notice the carving, the crushing, or the burning. When the Sons brought out lightstones, even the stars were denied him.

Erik answered their questions with silence when he could, and screams when he couldn't. But then they asked new questions. Who is the girl Nor, with her long hair and dirty nails? Where did she come from? Where is the armor she touched? Tell us what you know and we'll let her go.

Erik's stomach clenched and he fought back the urge to retch. They'd found Annor.

22

Annor crouched in an alley beside the river path. The two apples she'd eaten sat uncomfortably in her stomach. They hadn't been quite ripe, but she'd relished every tangy bite.

The river flowed swiftly in the moonlight. This was a good spot to swim for Bald Erik's island, but she'd have to fight her way across the current. Annor had already had one hard swim. If she dove from the bridge like last time, it'd be simple.

So, here it was again. A choice between a hard, safe route, and an easy, risky route. She gazed longingly down the path toward the bridge, then turned back to the river. Her parents had told her over and over she could do anything with Abba El's help.

Annor darted across the path, through the reeds, and into the water. The river was shallow close to shore, but quickly deepened. She kicked off and swam for the center with quick, strong strokes. She was gasping by the time she reached it.

By then the bridge had come and gone, passing over her head like a dark blot. The hard part over, Annor floated downstream, stroking and kicking just enough to keep her head up. Erik's island was a dark shape hunched beneath the stars.

Annor fought the current one last time to swim for shore. She sat limply on the rocky beach, catching her breath and listening to the murmuring river. She missed the evenings sitting on the shore of her island.

But she'd miss the nights giggling with Gunilla, too. Her friend. Hah. Annor tossed a stone into the river and struggled to her feet.

She decided not to pray in the temple. The green stone was too disturbing. Somewhere nearby would have to do. Bald Erik might have somewhere he liked to pray, but he'd be fast asleep. And she didn't want to wait. The Sons might be looking for her by now.

Annor picked her way along the rocky shore toward Erik's dock, careful not to turn her ankle in the uncertain light. She stopped short when she saw the boat.

She sank to her heels and forced away the panic. The Sons had come to pay Erik a visit. They weren't here for her.

She'd have to forget about praying, though. It was a stupid idea anyway. She'd just slip back into the river and let it carry her out of the Sons' reach. Supposedly people had headed west to escape the usurper. Maybe Mount Nevo lay that way, or even her own island.

A cry shattered the night, and Annor leapt to her feet. The Sons were torturing Eric. Before she could change her mind, she crept up the temple path. She couldn't fight the Sons, but she could be there for Eric when they left. Her right hand hovered over her knife. She'd never used it on another person, but she wasn't going back to prison.

A breeze blew through her damp clothes and toyed with her short hair. The temple loomed large and bulky against the fading stars, and light blazed from one of the broken windows.

Annor hurried off the path and across the broad plateau. She felt so exposed. When she'd rounded the far corner of the temple, she sank to the ground and fought to control her breathing. Panting like a spent deer would call the Sons down on her like a pack of wolves.

She jumped when a scream arced through the shattered windows above her. Erik's torture must be far worse than what the Sons had done to her. Annor bowed her head. "Please Abba El," she whispered, "let it be over soon."

The chill of the stone wall behind her seeped through her damp shirt. Soon. The Sons of Darkness would leave soon. Please, let it be so.

The sun peeked over the hill before her. Annor closed her eyes and rested her chin on her chest, willing the light to warm her.

Footsteps crunched down the steps on the other side of the building, in time with the Sons' joking, jubilant voices. Annor couldn't make out the words. Slowly, much too slowly, the voices faded into the distance.

She noticed her clenched fists and forced herself to relax. Anger wouldn't help Bald Erik, or herself. She rose to her feet and peered around the corner of the building. No one in sight. She crept along the side of the building until she could see the path.

Crouching, she left the haven of the wall and made her way to the edge of the cliff, inching the last bodylength on her belly. Before she peeked over the edge, a chill skittered down her back. She whirled to look back at the temple steps. They were empty.

Annor swallowed down the bile and peered over the cliff edge. The rowboat sliced across the river. One Son, hood flung back, faced her and strained at the oars. She didn't worry. The sun would be shining in his eyes. The other Sons faced Asseldam, hooded and anonymous.

Annor rolled away from the edge and crouched her way to the temple steps. She hesitated at the base. The green stone lay inside the desecration. But Erik lay inside, too, hurting and alone. She couldn't leave the island without trying to help him. She started to climb.

The sun shone through the hole in the dome and illuminated a circle on the side of the old altar room. Erik lay on the table in the room's center, his breaths raspy and weak.

"Erik?" She stroked his bloody hand. He smelled of death.

Erik frowned. "Annor?"

"Yes, it's me."

"But they said they had you, in the Black Citadel." He swallowed.

"I escaped."

He blinked. "You cut your hair," he said softly.

Annor shrugged and tried to smile. "They cut it."

"They have your hair?" Erik looked away. "That's not good."

"Let's get you out of here," Annor said. "You'll feel better in the sun."

"Wait. I'm sorry, but please. Could you hold the stone to my lips? I can't use it to heal myself, but you could do it for me." His voice was no more than a thread of sound. "It's just…." Shame clouded his face. "This time felt worse than usual."

Annor swallowed, eyeing the stone. It pulsed, green and malignant. "I just hold it to your lips and it heals you?"

"Yes."

Annor forced herself to pick up the stone, hefting it with both hands. It was sticky. Repulsive. Slimy. Her stomach clenched to hold down her nausea. She shouldn't have eaten those apples. But she could do this for Erik.

His anguished eyes had filled with longing. She touched the heavy stone to his cracked lips as softly as she could. His eyes closed, his body relaxed, and his face transformed from agony into bliss. She could see the pain leaving his body, absorbed into the stone bit by bit as if the green glow fed on Erik's suffering, sucking it from his tortured limbs and his battered torso. Even his clothes looked better, the awful stains vanishing into the stone.

The stone felt even slimier now, so that Annor worried it would slip from her grip and smash Erik's face. When she didn't think she could hold it much longer, she lifted it from his smooth lips and carried it back to the foot of the table. She scrubbed her hands on her pants. She wished she had boiling water to scald her fingers.

"Thank you," Erik said. He sat up in one smooth motion and smiled, his gaze almost impish. "This is the first time I've felt better after torture than I did before they started. I think that calls for a celebration." He laughed and slid off the table. "Let's get out of here."

The morning light made her blink after the gloomy temple corridors. Annor followed Erik northward along the plateau. When they rounded the corner of the temple, the sun beamed down like a gift. They sat together, leaning against the wall behind them, soaking it in. Upstream the bridge slashed across the river, but the Sons' taint couldn't reach them here.

Erik stretched. "Better?"

She smiled. "Much."

"You still look a little worse for wear. You must have had a rough time of it. I wish the stone could help you, but it's only tuned to me."

She shivered at the thought of the stone touching her lips. "Erik, why do they torture you? Are you an armor steward too?"

He bit his lip. "Not any longer."

"They learned your name?"

"They knew my name, but that's not something I can talk about."

Annor's mind churned. Which piece of armor had Erik had? Did he know who had the other pieces?

She shook the thoughts away. "I'm leaving Asseldam, but first I wanted to renew my commitment to Abba El. I thought you might know a good spot for that."

"Help me up and I'll show you where I like to pray."

Even though the stone had healed him so recently, when Annor tugged him to his feet a spot of blood soaked through his pants over his thigh.

Bald Erik led her further along the temple wall until it butted up against the hill beyond. It looked impassable, but Erik eased into a crack and vanished. Annor followed, finding him in a small hollow tucked into the base of the hill. An altar stood in the center of it, a pile of undressed stone meticulously arranged.

"You built this?" She touched the large, flat stone he'd set on top. "What of your wound?"

Erik grimaced. "I dragged a stone in here whenever I had the strength, which wasn't often."

"And the Sons haven't discovered it?"

"Here?" He chuckled. "I think Abba El hollowed out this spot just for me, a tender mercy. Would you like me to leave you alone?"

"No. Please stay." Erik kneeling beside her reminded Annor of all the times her father had joined her at the altar on her island. The thought brought peace to her heart instead of the pain of mourning.

Annor poured her heart out in silent prayer. "Forgive me, Father. I know I've fallen short, but I'll do better from now on. Thank you for the friends I've made. I give you my heart and my life. I know with thy help I can do more with it than I have on my own." She closed her prayer in the name of Ben El and sat back on her heels. Erik had long since eased himself off his knees.

The light grew brighter around them, blinding and white, until the Guardian appeared across the altar. Annor scrambled to her feet, surprised and elated.

"I accept your offering in the name of Ben El, Annor. And yours also, my son." The Guardian helped Erik up, and then embraced him. "You endure it well. Soon your torment may come to an end."

"I made the wrong choice," Annor blurted out.

The Guardian turned toward her.

"On my island, by the standing stone. I should have followed the route my father carved, and I'm sorry. I loved being around so many people. Not being alone any more. But I know it was the wrong choice. Maybe if I'd done what my father wanted, I could have gone to Mount Nevo afterward."

"What do you know of Mount Nevo?"

"Thaeri told me that's where the Puerán are, at least in his time. But I thought they might be there now, too. Or even back then. I mean, back when you gave me the choice."

"Yes, that's where they fled when they left Betavar." The Guardian smiled. "Would you like a chance to take the other choice? The Sons of Darkness have your hair, Annor, and the consequences of that can't be erased. Still, you'll find more joy on that path than the one you tread now."

"Yes, please let me take the path my father carved into the stone. I don't understand it completely, but it must be what my parents wanted for me. And well," Annor held out her bruised and mottled left hand, "my choice didn't turn out so well."

"Take what you have learned and move forward," the Guardian said. He rested his hands on Annor's head. Warmth spread from their weight through her scalp, down her neck, her torso, and her limbs. The warmth filled Annor with life. She felt reborn.

The Guardian stepped back and Annor gasped. She stood by her father's standing stone on her gloriously green island, so different from Erik's dusty, barren island. The morning sun glittered off the river. Her river. Her head had stopped aching, and her hand had healed.

"Thank you. Oh, thank you," Annor said. Then she realized. "But I didn't say goodbye to Erik."

The Guardian's eyes twinkled. "Learn to use the Gates of Horn and Ivory and you might see him again. Now, look at the stone and tell me the path you will tread."

Annor walked around the standing stone, reminding herself of the four carvings. "I'll cross the river and head upstream to the waterfall. I'll have to find the eye on the mountain, and then cross the mountain to the Shimmertree." She looked up at the Guardian. "Is that right?"

He tapped the eye on the standing stone. "For now, just find the eye. Your father left something there for you."

Annor smiled. "All right."

"One last thing." The Guardian waved his hand, and Annor was clothed in her leather pants and tunic, her chimney sweep clothes gone. "These will serve you better. Now, gather what's needful and walk the path. Go in peace, Annor."

And he was gone, blinking out so suddenly Annor caught her breath. The day was dimmer without him shimmering beside her in all his glory.

Annor inhaled the sweet air. She'd forgotten how good it smelled. She patted her father's stone, got a quick drink from the river, and ran down the path toward her cottage. She was home. Home! Thanks be to Abba El.

23

Leaves covered the worn path to her abandoned cottage. Some had pushed under the door to coat the floor, rising in a brittle cloud when Annor stepped inside. The table had a thick layer of dust. She sank onto the bed and a cloud of dust rose around her, like her first night with Gunilla. But it was home.

She strolled about the cottage touching the books on the shelf, her father's chisel, her mother's hair clip. Everything so familiar, but strange. She slid her hand along the rough wall. Her parents had lived in a stone castle in Betavar-that-was, with a myriad of streets, and a multitude of people. They couldn't have been content to live in a cottage after all that. But Annor's memories showed them happy in the simple life they'd chosen.

She went outside and followed the path that led to their graves, picking wildflowers along the way. She cleared the weeds from around the stones and traced her parents' names with her finger as she'd done so many times. Annor had shed many tears here. If Asseldam had done nothing else, it had healed her grief. She missed her parents, but the feeling no longer tore her apart.

"I love you," she said to their headstones. "And I'm going to get it right this time. Thank you for the example of your lives. I want to live mine as well as you did yours."

Back at the cottage, Annor planned what to take to the waterfall. Every inch of this one room held memories of her parents and their life together. She didn't want to leave it again. But she could come back. She'd know the way this time.

Annor gathered her fishing gear, her bow, and her quiver. But before she left, she decided to hide the king's gauntlets. The memory of the Sons asking about the armor haunted her. Maybe she'd let something slip during that awful night of torture that would lead the Sons to her island. Annor would hide the whole chest. The thought of Filip pawing at her mother's blue dress made her ill.

She used her father's chisel to pry up part of the floor, then shoveled out a mound of dirt. After lining the hole with rocks, Annor lowered the chest into the hole. She tapped the floor back into place and swept the cottage clean.

She took one last look around and spotted her father's sword hanging over the fireplace. He would be proud if he could see her now. She picked up her bundle of dried food and supplies, and shut the door firmly behind her. She took a deep breath. Time to follow the new path.

When she reached the riverbank, Annor stripped off her tunic and pants, and tied her satchel to a log. Holding the log steady in front of her, she kicked her way across the river.

Dressed again in her skins, Annor trudged through the forest. No real path existed through the dense fir trees. Sometimes she had to backtrack away from impenetrable thickets and steep drops. Other times she climbed over fallen trees and around boulders, trying always to keep the river within sight. The forest quieted as she hiked, birds and insects trailing off into silence. Bits of blue sky peeked between the leaves and branches overhead. It had been more fun traveling with her parents.

Annor heard the rush of the waterfall on the afternoon of the second day. Not long after that, she stood at the base of the pool and watched the river pour off the top of the cliff to thunder into the basin below. Gushing water and mist obscured the rocky cliff behind the falls. Annor stared at the falling water, willing herself to see something behind it that might be the eye her father had carved. But she saw nothing.

She found the shallow cave where her family had liked to camp, and cut herself a pine bough to sweep it clean. That had always been her mother's first task. Quite a contrast to her days of serving a queen.

Annor gathered a heap of fallen branches and quickly lit a fire in the same stone ring her family had always used. When she had the fire crackling, she sank to the floor and leaned against the cave wall. The journey had been longer than she remembered. She would just rest a while and watch the flames dance. The muted thunder of the falls soothed her. Her head slipped onto her satchel and she slept.

Annor awoke in the night and staggered out to feed the remains of the fire. She gazed up at the stars caught in the branches of the surrounding trees. "Thank you, Abba El," she whispered. "Thank you for my life, for my safe journey, for parents who loved me, and for hope." Sweet warmth filled her heart.

When she awoke the next morning, the sun had already begun to climb above the trees. Her stomach rumbled hungrily. She grabbed her little pot out of her satchel. The berry bushes might still have ripe berries. Her spirits rose when she made her way through the woods and found the bushes heavy with fruit. She gathered them swiftly, popping one into her mouth now and then between filling her pot. When she had enough, she licked her purple fingers and headed back to the cave for her fishing pole. She'd savor the rest of the berries while she caught a fish to complete her breakfast.

While she fished, she stared at the cliff face and thought about the weeping eye on her father's map. She couldn't see much through the tremendous volume of water roaring off the top of the cliff. Even if she found an eye, the cliff was damp and slippery. It'd be impossible to climb.

The pool held as many memories as the cave. Annor and her parents had spent days just floating on their backs, admiring the rainbows formed in the waterfall's mist. She'd learned her colors from rainbows. The water didn't entice her in today, but Annor watched ducks dive for food, their feathers flashing white against the deep blue of the pool.

Annor smiled when she spotted fresh deer droppings downriver from the pool. She grabbed her bow and quiver and silently followed the tracks where they vanished in among the trees. She almost lost the trail a time or two, but then she'd spot where the deer had browsed a patch of broadleaf seedlings, or rubbed up against a tree.

She spotted the deer's white rump and edged her way through the trees to where she could get off a clean shot. The deer perked its ears and sniffed the air, but it soon dropped its head to take another bite of the tender foliage. Annor drew her bow, aimed for the vitals, and took the shot.

She dragged the dead deer all the way back to the river to skin and butcher it. Annor's father had taught her how to dress and skin a deer as soon as she'd been old enough to use a knife. Maybe he'd had an inkling she'd be on her own some day, up to her elbows in deer.

Butchering was heavy work. Annor could barely crawl onto her fresh pine-bough bed that night. No doubt she'd be sore tomorrow. But she'd have a feast. She fell asleep smiling.

24

Annor had her feast on the shore of the pool. She'd ground arrowroot for biscuits and picked more berries. She'd tenderized her thick venison steak with a rock, and grilled it on a large, flat stone in the fire.

Water cascaded over the cliff edge, splashing and bubbling down the protruding ledges, chattering to itself, until it roared, foaming and frothing, into the pool below. Annor leaned against a boulder while she ate and watched the rainbows form. This was the best spot. The rainbows were uneven everywhere else, but here they formed a perfect arch.

The rainbow in front of her began in the mist on the left side of the pool, arced past the center of the cliff face, then faded off into the mist on the other side of the pool. It was beautiful. It was also right where the weeping eye should be.

Annor put down her half-eaten biscuit and stared at the cliff, willing herself to see something that resembled an eye. She squinted. Still nothing. Her mind flashed to when she'd sat on the riverbank in front of the translucent standing stone. To see the weeping eye, she needed Abba El to change her perception. She sent a silent plea heavenward.

The center arch of the rainbow reminded her of an eye. The splashing white water could be the white of an eye, or the tears. But an eye needed a pupil. Annor could faintly see a dark area in the center of the falling water, but that could be the cliff face behind the falls.

Too bad there weren't any paths to the top of the cliff. Otherwise she could tie a rope to one of the trees on the summit and lower herself down for a closer look. But the cliff was part of a mountain chain that stretched off in both directions. It would take Annor weeks to climb in and out of ravines and over ridges before she ever got near the top of the cliff.

Annor studied the cliff wall, glistening with moisture and emerald-green moss. No, she'd never be able to climb that. The center of the waterfall had larger ledges and protruding rocks that made it look like an easier climb, if not for the weight of the waterfall crashing down on your head. She remembered the dream she'd had all those months ago, about the cave behind the falls where her parents had warmed themselves in front of the Shimmertree. She could swim out and look. Just to be sure.

Annor stripped and dove into the water, swimming with strong strokes toward the boulder her father had named the king rock. She scrabbled on top of the rock, into the chill of the mist. The falls cascaded over the boulder behind the king rock like a curtain, splitting it in two.

She crawled over to the boulder and reached through the water. The falls pummeled her head and shoulders while she felt along the cliff face. Nothing. The cave in her dream didn't exist.

Back on shore she studied the trees on the cliff top, far above her. She could tie a rope to an arrow and shoot it over a branch. The rope in the back of the cave was plenty long enough. Once she had the rope over the branch, Annor could retrieve the arrow, tie the two ends of the rope together, and climb up to the dark spot.

She ran back to the cave for the rope and her bow. Standing beside the cliff, Annor tied the rope securely to an arrow and took aim. "Please let this work," she whispered.

She shot the arrow high into the air, the coil of rope by her feet unwinding rapidly as it chased the arrow through the sky, but the weight of the rope dragged the arrow down before it came anywhere near the branch. Glum, Annor fished the wet rope and arrow out of the water. She either needed a much bigger bow, or a much thinner rope.

Or leather cord. But cord would be too light to bring the arrow back down.

She chewed on her cold deer meat, turning the problem around and around in her mind. How could she make the arrow heavy enough to fall down the waterfall, but light enough to soar over the branch? Wet cord would be slightly heavier, but not heavy enough to drag the arrow down to the base of the falls.

She sat by her fire that night, staring into the flames. Her father must have known a way to get to the dark spot, but instead of being here to help her, he'd died. Annor didn't like being alone again. She wondered if Gunilla had her brother back yet.

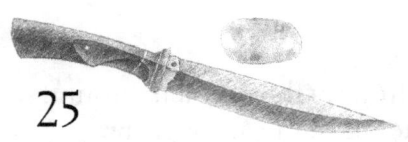

25

Annor woke with a jolt, dawn filtering through the trees outside the cave. The deer bladder!

She'd saved it when she butchered the deer. It only took a moment to rinse it in the pool. Annor carried it back to the cave and wrapped it around an arrow, tying it in place with a bit of cord. She set the wrapped arrow on a boulder. While she waited for it to dry in the sun, she ate and packed her belongings.

The deer bladder had stiffened by midday. Annor stood beside the cliff and nocked the arrow. It was such a simple plan, but the knots in her stomach told her how much she wanted it to work. She drew her bow, aiming above a protruding tree branch, and let the arrow fly.

The arrow had just enough momentum to glide over the branch before flopping down to hang in the spray of the falls. Annor sat down to wait. The arrow bobbed as the water splashed it. Slowly, oh so slowly, it sank into the water and vanished. She prayed that her plan would work, that the bladder had begun to unroll bit by bit and fill with water.

As time passed, the remaining coil of cord beside her played out in little jerks. When she thought enough cord had made it over the branch, Annor stripped and dove into the water. She swam toward the center of the pool, plunging under the surface to search. The churning water made it hard to see, but she spotted the arrow and the bladder and dragged them back to shore. She couldn't stop grinning. It had worked.

Annor untied the cord from the arrow and tied it to one end of her father's rope. She pulled on the dry end of the cord as the other end dragged the rope up the falls, over the branch, and back to where she waited.

She laughed. If only she had someone to share her joy. She looked around at the waterfall, the pool, the surrounding trees. This spot was just as beautiful and peaceful as when her parents were here with her. But after Annor's months in Asseldam, it felt lonely and isolated.

She'd finish walking her father's path, and then she'd go find the Puerán. Or maybe the Guardian would help her find Thaeri.

A fallen tree lay near the pool. She'd already hacked off most of the branches for firewood. Annor tugged and rolled it over to where the pool emptied into the river. She tied one end of the rope around the log. She took the other end and tied a loop for her foot, then wrapped a length of rope around her waist.

Annor hesitated before pushing the log in the river.

"Please Abba El, let this work."

She shoved the log into the water and ran back toward the cliff, positioning herself parallel to the protruding branch. She gripped the rope with both hands and waited.

The log was well on its way downriver when the rope dragged Annor to the water's edge. She dug in her heels, hoping she wasn't about to soak everything she owned. But then the rope lifted her into the air. She swung out over the pool, just missing the king rock. Dangling directly under the tree branch, the log gradually hoisted her up the falls.

She twisted around to stare at the cliff wall through the falling water. When she saw the dark spot, she swung forward and backward on the rope, pumping her legs. She built her momentum, then flung her head back and pointed her toes, shooting through the water into a dark hollow in the cliff behind it. Before the log could drag her back into the water, Annor grabbed the knife from her sheath and cut the rope.

She'd made it. She'd found the weeping eye.

26

Yevleh ground his teeth and punched the wall beside his bed, then paced restlessly, frustration and anger seething inside his chest. He'd like to shake the High Priest until his neck snapped. Yevleh licked his lips imagining Olaf's fat neck between his hands. How could he have let the girl Nor escape?

She was gone, her cell empty of all but her vomit. The other prisoners had been freed as well, though they'd been easily subdued and returned to their cells. But Nor, the only link the Sons had found to the king's armor in a hundred years, had vanished like a wisp of smoke. If Yevleh had been in charge, things would have gone differently.

He stroked his braid of office, still centered on top of his scalp. He'd been afraid to wake and find the Prince's visit a night dream, but the morning had been a dazzling awakening to his new life. Beloved of the Prince, and next in line to be High Priest. Yevleh punched the wall again on his next pass. If only everyone could see his golden braid and acknowledge his rightful place on the seat of power. They saw him as a lowly journeyman, months from ordination. But he'd earn the rank of High Priest. He would! No matter what it took.

Yevleh stopped abruptly, flinging himself back into his chair and picking up the manuscript. The Sons needed to actively hunt for the armor, as they had in Halvard's day. The idea had grown in Yevleh ever since he ate the fruit, and now it consumed him. Halvard had failed, of course. But he'd been stupid and shortsighted as the manuscript clearly showed, and the Hollow Altar had grown in power since Halvard's day. The Gates of Horn and Ivory had been discovered a generation after Halvard's rule. One of the apex horns had rested inside the altar ever since, imbuing it with more power than Halvard could have dreamed possible.

Yevleh leaned back and laced his hands behind his head. Maybe he could sneak into the temple and use the altar on his own. Getting past the guards and the wards wouldn't be difficult. Yevleh fingered his braid of office. If he found the rest of the armor, the Sons would have to acknowledge him as the rightful High Priest. Heyl El's wish would come true. The Hollow Altar would gain even more power with the full set of armor. The Sons of the Prince could even conquer the Puerán, wherever they hid. The whole world would belong to Heyl El. Just as it should.

Yevleh envisioned the convocation when he ascended to the seat of power, rank upon rank of black-robed priests and laerlings bowing down before him. He chuckled. Yes. Everyone would know he was beloved of Heyl El.

But what of the Ivory Gates? The fruit had given Yevleh so many insights while he studied the records. The brainless Olaf didn't realize the power within his grasp. Maybe Yevleh could use the power of the Ivory Gates to find the second apex horn before searching for the armor. Even without the second horn, the power of the Gates might be enough to propel him to the rank of High Priest. And then he wouldn't need to sneak around to use the power of the Hollow Altar.

Yes, the Gates were the key. He needed to pay another visit to the archives. Yevleh flicked Halvard's account dismissively. He'd search out every reference to the Gates. Their power would be his.

Yevleh covered his lightstone and climbed into bed. He stroked his mother's quilt. Instead of hiring a soos to visit his family after his ordination to priest, Yevleh would send a wagon to fetch them with all their belongings.

He'd have the whole world at his command.

27

Water plunged past the entrance of the rock cavity, roaring into the pool below. Dim light filtered through it and reflected off the water streaming along the floor and over the lip of the tiny cave. Annor didn't see an exit.

She fingered the end of her rope. Stranded. Somehow she'd missed that flaw in her plan.

But the water on the floor had come from somewhere. Annor dug her lightstone out of her satchel and squatted down to examine the back wall. Her legs buckled when she saw the opening at floor level. She let out a huge breath and sat in the running water, too relieved to care she was soaked.

Her lightstone shone on the misted side wall, illuminating a series of carvings. She smiled. Her father had been here.

Annor ran her fingers over the circles and lines. It looked like the maps he'd drawn when they were hunting. He'd drawn her a map of the cave and the tunnel. The circle nearest the waterfall had a line pointing toward the rear of the cave that branched in two. The line on the left petered out, but the line on the right continued and connected with another circle.

She grimaced. She didn't relish crawling into the little crack. But if her father had made it through, maybe it wasn't as cramped as it looked.

Annor fished her waterskin out of her satchel, took a long drink, and filled it in the shallow stream along the floor. She stowed the skin back in the satchel, then pushed it through the crack. Gripping her lightstone in one hand, she wormed her way into the tunnel.

She'd barely squirmed one bodylength in, when the tunnel split in two. She followed the branch to the right. It was blessedly dry.

Two more bodylengths and the narrow tunnel squeezed Annor's hips. Her father must have scraped off skin crawling through this. At least she had the lightstone. Worming her way into the depths of the cliff would have been horrific in the dark.

She continued to inch her way forward. One more bodylength, then two. The tunnel widened so Annor could crawl forward. A little farther and she stood hunched over, rubbing her sore knees.

Something glimmered on the wall. Annor raised her lightstone and saw a long, spiraling soos horn inset into a fissure in the wall. Annor set down her satchel and pried the horn carefully out of the crack.

Her father had forced her to burrow into the cliff's weeping eye to retrieve a soos horn. She hadn't yelled at her father very often, but if he'd been there, she would have.

Her stomach rumbled. Annor sank down and sat cross-legged on the floor of the tunnel, her leather clothes clammy and uncomfortable. She fished some deer jerky out of her damp satchel and chewed it thoughtfully, stroking the horn in her lap. The hollow horn shone translucently in the light from her stone.

Annor lifted the horn to look inside. The spiral intrigued her from this angle. She turned it in her hands, watching the spiral whirl around and around, never ending. She stopped turning, but the spiral whirled on its own, brightening before her gaze. A small plateau appeared inside the horn. A breeze rippled the grass, and a hawk flew silently past.

Annor looked around the tunnel, then back inside the horn, but by then the plateau had vanished. She was still irritated with her father, but the soos horn was more than it seemed. She tucked it into her satchel and started off down the tunnel, squishing along in her wet shoes. With any luck, she'd find the Shimmertree at the end of it.

Annor saw light ahead, and tucked the lightstone into her pocket. She hurried along faster. But the tunnel roof hunched lower and lower, and her back ached from stooping over. She crawled again for one bodylength before she burst through a screen of plants and into the afternoon sun.

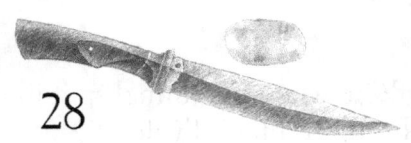

28

Before her lay the plateau she'd seen inside the soos horn.

Annor lay back against the hill and watched the hawk circle the plateau. A mountain slope reared abruptly at the far edge of the plateau, steep and high and crowned with snow, even in summer. The plateau dropped off sharply to either side of her, so the only way to get to this spot was through the tunnel concealed behind the waterfall.

She closed her eyes and soaked up the welcome sun. It felt glorious on her chilled limbs, and the plateau's waving grasses smelled like summer.

Her hand still clutched the spiraling soos horn. When Annor greeted her father in the spirit realm, he'd hear how annoying her last few days had been. Weeping eyes and impossible-to-scale cliffs, and no Shimmertree at the end of the tunnel. She frowned. Her father's path didn't make sense now.

The light brightened on her closed eyelids. She opened them to see the Guardian standing on the plateau below her. She scrambled down the small slope, grinning and holding up the horn. "I found it!"

The Guardian smiled. "Well done. Have you discovered how to use it?"

"I saw the plateau inside the horn when I was still in the tunnel. Is that what you mean?"

"That's part of it. The horn belongs at the apex of one of the Horn Gates. It will give you glimpses of the future or the past, but it takes practice to direct the scenes it reveals. If you rebuild the Gate and replace the horn at the apex, it'll be more powerful, giving you more details and options. But if you wish to walk through time and space, you'll need to rebuild both Horn Gates."

"Walk through time and space. That's what the Gates are for? But how do you travel without them?"

"Through the power of the Living Tree."

"Oh, right." Annor thought for a minute. "So, I could find the Puerán that way, and use the Gates to walk to where and when they are."

"Of course."

"And," she hesitated. "And Thaeri? I could find him too?"

The Guardian smiled gently. "If that is your desire."

"So, why me? Why didn't my father rebuild these Gates?"

"He had no need of them. He found his joy where and when he stood on his path."

Joy. Annor thought about the moment her fingers had brushed Thaeri's. The memory still sent warmth rushing through her, all these days later. "I can live wherever and whenever I want," she said, marveling.

"You need to find for yourself where and when you belong. It's your path to walk. But remember, both Gates must be rebuilt. You must retrieve the second apex horn to use the Gates' full power. Otherwise, you'll have glimpses of other times, but nothing more.

"Where's the second apex horn?" Annor held her breath, praying he'd say somewhere simple.

The Guardian tapped the horn in her hand. "Look and see."

Annor stroked it thoughtfully. "How do I direct it? Seeing the plateau was random."

"Focus on what you want to see, then open your heart and mind. It takes both."

"Both?" Annor held the open end of the horn to her eye. The sun shone through the wall of horn so that the spiraling length glowed with a richness and depth that had been missing before. Who knew a soos horn could hold so much beauty?

She focused on finding a second horn, and tried to open her mind and heart to the answer, setting aside her own desire for the solution to be simple. When she turned the horn, the spiral circled and expanded into infinity.

An image emerged. Annor found herself peering into a wooden box, black and large, so that a long soos horn fit easily inside. Other things rested in the box as well. One large, white object lay beside the horn and tried to catch her eye, but Annor feared she'd lose the image of the box if she let her gaze wander. She focused only on the second horn. Where was this box?

The image expanded to show the blackened box, wooden lid in place. It stood inside a many-sided room, stark and alone in the pale light. The room looked familiar, and Annor stared at it until the memory clicked into place. She'd seen this room from a different angle, when she'd peered through the chimney grates into the Sons' temple.

The Sons. They had the second apex horn inside their Hollow Altar. The horn dropped from her eye and she swallowed, dazed. Maybe she didn't want to rebuild these Horn Gates if it meant confronting the Sons of Darkness. She plopped down in the grass.

"What did you see?" the Guardian asked. His immaculate robe shimmered in front of her gaze, lustrous and brilliantly white.

"It's in the Hollow Altar, in that horrid black spider of a temple." She looked up and met the Guardian's eyes. "I don't have to go back there, do I? There must be another way to get the second horn. Could you get it for me?"

"That's not my path to walk."

Annor set the horn on the ground and rubbed her face with both hands. "Did my father know this when he carved the path into the stone?"

"The Sons hadn't found the Gates when your father carved the standing stone. He meant your path to lead you through the mountain behind us." The Guardian gestured toward the slope rising on the far side of the plateau.

"The Shimmertree is on the other side of the mountain."

"Yes."

"But why through? Why not over the mountain?"

"There is no safe path across the mountains that surround the Valley of the Shor where the Living Tree grows on its hill."

At least she didn't need to crawl beneath a mountain. But that didn't mean she wanted to go back to Asseldam. "Do I have to do this?"

"The path you walk is always your choice," the Guardian said. "You're tired and hungry." He flourished his hand and a loaf of fresh bread, a wedge of cheese, and a bowl of steamed vegetables appeared before her. "Eat and sleep, Annor, before you choose your destiny. I'll return in the morning."

And then he was gone.

The sun had sunk below the horizon while the Guardian had been with her, his glory dazzling her eyes. To find the day dimming into twilight surprised her. Yes, she was hungry and tired, but she doubted she'd be any more excited to return to Asseldam come morning.

The breeze had picked up with the setting sun, funneling cold air down the mountain, so that the long grass bent flat against the ground. Annor gathered her things and scrabbled back up the slope and into the tunnel entrance to eat in comfort. Nothing but wild grasses and a few scraggly bushes grew on the hill or the plateau. She'd have no fire tonight, but she could wrap herself in her deerskin and be warm enough.

She gazed at the mountain while she ate the food the Guardian had provided, watching the stars appear above its craggy white slopes one by one as the world darkened. The warm bread tasted sweet, with grain so fine it melted in her mouth. The vegetables dripped with melted butter. And the cheese! Annor had never tasted the like. It had such a delectable, pungent flavor that she savored every crumbly bite.

Annor brushed the remnants off her lap and crawled further back into the tunnel. Sleep took longer to come than she would have thought. Her tired body ached and her mind wouldn't be still. Thoughts of the weeping eye mingled with her dread of returning to Asseldam.

She'd have to hide from the Sons of Darkness. She couldn't go back to Gunilla's apartment. Gunilla had released her from prison, but first she'd betrayed her. If Annor asked the Guardian to send her directly to the temple furnace, maybe she could sneak into the altar room, grab the horn, and escape before the Sons noticed.

She'd have to find the Horn Gates before she could rebuild them.

The soos horn might show her the path. Hopefully it wouldn't lead her right past the Sons.

Annor shifted her position on the tunnel floor. Before she planned too far ahead, she needed to decide if she even wanted to rebuild the Gates. Her life would be much simpler if the Guardian sent her to the Puerán community, instead.

But Annor viewed simple options with suspicion. If she made that choice, she might be settling for less joy than she could find on the hard path. Annor didn't want to settle for anything. She wanted to grasp joy with both hands. She pulled the skin more snugly around herself and drifted off into sleep.

Annor stood on a shore beneath a full moon. Waves surged toward her across a pebbly beach, only to be sucked back into an endless, glittering sea. The pounding of the surf refreshed and exhilarated her. She'd never seen a sea before, but her father had described them during his stories of battle campaigns. He'd never mentioned the smell, though, and Annor breathed in deep lungfuls of the salty tang.

But the campfire and the shadowed figure beside it drew her more than the sea. Was this a dream or a not-dream? And was the figure friend or foe? Annor shrugged off her misgivings and stepped forward, her footsteps crunching on the pebbled beach while she approached the flickering flames.

The man sprang to his feet. "Annor."

She smiled. "Hello Thaeri." She settled herself beside his fire, an arm's length from where he stood. Touching had flung her back into her own life the first two times she'd seen him. This time she wanted a chance to talk.

"How did you come here?" Thaeri asked, settling back beside the fire.

Annor shrugged and shook her head. "I don't know. I went to sleep and here I am, just like before. Where is here, by the way?"

Thaeri chuckled. "Welcome to the southern sea. I've been building a boat here."

"A boat?"

"Yes, to get to an island a little way off the coast." He gestured into the darkness. "It's too far to swim."

Annor held her hands out to the fire's warmth and wondered if it warmed her body back in the tunnel. "What's so exciting about this island of yours?"

Thaeri smiled and shook his head. "My father thinks I seek the impossible, but I've heard there might be a seerstone hidden there."

"What's a seerstone?" Annor asked.

"A stone about so big," he said, circling his thumb to meet the tip of his index finger, "shaped like an egg, I think. A clear stone, like glass, but touched by the hand of Ben El to give us light and knowledge beyond all expectation."

"And your father thinks it doesn't exist."

Thaeri leaned forward and set another piece of wood on the fire. "Oh, he knows several exist, but he doesn't believe I'll find any of them. He thinks that if we're meant to have seerstones, Abba El would give them to us."

Annor studied his face. "But you don't."

"Abba El expects more of us than to stand with our hands out, waiting for gifts."

"Yes, I've noticed." It would be nice if she could hold out her hands for the soos horns instead of scaling cliffs and stealing from her enemies.

"Tell me of yourself, Annor," he said, tilting his head to one side and smiling shyly. "You are the greatest mystery of my life, intriguing and elusive."

She laughed. "There's not much to tell."

But his smile warmed her heart, and she found herself talking about her parents and growing up on the island, and then her awful year alone. "That's when I saw you for the first time," she said, "when you were hiking up the path on Mount Nevo."

Thaeri leaned toward her, intent. "So you go to sleep in your bed and appear in my life, but you don't know how or why."

"It just happens."

"Strange. What were you thinking about when you went to sleep?"

Annor thought back on that time. "I was lonely and frustrated, and praying for help."

He frowned. "What about the second time, when I gave you the glass of water? More than a year had gone by for me. Were you still alone on your island?"

Annor shook her head. "No, by then I'd come to Asseldam."

"Asseldam?" Thaeri's eyes widened. "I don't understand. Do you mean Betavar?"

She smiled wryly and shook her head. "No, it was definitely Asseldam."

"How could you come from the past?" Thaeri sat back and stared at the fire before turning toward her again. "You're even more of a mystery than I thought. And what were you thinking when you went to sleep that time?"

She shrugged. "I try not to think about that night."

"Someone hurt you."

"Yes."

"I didn't know what to do for you," Thaeri said. "You appeared out of nowhere, like a wounded bird that might fly off if I startled you too much. And then when I handed you the water...." He blushed.

So he had felt it, too. Thaeri's eyes met hers, and Annor smiled, a blush staining her cheeks. They stared into each other's eyes until a log shifted in the fire and Thaeri looked away. Annor let out her breath.

Thaeri poked at the fire, and gave her a quick glance before adding another log. "What about this time?" he asked. "Are you still in Asseldam?"

"No." She chuckled. "No, this time I'm in the middle of nowhere, sleeping in a dirt tunnel."

He leaned toward her. "And what did you think about when you went to sleep?"

She met his gaze. "I wondered if it would be worth it, to learn to walk in time wherever I wanted." She swallowed. "When I'm awake, I mean."

His smile blossomed slowly and his eyes grew moist. "Please do," he said. He scooted closer and took her hand.

And she awoke, sitting up in the darkness to bang her head on the tunnel roof. Annor smiled and rubbed her head. "I will," she whispered. When the Guardian returned, she would ask him to send her back to Asseldam, to retrieve the second horn.

29

"Erik!"

Startled, Bald Erik set down his fishing pole and watched Annor run down the temple path and onto the weathered dock. Why had the Guardian sent her back into danger? For her sake, he smoothed the worry from his forehead and put a smile on his face.

"My dear," he said, as she sat beside him, "I never expected to see you again."

"I know, but at least now I can say goodbye. I didn't get a chance before."

He smiled genuinely this time. "I don't believe you came back just to say goodbye."

She chuckled, and shook her head. "You're right, though I wish that were the only reason." She wrapped her arms around her bent knees and gazed at Asseldam. "Had any visitors lately?"

"No. Annor, why are you here? It isn't safe. If the Sons lay hold on you again they'll mutilate and defile you to weasel out your secrets. You won't escape a second time."

"I know." She twirled a strand of her cropped hair. "I had to come back. I need something they have. You see, there are these gates…."

"The Gates of Horn and Ivory," Erik said, the words heavy on his tongue.

"You know about them? Well, I found one of the apex horns where my father left it for me."

"Your father?" Erik's mind whirled, struggling to fit the pieces together while he studied Annor's face.

"Yes, but the Sons have the other apex horn, so I have to get it back before I can rebuild the Gates."

The pieces started to make sense. Erik shifted on the splintery dock, trying to ease his wounded leg. "So you'll be a seer."

"A what?"

"A seer. Able to understand the past and see into the future. The Guardian must be preparing you to take your place in history."

"My place?" Annor shook her head. "I'm not working for the Guardian."

"The Guardian? Don't you mean Abba El?"

"Whatever. That's not what the Guardian made it sound like. He offered me freedom, not dependence."

Erik smiled and shook his head. "It's in the service of Abba El where you'll find the greatest freedom. Freedom to receive all that He has."

"A seer," she said. "My father must have known all along, to carve the standing stone the way he did. And what the Guardian said about walking in time and space? That was to lure me onto this path."

Erik shifted again to ease his thigh. "What could be more glorious than expanding your mind to see as He sees, to walk as He walks? Why should you need to be lured to receive all that?"

She blew out her breath and shrugged. "You're right. I just wish someone had explained that before I chose which path to walk, glorious or not. It wasn't fair to make me choose without knowing where the path led."

"So you'd like to see past and future before you learn to see past and future."

Annor snorted. "That makes me sound silly, but you're right. My mother always said to put my hand in Abba El's and walk where He leads me."

"To trust Him to want the best for you."

"Exactly. Anyway, I guess I should get on with it." She gave him a fierce hug. "Goodbye, Erik. I'd hoped the Guardian would send me straight to their temple, but at least this way I got to see you again."

"The Sons' temple?" His heart constricted in his chest and his mouth was suddenly dry.

Annor rose to her feet. "Yes, and I want to start swimming as soon as the sun dips behind the hills, in case I need the whole night." She chuckled. "This better be the last time I have to swim across this river."

"You have a plan?" he croaked.

"Yes, thanks to my chimney sweep career. Goodbye, Erik. I hope you find your freedom soon."

"Thank you, Annor. Put your hand in Abba El's and walk in peace until you find that freedom of yours." Erik watched her pick her way northward through the rubble along the shore, until the curving temple hill blocked her from his sight.

He sank his head into his hands, too agitated to fish. He didn't feel hungry anyway. Their temple! Its groping corruption would assault her soul. Annor couldn't steal the horn from the Sons of Darkness without getting caught.

Erik feared for her life. If they caught her, if they tortured her as they tortured him, she had no cursed healing stone to bring her back from the threshold of death.

He frowned at the darkening heavens. Did he need to lose another person he cared for, because of the polluted Sons? At least he'd be spared the sight of her mangled, broken body. He tried to drive the dark thoughts and images from his mind. If she walked with Abba El, she would be safe. She'd succeed and find her freedom. He must believe that.

Freedom. If only he could die and find his own.

Annor would learn to walk in time and space while Erik sat on his island, forever doomed.

30

Yevleh smiled when Olaf announced Eskil had been executed. The altar room was crowded, packed shoulder to shoulder with black robes.

Eskil had deserved execution, the fool. Sneaking around behind the priests' backs, trying to set up his own power hierarchy. Thankfully Yevleh had known better than to join Eskil's pathetic little kingdom. The fool hadn't gained much with his ambitions. He'd briefly ordered around a few misguided journeymen and under-priests, and he probably enjoyed a few nights carousing. It couldn't have been worth it.

And now the other journeymen of Eskil's year, Yevleh included, had been gathered to witness the burning of Eskil's braid of office on the Hollow Altar. His mousy brown braid was pitifully thin, rather symbolic of his useless pretensions.

Eskil had paid the ultimate price for his treachery, his carcass eaten by rodents, his bones broken and flung in the river, his braid saved for burning. Nothing left for his family to mourn. Even Eskil's thoughts would be despoiled while they watched. Priests and journeymen ringed the altar in a series of graduated circles, all grateful their own braid of office still hung from their scalps.

A female heart-splintered vaettir stood beside the altar as the High Priest lit Eskil's braid on fire, the first woman Yevleh had ever seen within the consecrated bounds of the temple. She inhaled the acrid smoke with deep, ecstatic breaths, her usual dead expression transformed by aching desire. It was worth being here just to learn how heart vaettirs functioned, though Yevleh tried not to breathe any smoke himself.

He'd chosen a spot beside one of the many walls, as far as possible from the black altar, and took shallow breaths. Since the floor stepped down gradually toward the altar in the center, Yevleh had as fine a view as any of the others. Tomas had crowded into the circle closest to the altar, but he must regret that now, with his face all screwed up trying not to breathe. Essence of Eskil. Who but a vaettir would want to inhale that?

Olaf questioned the vaettir woman, probing for Eskil's thoughts. Who were his associates, besides those already discovered? What were the extent of his activities? What tricks did he use to manipulate himself into a position of power? Yevleh watched several journeymen squirm as their names were called out in the vaettir's euphoric voice. They wouldn't be killed, but they'd certainly be demoted and punished. Maybe even sent home mutilated and disgraced. Yevleh's eyes danced. Less competition for him, not that it mattered.

Yevleh resisted the urge to caress his own braid of office as Eskil's burned and dwindled. Olaf stood by the altar scanning sloppy notes while he questioned the vaettir woman. Someday everyone would see the braid of a High Priest centered on top of Yevleh's head. His braid grew thicker and longer than the older man's, and the golden hairs the Prince Heyl El had given him outshone the gold string or two Olaf had braided in with his white hairs.

Yevleh wondered what the priests had done with the abundance of hair he'd clipped off the girl Nor. They must have burned some of it by now. Yevleh wouldn't have been invited to such a ritual, of course, but he bet it hadn't been successful. Burning the hair of the living didn't give heart vaettirs access to their thoughts, just their emotions. Much less useful unless you knew how to manipulate the questions to extract the best information.

The fruit had given Yevleh some ideas, and the strand of Nor's hair he'd stolen would come in handy. He'd taken a piece from close to her scalp, so it would give him better information than the few scattered visuals the brain vaettir had gotten from the fudge party sample. And he'd use a heart vaettir, of course. Yevleh wanted to know where Nor was now, not where she'd been when she'd grown the hair.

He couldn't risk sneaking in here and burning her hair on the altar. Not after Eskil's fiasco. But Yevleh had a few places in mind that might work just as well. The trickiest part of his plan was gaining access to a vaettir. Yevleh hadn't been able to think of a way to avoid using one, since he had no desire to inhale the smoke himself.

With Eskil's braid nothing but ash, and the acrid smoke dissipated, the ritual came to an end. The vaettir's eyes had dimmed, her fervor faded back to apathy, as she frowned at the floor. Yevleh glanced back as he filed out the door with the other journeymen. There must be some way he could trick a vaettir into helping him, and a female might be easier to control than a male. He'd have to give it more thought.

31

Annor emerged dripping from the river into a dim and misty night. The mist was a tender mercy. Her leather clothes clung to her, clammy and heavy. The gap between the island and the shore had been narrower on this side, but the current had been swifter. Her dragging clothes had been an added burden.

Annor stood amongst the ruins she'd seen the day she and Gunilla cleaned the temple furnace. Gunilla had mentioned a guard patrol, though Annor hadn't seen one. Still, she'd be cautious in case guards watched even in the mist.

Annor headed for the standing stone where the Sons poured out the ashes of their dead. The stone wouldn't be guarded, and from there she could make her way between the spreading temple wings to find the steps down to the furnace. If she were quiet and cautious, she'd have a chance to hide from any guards before they spotted her. At least, that's what Annor told herself.

The mist swirled, uneven and patchy. She glimpsed a few stars before hazy fingers enveloped her once more. She shivered, more from trepidation than from the chilly air. She didn't want to be caught and dragged back to the bowels of the Black Citadel. Filip smirked in her memories, and her footsteps slowed. The temple windows glowed red and spectral in the night, floating above the ground like windows to Heyl. But she wouldn't let fear stop her. She wanted that second horn, and she'd get it.

Annor stopped short when she heard voices. She couldn't make out the words, but then the voices drew nearer. She crouched in the weeds, her hand hovering over her knife.

"… not like it makes a difference," a man grumbled. "Even if I did get a night off, I've got no money to enjoy it with."

"Saving up, are you?" a second man joked.

The first man spluttered. "Hah! The wife takes every spare coin for…."

The voices faded back into the mist. Annor waited for her heart to stop pounding. For a moment she'd thought the guards would tramp right over the top of her. But sound could be deceptive on a foggy night. She started off again, slow and steady, until she came upon the standing stone. Annor sank beside it and tried to clear her mind of the numbing terror that lurked, waiting to pounce. If she didn't want to get caught, she couldn't be paralyzed by fear.

She shifted onto her knees, giving the death stone a hesitant glance before bowing her head. "Please, Abba El," she whispered, "I need thy help. If you want me to do this, if you expect me to do this, let me go forward with thy blessing of comfort and peace."

When Annor opened her eyes, the red windows shining through the mist were less daunting. She fingered her father's knife, still strapped securely to her right thigh. The carved hilt reassured her further. Her father could never have dreamed she'd raid the Sons' foul altar. But he would have approved. He'd been on some interesting raids, himself, as one of the king's guards.

She snuck across the plain toward the temple, and threaded her way between two outstretched wings without meeting any more guards. Red windows gleamed above her on both sides now. Red eyes. But Annor focused on finding the steps to the furnace. She wouldn't have noticed if one red eye blinked.

32

The lightstones in the furnace chamber glowed, outlining the door. It'd been a blessing Sven assigned them to clean the Sons' furnace so that Annor had a route into the altar room. Her fingers hesitated on the door latch. A square of white light shining through the mist would alert a passing guard, or a priest chancing to look out a window.

Annor shielded the furnace door with her body and eased it open, praying the rusty hinges wouldn't screech. She didn't feel safe until she'd crawled inside and shut the door behind her. She crept through the chamber, and into the flue leading to the chimney, grinding soot into the wet knees of her leather pants.

It was darker in the chimney than it'd been on that sunny day with Gunilla. A misty night outside the top vent didn't illuminate much. Plus, Annor hadn't thought to reopen the grate covers after she'd swept her way through the chimney.

Annor had her lightstone wedged at the bottom of her pocket, but the Sons would notice if white light outlined the edges of the grates like it had the furnace door. She would have to climb in the sooty darkness.

Annor crouched at the base of the chimney shaft while her mind filled the air above her with the spirits of dead priests, fighting to keep her out of the altar room. She knew they weren't there, but that didn't make them less terrifying. Her heart pounded, she perspired in her clammy leathers, and her breath came in ragged bursts. Not the best way to sneak into the altar room unnoticed.

She drove away the image of dead priests with her memory of Thaeri sitting by his fire on the seashore. She focused on his gentle smile and pleading eyes. She could do this. She would do this. She stood and found the jutting bricks. Cautiously, she began to climb.

She came to the first floor grate sooner than she wanted. She heard only silence when she pressed her ear against it. A faint gray light outlined the grate. Annor gripped the cover, ready to slide it open. She pictured a semi-circle of black-robed priests staring at the grate, waiting for her to appear.

Ridiculous. She slid the cover to one side and peered through the slats. The room was empty except for the black box. Unless someone crouched behind the altar.

Don't be an idiot, she told herself. She'd swing the grate open, crawl through, lift the altar lid, grab the horn, shut the lid, and be back in the chimney in less than a minute, safe. Or, at least safer than in the altar room. She clenched and unclenched her hands, fighting down the panic bubbling in her chest.

Everything went as planned until she lifted the altar lid. The horn nestled beside a piece of the king's armor. The legs. She could take them, too. No, no, no. Just stick to the plan. She couldn't escape while dragging big, white legs. They'd act like a beacon, even in the mist. Still, it irked her to leave a piece of the king's armor with the Sons. Had the legs been Erik's stewardship?

Annor gritted her teeth, grabbed the horn, closed the altar lid, and scooted back into the chimney. Her pulse pounded in her ears, so she couldn't hear if anyone had walked into the altar room in time to see the cover slide shut. "Please, please," she mouthed. Don't let anyone have noticed. She tried to push away the grim, useless thoughts and get back in control. The temple had been assaulting her ever since she'd crawled into the furnace.

The horn was cool in her grip. Annor clutched it with her free hand and crept down the chimney, holding tightly to each jutting brick while the temple whispered in her mind that she'd fail. She'd lose her footing, tumble to the base of the chimney, and snap the horn beneath her.

When she'd crawled through the flue and into the lit chamber, she leaned against a wall and turned the horn in her hands. The temple pressed heavily on the low ceiling, darkening her spirits and sapping her energy. But she wouldn't let it beat her.

She needed a path to the Gates of Horn and Ivory so she'd know where to go next. Annor focused her thoughts on finding the Gates. How could she get there? How did the Sons get there? She gazed deeply into the horn's long, spiraling length as she turned it between her hands.

A picture emerged from the depths of the horn, and expanded. Annor saw the Ceremonial Road join the arching bridge, then her view went up and over the bridge. The city flashed by as the hill beyond it grew to fill the bounds of the picture.

One of the hill caves, just above a dead king's burial chamber, rushed toward her, closer and closer. Suddenly she was inside the cave turning right, left, in a bewildering series of turns until a solid sheet of shimmering white light blocked the width of the tunnel. But the vision didn't stop. It plunged through the light and out into a valley, showing her two red rectangles facing each other across an expanse of pavers.

Annor would never remember that series of turns. And what was the shimmering light blocking the tunnel? She dropped the horn from her eye and stroked it. First things first. She'd get over to the hill cave while it was still dark enough to hide, and worry about a path through the tunnel once she was away from the temple and its nest of Sons.

She crawled over to the furnace door, gingerly swung it open, and scrabbled out. Mist still shrouded the temple. Annor waited, listening, but all was quiet. She crept up the steps and out between the temple wings.

Waves of enmity radiated toward her from the black spider of a building. It reached for her, through the mist. Annor probably wouldn't be free of it until she stepped onto the bridge.

The red windows glowered as she slipped past. Except, one window was dark, like a black eye. Annor paused, her heart thudding. She was probably imagining the shadowed figure standing in the window, watching her. But he looked real.

Her every instinct screamed at her to run, but her feet were rooted to the ground. She clutched the long horn to her body. She had no way to hide it.

If a priest stood in the window, he hadn't alerted the guards. Annor shuddered and looked away. She forced her feet to move, and stole forward. Just a few more windows and she'd made it beyond the wings and onto the plain. She could hear the river rushing past, as eager to be away as she was.

That's when she heard the shouts. Annor broke into a run, straining toward the foggy bridge, and the alleys of Asseldam. Boots stormed behind her. A lot of boots. Annor pelted across the brittle grass, her breath coming in quick gasps. She couldn't go back to prison. And no matter what, she wouldn't let them get the horn.

Annor made it to the bridge and her feet thudded on the boards. The mist was no protection now, with all the noise she made.

A herd of footfalls erupted onto the bridge behind her and a guard called out for her to stop. Something whizzed past her head and thunked into the bridge beyond her. A knife. She passed it at a dead run. Her legs burned as she drove them faster. Faster. Just a little faster. Please, she prayed, let the guards all have lousy aim.

The next knife caught her in the back of her left arm. She gasped as the ribbon of pain shot through her. Annor hugged her arm to her chest. At least it wasn't a kidney or a leg.

She slowed, though she willed herself to ignore the searing pain of each jarring step. Annor refused to be caught. She wouldn't go back to the Citadel to be tortured. She skidded to the edge of the bridge, ducked under the railing, and launched herself into the river, clutching the horn in a death grip so the current couldn't rip it from her grasp. The water closed over her head.

Stupid river. Here she was, swimming across it yet again. The knife dug in deeper when Annor tried to take a stroke. So she gripped the horn with both hands and kicked. She'd made it past the center of the bridge in her mad dash, but at this rate she'd never make it to shore before the current swept her past the leat. The cries of the guards faded behind her.

The outflow from the leat engulfed her before she realized it, and Annor coughed and spat while she tried to keep her head out of the sewage. The putrid smell of the greenish-black scum gagged her. Bloated rat carcasses bumped against her bare arms. Her stomach roiled until she vomited out of her nose and mouth. If she could have breathed, she might have screamed. She didn't get her air passages clear until she'd passed through the outflow and into the cleaner water beyond.

With a few good kicks she'd be close enough to the riverbank to touch bottom, but dripping across the width of Asseldam would be foolish. Annor looked for guards running along the river path, but she'd outdistanced them. Or they'd been content to lose her to the river, not realizing what she had clutched in her hand. She let the river take her further downstream, past the southern half of the city, until the lights faded and only starlight bathed her face.

33

Annor crawled ashore and sat in the weeds. She shivered, the knife throbbing in her arm. The sun would be up soon. She needed to get away from the river and hide herself in the cave above the tombs. Still she sat, dripping and in pain. Her chin dropped onto her chest and she whispered, "Please help me. I can't do this on my own."

She lifted her left arm and rested her hand on top of her head. The knife stuck out of the back of her sleeve, smaller than her own and more suited for throwing. The hilt had been carved into a four-legged serpent. She gripped it with her right hand, but when she pulled, the hilt slipped in her grasp. Annor swallowed down a wave of nausea.

She gritted her teeth and tried again, choking back the nausea until her flesh released its grip. She dropped the knife into the weeds, shaking and hugging her arm. The blood flowed down to her elbow and dripped onto the dirt. Sweat trickled down her face and her clammy neck. She had no way to bandage her arm, but letting it bleed might cleanse the wound after her swim through the putrid flow of the leat.

Annor struggled to her feet. Asseldam loomed off to her right, still slumbering but due to wake soon. Before her and to her left stretched a rippling plain of grass, dotted with large white lumps. One shifted restlessly and her foggy brain clicked. A field of sheep. Downriver the black shape of a farmhouse was outlined against the night.

Annor picked up the apex horn and the guard's knife and trudged west. She'd need to veer north at some point. For now, she wanted to get as far from the river as she could before the sun rose.

Her leather sleeve was sticky with blood, but the trickle down her arm had stopped. Annor's legs felt shaky, and her stride faltered. She was thirsty. She had no waterskin, though, and no food to fuel her dwindling energy.

The sun peeked over the horizon and the sheep stirred. Annor glanced back toward the farmhouse and bit her lip. If the sheepherder rode out to check on his flock she had nowhere to hide in the short-cropped grass.

Annor's head spun from the blood loss, but she spotted a fence off in the distance. A little farther and she'd be beyond the sheepherder's notice.

The sky brightened as she plodded on. Walking felt like floating, until she forgot to watch her feet and tripped. The jarring pain brought her back.

Annor cracked open her wound clambering over the fence. She leaned against the far side of the fence trying to drum up moisture in her dry mouth. Her tongue stuck to her teeth.

She pushed herself off the fence and headed for the hill behind the city. Gunilla was somewhere in that city, probably talking to Sven at the Guild right now. Annor thought her loneliness had ended when she and Gunilla became friends. But now Gunilla had her brother back and Annor had no one.

A yellow-brindled dog barked and ran toward her across the plain. Annor had seen a few dogs in Asseldam. Scavengers, mostly. It circled her, sniffing between barks, then sniffed along her back trail and licked a blade of grass. Blood had been trickling down Annor's arm and dripping off her fingers ever since she'd climbed over the fence.

Annor plodded on and the dog trotted after her. She ignored it. Just moving forward took all the energy and focus she had.

By mid-morning Annor made it to an abandoned quarry site. She was stumbling with weariness by then. When she stared at a pit in the ground it blurred into two holes, then back to one. A rope tied around a nearby boulder vanished down the hole.

Annor blinked and sat down, licking her dry lips. She could hear the cutters working in the distance. She needed to hide, but she was so thirsty.

The hole might be a well. She crawled over and peered in, but shadows hid the bottom. Annor set down the horn and hauled on the rope, cracking open her wound yet again. It was worth it, though, when the old, wooden bucket reached the top brimming with cold water. Annor drank until her stomach sloshed, spilling water down her tunic. She set the half-full bucket beside her.

The dog appeared and Annor jumped. She hadn't realized it'd been following her. It ducked its head in the bucket and noisily slurped up the remaining water. Then it raised its dripping nose and studied her.

Annor picked up the horn. She dropped the bucket back down the well and stumbled over to a pile of rubble at the base of the hill. Stonecutter rejects. Shaking with fatigue, Annor knelt behind the rubble. It would have to do as a hiding place. There was nowhere else.

She curled up and hugged the horn to her chest. When she closed her eyes, the world stopped spinning. She'd sleep until dark, and then she'd head to the cave. She'd feel better after she slept. She shivered again. The water sat cold and heavy in her stomach.

Something warm settled down into the curve of her legs. She raised her head and blinked blearily into the eyes of the dog. Her head sank back to the ground and she slept.

Annor opened her eyes to darkness. The dog had gone. She stretched and staggered to her feet. The sleep had refreshed her, but her stomach ached with emptiness. She hauled up another bucket of water and drank her fill. It didn't ease the hunger.

She poured the remaining water on the ground and stirred it into the dirt, then coated the horn with mud. Now it wouldn't shine in the moonlight at least.

Annor walked north along the base of the hill, letting it lead her toward the city. Asseldam lit up the night, more beautiful than it ever was in the day. Crumbling wooden houses crowded up against the hill. She threaded through the dark alleys, sliding her knife out of her sheath and gripping it in her good, right hand. She wouldn't go down without taking someone with her, no matter how weak and dizzy she felt. None of the people she passed gave the muddy horn a second glance.

She got a second wind when the amphitheater came into view. Not much farther now.

Annor counted tombs and paused when she came to the fifth. She couldn't read the inscription in the darkness, but she didn't remember whose tomb this was anyway. She slid the muddy horn down the back of her tunic and tucked it into the waistband of her pants. It poked awkwardly through the neck of her tunic, higher than her head, but she'd need both hands to climb the hill behind the tomb. If only she weren't so tired.

She listened to the night. A thin strand of music met her ears, but no voices marred the quiet. The city slept.

She scrambled up the slope and onto a ledge in front of a cave opening. Her head buzzed and her arm ached. Annor pulled the horn out of her tunic and ducked into the cave.

34

Darkness cloaked him as warmly as the black hood he'd drawn over his head. Yevleh stood outside the tomb of King Avar, first king on this side of the river.

He'd lain under his mother's quilt many long nights, debating where to burn Nor's hair. Any lingering thoughts of burning her hair on the Hollow Altar, in spite of Eskil's death, had fizzled with the theft of the apex horn. Guards had been installed outside the altar room to watch it night and day, like shutting a gate after the soos have escaped.

The High Priest was as much of an idiot as ever. Even if the man had thought to burn some of Nor's hair by now, Olaf probably had no inkling that she'd stolen the horn. But who else could it be? For the first time in Asseldam's history, they'd captured someone who'd touched the king's armor. But she escaped, and then the horn vanished, as well.

She'd escaped from the Black Citadel. Nor couldn't have randomly touched the armor. She might even be an armor steward. And now she'd dealt the Sons of the Prince a heavy blow by stealing the apex horn and weakening the power of the Hollow Altar. The intriguing question was why she hadn't stolen the king's leg armor as well, weakening the altar even further.

Yevleh fingered the packet of herbs in his pocket and stared down into the darkness of the tomb entrance. Just as he didn't dare burn Nor's hair on the altar, he'd decided it was too risky to involve a vaettir. Instead, he'd bought the herb packet from a shady dealer he sometimes employed. The man swore the herbs would let

Yevleh experience all that a heart vaettir would, even without being embedded with a splinter from the Hollow Altar. If the dealer had lied, Yevleh would slit his throat. This was too important to get wrong.

King Avar's tomb was the most potent unguarded place Yevleh could think of in all of Asseldam. He rubbed the inscription over the entrance for luck, shrugged off his misgivings about entering the realm of the dead, and ducked under the lintel. He didn't dare shine a lightstone. Not yet. He trailed a hand along one wall as the passage led him down beneath the ground. But then the ceiling lowered, forcing Yevleh to crawl on all fours.

He found the stone door with one reaching hand, and braced himself to crack the seal and push it open with his feet. He held his breath, fearing the smell of decay. But the air just smelled stale. Maybe he wasn't the first to venture here.

Yevleh crawled into the burial chamber and pushed the stone door nearly closed behind him. He didn't want to be sealed in. For a moment, he envisioned himself trapped, his dead body keeping the king company as they both rotted into dust. Success never came without risk.

He pulled a lightstone out of his pocket and set it on top of the stone coffin. The rounded walls and ceiling encompassed him like a sphere. Only the floor was flat. A spiral had been carved into the coffin's heavy stone lid. He sneered. Puerán primitives.

Yevleh pulled the coil of Nor's hair out of his satchel, and tucked the strands into the spiral, all along its length. He poured the herbs on top of the spiral, drew out his pestle, and ground the herbs into the hair. Lastly he took out his tinderbox.

"Burn," he commanded. "By the flame of my devotion and the power of Heyl El." He struck several sparks before Nor's hair caught fire. He blew on it gently. The herbs smoldered, potent in the small tomb.

Yevleh bent over the coffin and inhaled deeply, closing his eyes and begging Heyl El for a boon. "Prince below, open my mind, feed my vision. Please, my Prince, god of my heart." He inhaled again and again, dizzy from the smoking herbs and the choking smell of burnt hair while he reached for the emotions of the girl Nor.

Enclosed. Trapped. Pain, hunger, and fear. The foreign emotions swept over him in a giddy wave of otherness. The dealer had been right. Underneath Nor's feelings raged his own triumph and a delicious sense of power. Yevleh tamped down his awareness of himself and focused on Nor.

Fear of what? He hunched over the burning herbs and hair, inhaling until a smoky haze enveloped his brain. What are you afraid of girl? Dark corridors and enormous droppings, some dry, some moist and fresh. Skittering sounds that echoed down the corridors.

Yevleh inhaled again, but the hair had burnt into a spiral of ash, and the otherness slipped from his mind leaving him trembling. He crouched on the stone coffin and stared at the ash, grinning like a madman. Success. Yevleh had recognized that fear. He'd felt it himself not far from this tomb when he'd been sent as a laerling to feed the monstrous horror guarding the way to the portal. Nor was in the caves, headed for the Gates of Horn and Ivory. Of course! What else could she want with the apex horn?

35

Bald Erik tried to ignore the pain. This time the Sons had come during the day. The hole in the dome above him shone as a bright circle of light. He tried to lose himself in the light, but the High Priest kept bending over him and blocking Erik's view. Irritating man.

The priest was especially vicious today, as if he could torture Bald Erik enough to solve all his other problems. He cackled in Erik's face asking endless questions, but Erik let the sound wash over him. He had nothing to say today. After all these years, how could Olaf expect any new information to come out of Erik's mouth?

Light. Olaf had moved back out of Erik's line of vision. Now he could see the sky and get lost in that distant haven. But the word "horn" caught his attention and dragged his mind back into his hurting body. It hadn't been the High Priest who'd said it, but one of his black-robed minions. They stood in a clump near Erik's feet, handing Olaf the blood-stained tools.

The lesser priests all had their hoods drawn, shadowing their faces. Erik couldn't tell one from the other. But one of them continued the discussion of the horn.

"No one could have taken the apex horn without the blessing of the Prince. Someone entered his temple and lifted the lid of his altar. It must be one of us that the Prince has blessed with his favor. We just don't understand why yet."

The High Priest snapped at them to quit their gossiping and plucked a chisel from the outstretched hand of the nearest Son.

Annor had done it! Somehow, some way, she'd stolen the horn out from under their noses, and the Sons had no idea how or even who had robbed them. He grinned in spite of the agony from his recently crushed fingers.

"So you know something of the horn," Olaf said to Erik.

"Yes," Erik said. "I know it's been stolen out of your unholy altar. Is that why you're so grumpy today?"

Olaf growled and slammed the chisel straight down, crunching Erik's sternum and puncturing his lungs.

Cold flooded Erik's chest and he couldn't breathe. The fountain of blood was eerily beautiful until the soaring pain overwhelmed him.

"Please let me die," Erik whispered to the light above him.

But no. One of the lesser priests rushed to hold the green stone to Erik's lips and the ecstasy of healing began. The cycle would never end. Never. Erik groaned and lost himself in the stone while he could.

36

Annor had been worried she'd miss one of the turns she'd seen in the horn. Everyone in Asseldam had a cousin who'd gotten lost in the hill caves. They wandered the dark, twisty passages until they died of thirst. Or so the stories said.

But even though the rough walls all looked the same, the Sons had marked a path through this tunnel with luminous paint that shone in the glow of her lightstone. It'd be hard to get lost. If anyone had wandered into this cave, they hadn't died of thirst. They'd been eaten.

Annor held her fingers curled loosely over her lightstone to dim the light, but even so she had no trouble following the markings. She could have raced along the dark tunnels if she hadn't needed to hide from the beast. The creature reminded Annor of the four-legged serpents she'd seen swarming the temple's throne room. Only massively larger. And with more legs. The brief glimpse she'd caught of it, following her trail, had sent her scrambling into a side passage off the marked route.

The beast was long, so long that it took an eternity for its sinuous length to pass the opening of the tunnel where she crouched, trembling. Annor would get lost if she ventured any further off the marked path, and the beast only guarded the marked parts of the cave. It had sniffed along her trail with its broad head skimming the ground. But when Annor's scent turned off into this side passage, it had hurried on without a glance.

Annor had heard the beast skittering along in the distance long before she'd seen it. That had been her first hint she wasn't alone. She'd hoped it was only the sound of rats echoing through the passages, and kept trudging, deeper and deeper into the heart of the hill. When she'd come across the enormous droppings she'd realized that even if it were only rats, she didn't want to meet them.

The tunnel pressed down around her. She was trapped. The stifling darkness was worse than any chimney, going on and on without relief. Annor closed her eyes and pictured herself back in the field with the sheep, with the limitless sky above her. It eased her panic, but when she opened her eyes she was still trapped.

The horn might be able to show her a different route. Annor scraped the horn as free of mud as she could. She set her lightstone in front of her on the cave floor and held the horn up to her eye. Before Annor turned it, she thought carefully about what she wanted to see.

"How can I get past the beast and walk through the wall of light?"

The spiraling horn filled her vision and her mind. She saw the shimmering sheet of white light stretching across the width and height of the cave. Only, this time the beast lounged in front of the light. Its enormous head lay sunk on the floor, but wide and unblinking eyes glared down the passageway.

It lay in wait for her. "This isn't helping," she said. "How do I get past it?"

The beast faded into an insubstantial outline while the shimmering light and the cave remained vibrant. Annor saw herself walking toward the light. The beast brightened and dimmed as if struggling back into life, but the Annor in the horn walked steadily onward and vanished into the light.

She let the horn drop from her eye and stared at it, puzzled. The cave beast guarded the wall of light, but somehow Annor was supposed to ignore it and walk right through the spot where it lay in wait. She wondered if the Sons ever fed it, or if the giant piles of dung were the remains of everyone else who'd tried to get past.

Her empty stomach ached, she was so hungry, and her arm throbbed. Her head slumped down on her chest and her eyelids grew heavy. She'd been wandering the tunnels for hours. She curled on her side and let her eyes close. Her pain faded as she slept.

Annor's eyes felt gritty when she woke, and her stomach rumbled, but it didn't matter because she knew what to do. The Guardian had told her the Gates would help her walk in time and space, just like he did. So she needed to walk in time to pass the beast. Even if it still crouched there, waiting for her, Annor could walk through the wall of light at a time the beast wasn't there.

At least, it had made so much sense when she first awoke. But as Annor stretched and rubbed the grit from her eyes, she wondered what she'd been thinking. She didn't know how to walk in time.

Her wound throbbed and she peeled back her stiff sleeve to take a look. The whole back of her arm was puffy and red, except for the wound itself, which was a sickly green. She could puncture the edge of the wound and squeeze out the pus, but she felt so befuddled she might cut too deeply and make the wound worse. Best to let it be for now until she found something to eat and drink, and could bathe her knife blade in a fire.

Was she feverish? That could be why she'd thought she could walk through time. But it fit with the picture the horn had shown her. Annor crept toward the marked part of the cave system. She paused in the tunnel opening, listening hard.

She saw nothing but a rough, dark passage stretching off to the right. The wall of light was in that direction. The tunnel to her left, back toward the entrance, was just as empty. Annor heard nothing but her own breathing.

She closed her eyes and tried to clear her mind of doubt. "You can do this," she told herself. "There's no other way to get to the Gates." And if she didn't make it to the Gates, she'd never be with Thaeri.

Walk in time. Walk in time. She stroked the horn and pictured a time in the future when the beast would be near the cave entrance. It would have forgotten about her, thinking her long gone. If Annor could get to that future time, she could better serve Abba El.

She held that thought in her mind a long while, striving to make it her reality. The intensity of her focus left her shaking and dripping with sweat. When she opened her eyes, the dark cave looked just the same. Except, something lay slumped down the tunnel to her left, glittering at the farthest reach of her lightstone.

Annor tiptoed toward the shape. Whatever it was, it didn't move. It wasn't until she crouched next to it that she realized the beast had shed its skin like a snake.

She'd done it. She was in the future. At least, she hoped so.

She snuck down the tunnel, toward the wall of light. The cave walls enclosed her while darkness crept up behind her. She followed the markings, turning down one side passage after another, to the left and then the right. They were as dark and twisty as the parts of the cave she'd already passed.

Holes in the floor had been covered by large metal plates. Steps had been carved into steep, sloping passages, and a railing along one short bit protected her from a drop into infinity.

Twice she came to large caverns with multiple exits, but each time the Sons' markings pointed her way to the light. She passed a locked metal gate blocking a passage that led into more darkness, a few passages that had been bricked off, and a pile of debris spilling in from another passage that had collapsed. Annor made a sharp right, then a left, following the markings down a slope, up steps, past more covered holes, some black outcroppings, then a drop through a hole into a lower level.

She worked to keep her mind focused in this future time, and to keep fear from distracting and swallowing her. But then she saw the wall of light ahead, shining through the darkness. In her own time, the cave beast lounged there, enormous jaws waiting to crunch her bones and eat her for supper.

Annor pocketed her lightstone and stepped toward the light. "The beast is near the entrance," she whispered. Her breath came in short gasps, and she whispered frantically. "The entrance." But her fear told her it wasn't true. The air rippled and she saw the outline of the beast lumber to its feet. Its gauzy black eyes met Annor's and her knees weakened.

"It's near the entrance," she said. "I'm in the future!" She took another step, and another. But the cave beast only looked more solid. In the horn she'd walked safely past the beast and into the light. But the horn might have been showing what was possible, not her actual future.

She heard the beast growl, and she watched it gain color and substance. Annor shut her eyes and took another step. "I'm in the future. The beast is near the entrance. Please, Abba El, let it be so." She switched the horn to her left hand and pulled the guard's throwing knife out of her sheath.

The air blew warm and stale around her. The beast's breath. No. She was in the future. Light burned red through her closed eyelids, like the midday sun.

Annor opened her eyes and found herself face-to-face with the slavering beast. Its breath reeked of decay and sorcery, its teeth gleamed black in its wide jaws. She tried to breathe and choked instead. She was going to die. All of it had been a waste. The torture, climbing the falls, stealing the apex horn, her not-dreams of Thaeri.

"No!" Annor shouted into the beast's gaping mouth. "I will live!" She reached up and jammed the knife into the beast's eye, sinking it up to the hilt so that noxious green liquid splashed over her hand.

Then she leapt past it and ran for her life. A piercing scream shattered her ears. The beast whirled, thrashing in the tight passage. Another step. Another. She'd almost reached the light. She forced herself not to look over her shoulder. Another step. Sobbing in terror, Annor lunged into the light.

She'd been expecting warmth, but she'd leapt into a portal to nothingness. The Guardian had always sent her traveling with a blissful sense of peace and reassurance. Here she felt empty and abandoned. She kept moving forward, but she couldn't feel the ground, couldn't feel her feet. Gritting her teeth, Annor pushed through an unseen barrier that tore around her. But she found another layer, and another beyond that.

The light had dimmed or her eyes had grown accustomed to the brightness. All she saw was white. White nothingness ahead, above, beside her. White beneath her feet that were no longer there. She ripped through another layer, gripping the horn in a hand she couldn't see. And then the last layer tore.

Annor fell out into a circular valley. Green grass and impassable cliffs ringed the valley, reaching up and up into an impossibly blue sky. Two red, rectangular slabs faced one another in the center, from opposite sides of a paved square. She'd found the Gates.

The portal where she'd emerged shone feebly at the base of the cliff. Annor stumbled away from the cliffs and over to the grass. She sank to her knees and ran her hand through the green, plush carpet. She felt reborn, liberated from the darkness of the caves and the terrors of the cave beast into a newness of joy.

The red Ivory Gates puzzled her. There was no way to walk through them, and they didn't open like doors. She rapped on one with her fist. Solid.

A basket sat centered on the paving stones, between the Ivory Gates. The apex horn she'd given the Guardian stood upright on the edge of the square where its Gate must belong. The basket and the horn hadn't been there when she emerged from the portal.

Annor's mind drifted dizzily after her ordeal. She was safe, but still thirsty, still hungry, and still wounded. Her arm throbbed in time with her heartbeat.

She stepped over to the basket and looked inside. A small glass bottle brimmed with water next to fluffy, little cakes. Not enough to satisfy her thirst or her hunger, but better than nothing. Annor lifted the glass bottle to her lips and drank. The water startled her, sweet and pure, unlike anything she'd ever tasted.

She nibbled one of the white cakes. It was freshly baked, slightly warm even, and melted in her mouth. It tasted nutty, with a hint of citrus and the sweetness of honey. Her thoughts cleared as she savored each bite of the little cakes, eating one after the other between sips of pure water until the bottle was empty and the cakes were gone. Annor felt refreshed and satiated, as if she'd feasted at one of the king's banquets her mother had described so many times.

Now she needed to deal with her wound before the infection took her whole arm, but she had no way to purify her knife blade. Unless… Annor approached one of the Ivory Gates. The white ivory framing the red slab shone bright and flawless, while the red looked false and wrong. She hesitated, but then scraped at the red with her knife. It flaked off revealing a thickly mirrored surface beneath. The Sons must have painted the surface of the Ivory Gates when they destroyed the Horn Gates.

Annor pushed the tip of her father's knife into the cleared section of the Gate. The radiant surface swallowed her blade up to the guard. When she pulled out her knife, the blade shone like crystal. She smiled. Too bad she couldn't slide her whole body into the Gate. She'd never felt so grimy.

37

Annor sat in the grass and squeezed green pus out of her wound until her arm bled cleanly. When the bleeding slowed, she stepped back to the Ivory Gate and scraped off more paint. She wanted to return the little valley to what it'd been before the Sons tainted it.

The paint curls vanished in puffs of smoke when they touched the pavers. Blood red paint. She shook her head. The Sons hadn't figured out how to use the Ivory Gates, so they'd painted them to keep anyone else from using them.

The surface of the Gate was smooth and unmarred, with no sign of where she'd slid her knife blade into the crystal. The mirrored aspect disconcerted her. As Annor cleared a broader swath of the Gate, her face stared back at her. Behind that was yet another reflection of her face. When she'd scraped off the last of the paint, her reflection was cast back again and again, innumerably.

Annor stepped over to the other side of the square and scraped a red circle of paint off the second Ivory Gate. She stared at the mirrored surface, puzzled. Instead of her face, she saw the back of her head. These Gates were strange. She fingered her chopped hair. It looked pretty awful. Her mother would have been sad to see her like this.

Annor went back to scraping. When she'd cleaned off the last bit of red paint, the light brightened in the little valley, like the sun had emerged from a cloud. But the blue sky was empty of both sun and clouds. The cliffs cast no shadow, and neither did the Gates. No sun?

Annor must have left the bounds of her world when she stepped into the wall of light. Maybe it should have felt eerie, but it didn't. She felt at peace here.

She stood in front of the cleaned Gate and frowned at the reflection of her back. Behind that was another reflection of her back, and another, and on and on, the reflections sinking deeper into the Gate the farther back they went. Puzzling.

Annor turned and considered the two apex horns, standing alone on the pavers. She'd placed the second apex horn opposite the first, but there were no other horns in the circular valley. She was in trouble if the Sons had taken the horns back to a storage room in the Black Citadel.

Gazing into one of the apex horns might show her where the rest of the horns had gone. But after scraping the Ivory Gates clean, Annor wanted to learn how to use them. She examined her reflection and stroked the mirrored surface.

Her father might have known how to use the Gates. He'd been entrusted with one of the apex horns. He might have come to this little valley, through the tunnels, just like she had.

Annor stared at the second reflection in the Gate while her mind wandered, remembering life on their island while her parents had been alive. They'd been so happy in their simple life. All Annor wanted was to find a little piece of that happiness again.

Her mind quieted, and the second reflection expanded to fill the ivory frame, like a vision in the apex horn, but larger. Annor watched herself walk through the dark city of Asseldam until she reached the fifth tomb. She scrambled up the hillside and entered the cave.

Annor whirled away from the Gate and faced the cliff, not wanting to relive her encounter with the cave beast. The Ivory Gates showed past and future like the apex horns. Focusing on the second image had shown her one day ago. A hundred images back might show her a hundred days ago. If so, maybe she could go back to the day when the Sons of Darkness dismantled the Horn Gates. That had been closer to a hundred years than a hundred days, but the images in the crystal mirror were as endless as time.

Annor turned and let the string of images fill her gaze, farther and farther back. They streamed past her notice as she delved deeper into the Gate.

She found her eye drawn to one reflection, far back in the Gate. The other images had been static, but this one quivered. As Annor focused on it, it expanded to fill her vision. She saw the square behind her swarming with black-robed Sons. She turned, startled, but the actual square was empty.

Annor rubbed her hand across the Gate's crystal surface. The image looked so real, more like an open doorway than a mirror. When she focused harder, she could hear the Sons' voices. One of them was the High Priest. He yelled at the other Sons, telling them to dismantle the Horn Gates.

The green amulet strapped to the High Priest's forehead glowed with anger. His necklace had fewer finger bones than the one Annor had seen in her cell, but this man was twice the servant of Heyl El. A Son of the Prince who oozed darkness.

Annor glared at his image even as his voice set her teeth on edge. He scared her, but he was long dead, lost in the past. And today she'd reverse all the damage he'd wreaked on the Gates.

The High Priest told the Sons to paint the Ivory Gates. He sent other Sons to hide all the horns under a rock fall at the base of the cliff. They'd only found one apex horn.

Annor smiled. Back in this long ago time, her father had already taken the other apex horn and hidden it in the passage above the waterfall, far out of the Sons' reach. Her father had thwarted the Sons, and she would, too. Annor turned away from the vision and crossed the grass to the base of the cliff.

The rock fall was easy to find, but shifting the rocks and carrying the horns back to the paved square depleted all the energy Annor had regained from the water and the cakes. When she'd finished, she lay on the soft green grass and gazed into the perfectly blue sky. Annor felt cradled by the surrounding cliffs. Protected. Nothing could hurt her here.

After her rest, she sat in the center of the square and studied the pile of horns. Thankfully she'd seen how the Gates looked before the Sons dismantled them. Unlike the rectangular Ivory Gates, the Horn Gates arched at the top. And since they didn't have mirrored slabs, she'd be able to walk through them instead of just seeing images. She smiled when she imagined herself walking through a Gate into Thaeri's time. Could it be that easy?

She spread out the horns and tried to understand how they fit together. The horns had come from a greater variety of animals than Annor could fathom. She found only two of each kind. Some of them might have been gathered from animals in faraway lands of her own world, but surely not all of them. The Gate builder might have collected horns from all of Abba El's worlds.

Annor divided them into two piles, separating the pairs, but she didn't know what to do next. She fidgeted with the horns for a while, trying to intertwine the prongs, but nothing seemed right. If she built the Gates wrong, they'd be useless.

She set the horns down and got on her knees. "Abba El," she prayed, "Thank you for helping me pass the cave beast. Thank you for the basket of provisions, and for showing me how to find the hidden horns. Please, enlighten my mind now so I can know how to recreate the Horn Gates, that they might be of use to Thee once more."

She closed her prayer in the name of Ben El and sat back on her heels, focusing on the edge of the square where a Gate belonged. She waited until her heart felt peaceful and her mind calm, then turned to the heap of horns beside her.

Slowly the Gate took shape in her mind. She could see it form, horn by horn. They fit together beautifully, and somehow inevitably. When she'd watched every last piece take its rightful spot, Annor grinned and got to work. Her hands were clumsier at building than her mind had been. And yet after she'd tweaked and shifted each horn into the correct position, the Gate grew beneath her touch.

She built up the left side, and then the right, and stood on tiptoe to gently form the remaining horns into an arch, joining the two sides together. Lastly, she slid the apex horn into position, locking all the other horns in place. Before that moment, Annor had been afraid she'd bump the fragile structure and bring all her effort crashing down. The apex horn solidified the Gate, making it as immovable as the encircling cliffs. She stared at the empty space beneath the arch, waiting to see something. The Horn Gate radiated power, but it was empty.

She shrugged and stepped over to the other side of the square where the second heap of horns waited. It was easier the second time.

Her hands were more sure, her vision clearer. The Gate soon rose from the pavers, a twin to the first.

Annor held the second apex horn in her hand, ready to maneuver it into place. Joy washed over her. She'd done it. She'd overcome so much, and this would be a new beginning. She slid the horn into its spot. The Gate vibrated with power and the light in the valley brightened even more.

38

The palpable power of the Horn Gates surged across the square as they reached toward one another. But Annor saw nothing beneath their arches besides the valley's green grass and the cliffs beyond. She wanted to access the Gates' power and have them take her to her future. To Thaeri. She was so close.

All four Gates belonged to Abba El. She'd only be able to walk in time if she used them to benefit others. That's probably why the Sons couldn't get them to work. All of her self-centered requests would be meaningless to the power they channeled. "Thy will, not mine," Annor whispered.

She'd seen Asseldam in all its decadence. She'd had a glimpse of the future Betavar from her cell in the Black Citadel. Thaeri's people had worked to restore the city to the glory of the Betavar-that-was. If Annor wanted to help them, she needed to know what the city had been like under the rule of King Beraqel, the last king. Then she'd have something to offer Thaeri's people. She wouldn't just be a refugee escaped from the Sons.

Annor stood in front of the first Horn Gate she'd built. The Ivory Gate to her left reflected her face. The Ivory Gate to her right reflected her back. The future and the past.

"Please," she said, "if it be Thy will, show me Betavar in my parents' time. Let me understand how the city helped its people, and how that can help the people in Thaeri's day. I can't change the past, but let me learn how to bless the future."

The air flickered beneath the arch and a blur of color appeared. Annor glanced behind her. The other Gate framed the same image.

The blur gradually came into focus, the white and blue and brown separating into distinct shapes.

The temple on Bald Erik's island. But this was no shattered wreck of a building, abused by the malignant Sons. The temple's unbroken windows sparkled in the sun. The polished steps gleamed, and railings led up to a magnificent front door.

Her view passed into the door and through it. Annor gaped when she saw the beauty that lay beyond. A multitude of lightstones lit the corridor with a brilliance that made the passage feel like a path to Abba El.

Her view traveled down the corridor and turned toward the large, circular room that in her time housed the battered table and the green stone. Annor cringed.

The room burst upon her with a radiance that had her gasping. Sunlight pouring through the dome shone on a stone altar. Not a rough pile of rocks, but an altar of cut marble. The polished marble reflected the sunlight, blinding her. The cushioned chairs and the enormous wall hangings were impressive, but nothing in that lofty room could match the glory of the altar.

The shape of the altar reminded her of the Sons' black box. The Hollow Altar must be the Sons' dark copy, just as the Sons of Darkness were Heyl El's copy of the glory of the Puerán.

So this was what it was like in an altar room dedicated to Abba El, so different from the Sons' black temple. Their altar room had been disturbing and suffocating. This room filled her with reverence and light. She would have lingered there, looking at the splendor, but her view drew rapidly back, out the door, down the stairs, and along the path toward the edge of the hill, where it paused once more.

Across the river lay the city of Betavar, so different from the city she knew. It was smaller, for one thing, with not nearly as many buildings. The castle crowned the north end of the city, and no Black Citadel marred its center. The leat sparkled in the sunlight, bringing clean water to the western edge of the city before turning to flow into the river. The greatest difference though, lay in the ambience she could feel even this far away. Betavar was clean, beautiful, and inviting.

A small white stone lay on the path, just beyond the edge of the
Gate. Annor reached into the Gate and picked up the stone. She
held a piece of the past in her hand. If she wanted to, she could step
through the Gate and into the past, walk through Betavar-that-was,
and see her parents. She shook her head. No, if she stepped through
she might be stranded in the past, unable to see the Gate.

But she could make her way through the caves again, and get back
to the Gates that way. No cave beast lurked in the passages, waiting to
devour her.

Yes, but the Sons hadn't marked the route to the portal yet. She'd
get lost. And what if someone had already taken the apex horn? Even
if she found her way through the caves, the Horn Gates would be
useless. Annor would be trapped in the past with no way to get to
Thaeri. And the usurper was coming shortly, to conquer the city.

No. She would look and learn, but that was it.

The view through the Gate moved past the edge of the hill and
out over the river. Annor watched the water flash by beneath her as
she sped toward the city, angling toward the castle. The castle was
a perfect balance to Abba El's island temple. Spiritual and secular
working together. Annor's breath grew tight in her chest as the city
flashed by and the castle grew larger. She might get to see her parents.

Her view passed through the castle wall into an enormous hall, two
stories high and filled with people. They looked cheerful and excited,
as if waiting to hear happy news. Their bright clothes, their long hair,
their radiant smiles, were strikingly unlike the beaten-down people of
Asseldam. The king sat on his throne, his pregnant queen to his left.
The king's guard lined the west side of the hall, gleaming in their mail
and blue capes. The queen's attendants lined the east wall.

Annor's view surged down the center of the hall toward the king
and queen too quickly to pick her mother out of the line of attendants.
But as captain of the king's guard, her father was easy to spot. She took
in his laughing face, so young and free of worry. But soon he was out
of the frame, and all she could see was the king sitting so near that she
could have leaned through the Gate and touched him.

The king outshone everyone else in the hall with the magnificence
of his white armor. He wore his crown instead of his helmet, and his

blue cape matched that of his guards. The amulet on his chest winked in the light, a miniature Shimmertree with blazing, white fruit.

Annor smiled when she noticed the gauntlets on his hands. She'd held them, tried them on even, and in her time they rested safely in the chest under her cabin floor. How strange. His armored legs, on the other hand, lay inside the Hollow Altar. Seeing them on the king made Annor regret leaving the legs behind even more than before.

He stood and spoke, congratulating the people. Annor couldn't make out his words, but his pleasing voice flowed over her. His eyes were so kind, so loving. She would have served this young king as faithfully as her father had, and would have mourned his death just as deeply. He ruled with integrity and humility. He'd been all the things the Sons of Darkness weren't. And they'd killed him for it, slaughtering him on that magnificent altar in Abba El's temple.

Her arm throbbed, and Annor wondered if her father had brought his pouch of herbal salve to this ceremony. He'd always claimed he wouldn't go anywhere without it. She'd cleaned her knife wound as thoroughly as she could, but her father's salve would fight the infection.

"Please, Abba El," she whispered, "may I get the salve? If I'm healthy I'll be better able to serve Thee." The view shifted away from the king and toward the captain of the guard who stood in parade stance, listening to King Beraqel's speech. Her father radiated strength and looked invincible. No wonder the king had trusted him to keep the gauntlets safe.

And yes, he wore the pouch on his right hip. She could see it hanging from his belt, just under his cloak. She knew her father would gladly give it to her if she could explain. But his daughter was a pampered little girl a year or so old, while Annor was grown, and dressed in grimy skins.

She wouldn't be able to untie the pouch without him noticing, but she could cut it free. She slid her knife out of its sheath. Her father's knife. She held it in her hand, yet she could see it in the sheath on her father's leg.

She licked her lips, praying the hall full of people wouldn't notice her disembodied hands. Crouching at the level of the pouch, she reached through and flicked her father's cape out of the way, cupped the pouch in her left hand, and cut the leather tie. The pouch dropped into her hand. She began to ease it back through the Gate, when she felt her father's eyes on her face. She'd leaned too far forward.

Annor looked up, her own eyes wide, expecting him to shout, to grab her wrist, to yank her through the Gate.

Her father looked puzzled. His eyes dropped to her knife, and then to the knife in his sheath which looked strangely insubstantial. He looked back at Annor just in time to see the tear trickle down her cheek.

"I'm sorry, Papa," she whispered, "but I need your healing salve."

He sucked in his breath. "Annor?" he whispered.

She nodded, and the hall erupted with cheering. The king had finished his speech. Her father looked up, startled, and Annor moved back, away from the Gate and the past. Her father's eyes darted, searching for her while he held his military stance.

"I'm sorry, Papa," she whispered again, wiping her face. The image in the Gate faded and then vanished, so that the arch framed nothing but the grass and the encircling cliffs.

The salve felt glorious when she spread it on her wound, cool and numbing. The feeling reminded her of the many times her father had taken care of her nicks and scrapes. She tucked it into her pocket, and patted the lump it made.

"So you know how to use the Gates."

Annor leapt to her feet and whirled to face a black-robed Son of Darkness. "Hey," she said, "you're the one who cut my hair."

He flourished one arm and nodded regally, though his blue eyes never left her face. "My name is Yevleh," he said. "And you have just elevated me to my rightful position."

39

Annor and Yevleh faced one another, both wary, both waiting for the other to make a move. Annor crouched a little, staying light on her feet. Her right hand hovered over her knife.

Yevleh circled toward her. "I'm not going to hurt you," he said. "Let's relax and talk this out."

Annor circled away. "You're right. You won't hurt me. But that doesn't mean you won't try."

She glanced toward the portal at the base of the cliffs. She hadn't thought to keep a watch on it. And now a Son of Darkness profaned her refuge.

Slowly, they circled one another.

Yevleh spat on the pavers and bared his teeth. "Fine, we'll play it your way."

How had she ever thought him handsome that day in the glass factory? Annor's hand still hovered near her knife. If Yevleh had a weapon, he would have been threatening her with it by now. She could take him down with her knife, but he was unarmed.

What other choice did she have? She'd never wrestled anyone but her father, and she'd only beaten him when he let her. She didn't know how her skill would measure up against this man. He had a longer reach, besides having the weight advantage. Too risky.

The portal crossed her gaze again as they circled, but that was no escape. Annor never wanted to confront the cave beast again. That left the Horn Gates, but Yevleh would be onto her the moment she stopped to focus on a Gate.

"Thank you for the dance," he said, "but it'd be more fun with music. Come with me and I'll show you the pleasures of Asseldam."

Foul man. "I wouldn't go anywhere with you."

Yevleh stopped circling and held his hands away from his body. "Nor, you must see we're accomplishing nothing. I don't want to hurt you. I just need to take back what you stole."

"Can't steal from a thief," she said.

They'd stopped directly between the two Horn Gates. Annor focused on what she could see of the Gate over Yevleh's shoulder. "Abba El," Annor whispered under her breath. "Grant me passage to another time and place. I only want to be free to serve Thee and build up Thy kingdom."

The air flickered beneath both arches. Yevleh gasped, staring behind her. Annor charged forward, driving her shoulder into his midsection and yanking up on the backs of his knees, forcing him off balance and onto his back. His head hit the pavers with a satisfying crack as she scrambled to her feet.

She stood in front of the Gate, tensed for a blow from Yevleh, her heart pleading for a way out of the valley. The archway fogged, then cleared to show Thaeri standing just beyond the Gate's frame. Elated, she stepped toward him, her body halfway through the Gate when Yevleh grabbed her from behind and dragged her back into the valley. Thaeri's eyes widened. He said something, but Annor couldn't hear him.

Yevleh clutched her in a choke hold, blocking her airflow. Pinning her right arm behind her, he jammed it upwards. Pain seared through her shoulder. Annor clawed at his black sleeve, fighting to breathe. Thaeri vanished in a swirl of shadow.

Annor tried to shift her hips and get a leg behind Yevleh's. He pushed up harder on her arm and the spike of pain held her in place. She fumbled for her knife with her left hand, but she couldn't get a grip on it. She elbowed him hard instead and caught him in the ribs. Her wounded arm stung from the effort.

Yevleh flinched but his hold didn't loosen. "Stupid wench. Enough of this. I'll spare your life if you tell me what piece of armor you have and where it is."

She didn't want to die. She'd hardly lived. The space within the Gate still spun, murky but unformed. Annor ached for air. Her lungs burned and blackness lurked at the edges of her sight. Then her eager fingers slid her knife out of its sheath. She slashed Yevleh's leg, weakly, but the sharp blade sliced through his robe and scored his flesh. Yevleh bellowed and let her go.

Annor dove into the swirling darkness inside the Gate.

40

The girl vanished into blackness and the empty arches of the Horn Gates framed nothing but grass and cliffs. Yevleh lifted his robe to inspect the stinging slash on his thigh, the blood trickling down his leg in a small but steady stream.

Yevleh cursed and smacked his fist into one of the uprights. The Gate didn't even quiver, but his knuckles cracked and bled. He still had two apex horns to bolster the power of the Hollow Altar, but any chance of getting Nor's piece of the king's armor had vanished with her through the Gate.

Yevleh smirked. He would have enjoyed persuading Nor to tell him about the armor. Stupid Filip, using such potent fudge on a non-addict. Yevleh would have given her just enough fudge to loosen her inhibitions, and then introduced her to a few pleasures.

Yevleh patted the Horn Gate. With both apex horns he'd still be able to seize control of the Sons of the Prince, even without Nor's piece of armor.

He tore a strip off the bottom of his robe and wrapped it around his thigh, tightening it until the bleeding stopped. The miracle healings worked fine on stage, but they just masked the problems. Yevleh wanted his wound to actually heal.

He crossed the square and stood in front of an Ivory Gate, admiring his reflection. The endless repetitions were unnerving, but he'd never seen such a clear reflection of himself. His braid of office glinted gold on top of his head, like a crown. The rightful High Priest. The Prince Heyl El had honored Yevleh with his visit and his trust, and soon all the Sons of the Prince would know it.

He crossed back to the Horn Gate that had swallowed Nor. The records said the apex horn was simple to remove. He was glad he didn't need to perform a silly Puerán ritual to free it. Yevleh grabbed the soos horn and gave it an experimental tug. At first it was as immovable as the rest of the Gate, but when he tugged harder the horn loosened. He drew it carefully out of the top of the arch until it slipped out from the tangle of horns and into his waiting hands.

Yevleh turned the horn, looking at the tip, the twisty length of it, and the hollow interior. He'd never examined the horn while it rested in the altar. All he knew of it came from rumors and his study of the old records. One rumor whispered that the holder of the horn could see visions within its spiraling length. But many Sons had stared into the horn for long hours and seen nothing. Too bad. Yevleh would have enjoyed using it to spy on the other Sons.

The Gate was fragile without the apex horn. He pushed on it with his free hand and watched it rock on the pavers. Yevleh glanced down at his bloody knuckles. He'd love to knock the Gate over and tromp the horns to bits. But if Nor had learned to use the Gates, he could, too.

The second apex horn yielded as easily as the first. Before he left, Yevleh stood beside the portal and gazed around the little valley. The sunless sky enclosed the circle of cliffs like a protective blue lid. This place appealed to him. It could be his own private retreat. He'd invite a trusted advisor now and then, or maybe a woman, but mostly it could be a place to meditate and plan his triumphs.

One thing was certain, the valley needed more protection than the cave beast. If Nor had slipped past, then anyone might. One of his first commands as High Priest would be to station guards outside the cave entrance.

Yevleh turned and stepped into the portal, welcoming the unending whiteness and the glorious sense of oblivion. It stripped him of doubt so that when he stepped into the dark cave beyond, clutching a horn in each hand, he felt like a conqueror.

The beast sniffed him, but let him pass. Green fluid leaked around the knife lodged in its right eye. Nor must have snuck past on its blind side. Yevleh considered pulling the knife out. But if he left it until he came into power, the knife would still be there to convict the guard who'd owned it.

Winding his way back to the cave entrance, Yevleh plotted how to use the increased power of the Hollow Altar to find the rest of the king's armor. He grinned. The first piece he searched for would be Nor's. With her wandering around, it was bound to be unguarded. And each piece of armor he collected would bolster the altar's power. Halvard's skull would be grinding its teeth in the High Priest's office.

When Yevleh found the breastplate, he'd declare war on the Puerán. And if he learned how to use the Gates of Horn and Ivory…. Yevleh smiled. He'd be unstoppable.

He ducked through the cave exit and out into the light. He paused for a moment on the ledge outside, surveying the city. The Sons would be his, Asseldam would be his, and once he'd conquered the Puerán, the whole continent would be in his hands.

Thanks be to the Prince Heyl El!

41

More tunnels?

Annor sat in the glow of her lightstone and choked back her frustration. She'd seen Thaeri. She'd been so close. And now she was here. Nowhere. Buried alive.

Annor stood, her head scraping the ceiling so that dirt rained into her cropped hair. The earthy air pressed against her face.

Annor shuddered and started off, stooping in the low tunnel, but hiking briskly upwards, wanting nothing more than a way out. Without meaning to, though, her footsteps slowed until she stopped, rooted to the spot. Her thoughts were sluggish, her heart unsettled and depressed. Silence pressed against her ears.

She turned and looked back the way she'd come. Upward felt wrong, even though it made the most sense.

Annor sighed and started back down the tunnel, slowly at first. She picked up speed as her confidence increased. She didn't know why, but Abba El wanted her deeper underground.

Her tunnel fed into a bigger tunnel, and she hesitated. Right, or left? She turned left, but five paces later a giant crack stopped her in her tracks. Fine. She turned around, passed the branch of the tunnel she'd come from on her right, and then came to another branch on her left, a black gap in the darkness.

She shone her lightstone down the branch. Not much to see. She shrugged and kept walking straight. She passed another branch on the left, then one more. About half an hour after she'd fled though the gate, the tunnel branch ended in a wall of dirt.

Annor turned and looked back. She rubbed her eyes and shook the dirt out of her hair. Her mouth was dry, but she had no water. She patted her pants and found nothing but her father's salve and her knife.

"Standing still won't take you where you're going," she said aloud. She'd hated it whenever her father told her that.

She started back the way she'd come, puzzling over which tunnel branch to follow out of the three she'd passed. She stopped at the first one and sniffed. Something smelled nasty.

She turned down the second branch instead. About twenty paces in, she heard a murmur in the darkness, a rhythmic steady whispering. Flowing water. She licked her dry lips and turned in a circle trying to find the source of the sound. She got down on her hands and knees and listened at a small crack in the tunnel floor. The whisper grew louder, steadier, but she didn't know how to get to it. She stood and stretched her aching back, trying to think.

The animals who'd dug this burrow needed water as much as she did. Based on the way this tunnel branch angled, the crack probably met up with the smelly tunnel.

Annor frowned. She didn't want to stumble into the tunnel diggers, but she was so thirsty. She walked back up the tunnel, turned left in the cross tunnel, then left again down the smelly branch.

Her steps slowed and she held her lightstone out at eye level. The air became steadily fouler, with a rank, musty odor that itched inside her nose. The tunnel widened and formed an alcove to her right. Annor coughed and covered her nose and mouth with her free hand. The floor of the alcove was higher than the rest of the tunnel, and filled with piles of droppings. Black mold grew in a thick wavy layer over the droppings, and the stench threatened to choke her, like a rotting carcass. She sneezed and her empty stomach roiled.

Annor sped further down the tunnel and away from the alcove. A damp breeze cooled her cheeks and played with a strand of her hair. Five more paces and the tunnel roof lifted and ended in a cavern. The nest, but empty.

The dirt thrummed under her feet, and the water's whisper had grown into a growl. Another tunnel led out of the nest, and Annor scurried down it, the air damp on her cheeks. The river roared in her ears.

Water droplets spattered her dirty skin. The smooth tunnel floor gave way to an uneven trail that led her down, down, until the water drops became a spray, and the river came into view.

She pocketed her lightstone and knelt on the bank while she buried her face in the river, washing away the dirt, the smell, and her nausea. She drank deeply, and the river water tasted glorious. Pure and sweet.

Annor stood and shook the water out of her hair. But her shirt was already soaked and her pants were wet from the spray. She shivered.

She'd reached an impasse. The only tunnel in the burrow that led up, and so out, was the tunnel where she'd arrived from the gate. And Abba El didn't want her hiking up that tunnel.

She'd seen a large gap between the river and the channel roof. Maybe she could float her way out. But if the gap vanished downstream, she'd drown.

She rubbed her eyes. Maybe this would make more sense after she'd slept. Annor reached for her lightstone, but paused with her hand in her pocket. Upstream a glimmer of light shone steadily on the rushing water. She took out her lightstone, hoping to see a path along the riverbank, but there wasn't one. She'd have to swim, in a deluge, in the dark. She might as well be back in the Black Citadel. And even if she made it to the light, it might not be a way out.

Annor sat on the bank and rested her forehead on her bent knees. Why couldn't something be easy?

Might as well get it over with. She wouldn't be able to sleep without knowing if the light led anywhere. And she was already wet. Before she could change her mind, she jumped to her feet and dove into the river.

The current was as swift as she'd feared, the water dragging her downstream. But Annor fought it with all her strength, swimming with her head out of the water so she could keep an eye on the spot of light.

Her muscles burned and her clothes pulled against her. But she thought about how angry Yevleh made her, and the anger gave her strength. She kicked fiercely, and one of her shoes slid off into the water. Annor kicked off the other one and swam harder.

At least she was making progress. The glimmer of light was closer. She swam furiously, and kicked through the water like Heyl El himself was chasing her.

The light shone almost overhead and lit a knobby outcropping to her right. She grabbed on to the bit of rock, and clutched it, gasping and panting for breath. Her heart pounded in her chest, and she shivered in the flow of chilly water.

Beyond her knob of rock, and a bit higher, a step had been carved into the side of the river channel. A tear joined the water streaming down her face.

Annor pushed off from the rock and launched herself toward the step. Someone had set a hook into the top of the stone step, giving her something to grab onto. Her toes scrabbled along the wall and found a carved indentation. And then another.

Before long Annor sat on the step, hugging her arms to her chest while the river rushed past below, spraying her when it could. She'd beaten it, but the river hadn't given up.

42

The light Annor had seen didn't come from up the steps behind her, but from a circular aperture carved into the ceiling of the river channel. Annor smiled. She'd found people.

When her muscles stopped feeling like jelly, she fished her lightstone out of her pocket and started up the steps. The people who'd hacked the steps out of the rock might know about the animal burrow, but they'd still be surprised to see her climbing in their tunnels. Hopefully they'd be friendly, even if startled. But just in case, Annor loosened her knife in its sheath and held her lightstone in her left hand.

She came to a stair landing with a small room on the left. The room was empty except for a discarded bucket. She climbed the next flight of stairs and arrived in a large, stone room. Also empty. Stone pillars had been left to support the ceiling when the builders hollowed out the space.

Annor stood next to a pillar and studied the room. Small slots in the ceiling might have held lightstones once. A dark, low shape lay at one end. Annor stepped closer until her lightstone illuminated what could only be an altar. She brushed her fingers over the dusty altar stone. Followers of Abba El. Maybe some refugees from Betavar had built this place. She might be closer to Asseldam than she'd thought. Of course, even if she found her way back to the city, she'd still have to clamber through the tunnels behind it to get back to the Gates.

Annor closed her eyes and pictured the little valley with its four Gates, the green grass, the intensely blue sky. Her haven. The thought of Yevleh destroying the Gates or defiling the peace of the valley made her sick. She had to go back and find a way to protect the Gates from the Sons of Darkness.

The gathering hall had two exits. One led to a privy with an opening straight down to the river. The other led up more steps.

Annor climbed, shining her lightstone into small rooms she passed. All empty.

A stair landing had a larger room off to one side. Empty. She climbed more steps and came to a long hallway. Empty stone rooms opened off on both sides the entire length of it. A large, circular stone had been rolled across a smaller opening halfway down the hallway. Maybe the tunnel builders had left some food stores behind. Annor put her lightstone in her pocket and dug her bare toes into the unyielding stone floor. She heaved against the stone. It rolled easier than she'd expected, and she landed on her bottom with a grunt.

With her lightstone in her pocket, it should have been dark in the tunnels. Instead she saw a circle of light at the far end of the hallway. She tiptoed toward it, fingering the haft of her knife. They must have heard her shift the stone, but maybe people rolled it back and forth all the time.

She heard a whispering sound, the closer she came to the light. A murmuring hum. And the light didn't look right for a lightstone. She snorted. That's because it was an air shaft. Annor ducked her head inside it and looked up, up through endless rock to the faraway sky. The bottom end of the shaft opened to the river, rumbling along far below her.

She took out her lightstone and trotted back to the stone she'd moved, her stomach growling hopefully, but when she illuminated the space behind the stone, all she found was another flight of steps. She rubbed the front of her aching thighs and started up.

Annor passed more hallways and more empty rooms as the stairs switchbacked through the heart of the mountain, up and up. She passed the air shaft several times. The day above was waning, the the light dimmer each time she poked her head in the shaft and looked longingly toward the unreachable sky. Then, no more stairs, just a hallway so long that she couldn't see the end of it within the glow of her lightstone. She followed it past empty room after empty room and still hadn't come to the end.

Annor's legs trembled with fatigue, so she sat on the dusty floor and leaned against the wall. She rubbed her toe where she'd stubbed it on an uneven step, then put her lightstone in her pocket and closed her eyes.

Her clothes had dried on her upward journey, and her hunger had grown. Thirst had begun to haunt her. The tunnel dwellers had used a pulley system to fetch water from the river, but they'd taken all the buckets except for the one she'd seen in the first empty room. She regretted not grabbing it, but she'd thought she'd find people, not an abandoned town. The tunnel builders had packed every crumb and left.

She slid down and curled into a ball. The floor was cold and hard, but Annor was so tired. It felt good to lie there in the blind dark, motionless. She was tired of tramping around in the darkness. Tired of being hungry and thirsty. Tired of being alone. She'd have been better off staying on her island.

Annor slept deeply, not waking until a ray of light warmed her face. Blinking, she sat up. A small patch of light gleamed farther down the hallway. She feasted on it, willing her legs to find the strength to move. A beetle scuttled past her feet.

She walked toward the light and stepped through a screen of plants into a new day. The blazing sun brought tears to her eyes and she blinked to clear them.

A slab of rock served as the tunnel builders' front porch. A circular stone leaned off to one side ready to seal away the tunnel's secrets. Steps led down the mountain slope to a valley below.

43

Bald Erik heard the clomp of feet long before they came to wake him. The footsteps reverberated in the empty temple, echo upon echo, as they neared his sleeping chamber. He'd never had this many Sons gather to torture him before. Olaf must have something special planned for tonight.

The Sons entered his room in a blaze of lightstones. "Good," one of them said. "You're awake. Come along then and join the celebration."

Erik staggered to his feet, his leg throbbing, and shuffled between two of the black-robed Sons down the hallway toward the former altar room. He'd been having such a nice dream. He struggled to hold onto it. His wife's smiling face, the laughter of his little son toddling toward him, hands out for balance.

The Son behind him prodded Erik in the back. "Move along, old man."

Erik blinked when he entered the desecrated altar room. The waiting Sons had placed lightstones all along the floor's perimeter. The light blazed upward, lengthening the Sons' shadows so they stretched to the domed ceiling above. The room was as full of priests as he'd ever seen it in these long years. A group of vaettir stood behind them, crowding the room further.

The green stone sparkled at the end of the table. Erik swallowed his anxiety. He wouldn't allow these vultures to see his fear and feed on it.

"Don't be shy," one of the Sons said. He stepped out from the crowd of black robes and flung back his hood. "Such a pleasure to meet you. Of course, I've read through all my predecessors' notes, so I feel we're already acquainted."

Bald Erik frowned. He'd never seen this young Son of Darkness. But the man wore his braid of office centered on top of his head. The braid glittered gold in the light, and with the amulet strapped to his forehead and the necklace of finger bones around his neck, there could be no doubt. "Congratulations on your elevation to High Priest."

"Thank you, Erik. My name is Yevleh, but you may address me as Heir to the Prince."

Erik chuckled. "You're reaching a little high for someone so new to the office."

"No, indeed. All my colleagues recognize me as such." Yevleh gestured to the sea of black robes. The Sons inclined their heads, murmuring, "Yes, Heir."

"See?" Yevleh smiled and snapped his fingers. "Bring him to the table."

They prodded Erik in the back until he crossed the room. He sat on the tabletop and swung his legs up and on, as usual.

"Not so fast," Yevleh said. "We're doing this a little differently tonight. Strip off your clothes, and then get on the table."

Erik shrugged and pulled his ragged shirt over his head. His chest hair had begun to grow back. He must be in for another plucking. He unstuck his pants from his thigh wound and let them drop to the floor beside his shirt. Blood ran down his leg. His leg hair was growing back, too. Definitely harvest time.

Erik smiled to himself, thinking of the Sons as crazy farmers, and settled back onto the table. The chill of the tabletop on his bare flesh sent a shiver through his frame. This young demon might think he trod new ground, but Erik had endured it all through the years.

"Tie him down," Yevleh said. Several Sons stepped forward with coiled rope.

They hadn't tied Erik for many a long year. He'd never struggled, so someone along the line had decided it was a waste of time. Much more entertaining to torture a willing subject.

Yevleh stepped closer, smiling. The green amulet on his forehead glinted in the brightly-lit room. "I think I may know a friend of yours. A girl called Nor. She had long, brown hair when I first knew her, but I had the privilege of trimming it."

Erik's eyes widened, but he didn't speak.

"Ah, you do know her. In gratitude for her new haircut, Nor led me to where the two apex horns waited, at the Gates of Horn and Ivory. I was saddened I had to send her into oblivion."

Erik's jaw ached from holding back his despair. What had this fiend done to Annor? And now the Sons of Darkness had both apex horns. No wonder the other Sons bowed to this young one's leadership.

"So sorry to have to break the news to you." Yevleh smiled again. "But let's get started." He set a small cage on Erik's chest.

"Are you sure this is wise?" one of the Sons asked. He stepped closer and pulled his hood back onto his shoulders. He was an older man, his braid of office thick along the side of his head with a red cord braided along the length of it.

"General, you know the venom isn't always fatal. And if he comes too close to death, we'll use the stone to bring him back. I'm surprised Olaf never tried this."

Erik swallowed. What was in the cage?

Yevleh unlatched the cage door.

Erik waited, craning his neck to stare into the dark opening. A tongue flicked out of the darkness and into the light, and then the creature cautiously followed, blinking. A four-legged serpent.

Yevleh was correct. The creature's venom wasn't always fatal. After inflicting excruciating pain, the venom induced a coma. A few victims awoke from the coma, their minds obliterated. But most died within several hours. A serpent bite was a favored method of capital punishment in Asseldam. The few who survived were given their freedom, much good that it did them.

The serpent's claws dug into Erik's bare chest as it stretched toward his neck, nostrils flared wide. And then it struck. Lightning fast, the fangs entered his throat. A wickedly cold sensation streamed into Erik's chest and out to his limbs, growing colder and more painful with every beat of his heart.

Erik's body convulsed. The straps holding him to the table kept him from flailing onto the floor. He didn't know how long the harrowing pain lasted, or how long he strained, back arching, against the ropes that held him down. He might have been screaming, but with his brain on fire, he couldn't be sure. Light pierced his clenched eyelids until, mercifully, blackness overwhelmed him.

"Will he bleed out? His wound is gushing after that little demonstration."

"He'll be fine."

The voices came from so far away Erik wasn't sure he heard them, or imagined them. The sound of footsteps shifted around him, and someone commanded the vaettir to step forward and surround the table. The general, no doubt.

"First we'll insert the splinter into his heart." That was the little demon. What was his name? Yevleh.

"Why wasn't he given a splinter long ago?"

"They tried and failed. His resistance was too great. But with him hovering near death, it should slide right in."

Yevleh sounded quite full of himself, but maybe he was right. Halvard was the one who'd tried giving Erik a splinter from the Hollow Altar. But the splinter couldn't penetrate Erik's skin, no matter what the man tried. Erik had resisted it, certainly, but that long ago he'd been less sure what he was capable of.

Out of the darkness a sharp pain pierced the flesh over his heart. If he were in a coma, he shouldn't be able to hear and feel. And think. But it couldn't last much longer. The venom must be eating away at his mind even now.

"Abba El," he pled in his heart, "haven't I been patient? I've suffered under the hand of wickedness these many long years. My family is gone. Scattered, or slain. My body is a plaything for whatever their twisted minds can devise. I've watched the city decay and the people degenerate with it. And now the spark of hope Annor brought has been snuffed out as well. How much more will you ask of me? How much longer must I endure?

"My life is a willing offering in thy hands. I've waited, I've suffered, according to thy will. For what purpose I know not. But please, dear Father, can it end? My freedom or my death. Either would be welcome. Thy will be done, in this as in all things."

A sweet peace enveloped Erik as he lay helpless on the table. It surged through him as the venom had, radiating from his heart to every element of his being, burning and healing in a moment of glorious joy. A tear leaked from beneath his closed eyelids. The righteous need not succumb to poison. The Puerán had taught that and lived it, and now Erik knew for himself that it was true.

As the venom fizzled into nothing, Erik lay motionless, waiting for his faculties and strength to return. He could feel the splinter boring into his heart. He'd have to do something about that as well, but not right now. He knew it was urgent. He'd seen too many people killed, and reduced from defiance to willing, drooling slaves, to doubt that. But the poison had left him feeble and exhausted.

The Sons of Darkness still believed him comatose. They busied themselves preparing his next ordeal, whatever that might be. He heard them clearly now, moving around and ordering the vaettir into position. Position for what?

Someone sprinkled Erik's body with powder. "Are you sure it will be more effective this way?" Yevleh asked.

"Oh yes," the general said. "We'll get a much stronger reading with the hair still attached at the root."

The general invoked the name of Heyl El, commanding the powder to burn and ignite Erik's body hair. "Inhale," the general told his vaettir. "Discover his secrets. Reveal the remnants of all he holds dear."

Not this time. Erik commanded a wind to blow in the name of Abba El. It was a mental command, and Erik was weak and disoriented, but he invested it with all the spiritual resources he could gather. And it blew. A wind swept through the dome, brushed his skin, and snuffed out the flames.

Erik opened his eyes and sat up, the binding ropes crumbling into fragments. He looked down at his smoking arms, chest, and legs. All a shocking red, though unblistered. Then Erik raised his hand to the starlit dome above and drew a spiral in the air. "More," he commanded, his voice firm and penetrating.

The ensuing wind blasted the vaettir away from the table. They staggered back, arms hiding their faces, whimpering and moaning. Gusts ripped the hoods from the Sons' heads, leaving them exposed and vulnerable. The gale strengthened, driving the general, Yevleh, and all the rest, to their knees. Their anxious cries joined those of the vaettir.

Erik slid out of a pool of his blood and off the table. The blood flowed toward the green stone in a steady red stream. Erik stood in the midst of his enemies, the wind holding him sheltered in a circle of calm. And then the wind died. Erik scanned the desecrated altar room, the weeping Sons, the wailing vaettir, all kneeling as if in supplication. "Abba El," he whispered, "thou art mighty to save."

Yevleh staggered to his feet. "Get him," he called to the others. "Hold him fast. We need to put in more splinters. The heart splinter wasn't enough. We'll stick one in his brain and another in his hand."

The Sons wiped their eyes and noses on their sleeves and surged to obey.

The general stepped forward, clutching a small wooden box. "But three splinters will make him catatonic."

"Him? Ha! He'll become the most powerful tool in our arsenal." Yevleh chuckled. "Look at him, healed even without the green stone. With the stone, we can do whatever we want to him."

The priests pressed upon Erik, forcing him back to the table, but Erik wouldn't go easily. Not any more. He raised his right hand toward the ceiling and the temple shook. The priests murmured and retreated.

"Find more rope and bind him back on the table!" Yevleh shouted. "Bring the other splinters! We'll use them all."

Black robes surrounded Erik, some priests grabbing knives and saws and chisels stained with his dried blood. The vaettir had moved back to the walls. Erik looked up at the circle of sky. How long until dawn? The night was unending.

He aimed his palm through the crowd of black robes, to the small wooden box in the general's hand. Lightning flashed from Erik's hand and the box burst into flames.

The general shrieked, dropped the box, and watched it burn, horrified. The vaettir nearest the general clutched at his chest and screamed, then collapsed to the floor. The general knelt beside him, frantically shaking him. The vaettir's shirt burst into a circle of flames over his heart. "No," the general cried, "we have so few left!"

The priests stepped back, fear widening their eyes. A few glanced to the doorway, planning their escape.

"Stop!" Yevleh commanded them. He pushed one Son out of his way and stood in front of Erik, eyes blazing. "You will submit to my will, or I will crack the stone so it will never heal you again. I've read how Olaf liked to turn you into a pile of gore and broken limbs. Don't think I'm afraid to do the same. Are you willing to live forever as my broken, bleeding toy?"

Erik looked into Yevleh's eyes and chuckled. "Do you think I fear you? Any of you?" He smirked at the priests with their bloody weapons, the general, the vaettir beyond. He clenched his hand into a fist and the temple shook again, stronger. Fiercer. The floor rolled beneath their feet.

The priests dropped their weapons and fought, pushing and shoving, to get through the doorway and out of the altar room. The general shouted to his remaining vaettir, "Flee! Run!" The temple shook harder.

Soon, only Erik and Yevleh remained. "I can bring this whole temple down upon you," Erik said, "if it be the will of Abba El." He dropped his arm and the temple shuddered into stillness. "But the time is not yet. The iniquity of Asseldam isn't quite ripe."

Yevleh scowled, his breath coming in short, angry gasps. "Kneel before me! I am the Heir to the Prince Heyl El. That splinter in your heart means you must obey. Kneel!"

Erik held his right palm in front of his chest and took a deep breath. Lightning sparked from his palm and entered the blackened hole above his heart. The splinter fought to tear itself out of his chest. The agony brought tears to his eyes, but Erik stood firm. "Be gone," he whispered through gritted teeth.

The tip of the splinter appeared at last, singed by the thread of lightning still radiating from his palm. Slowly, painfully, it squirmed out of his chest and fell to the floor where it burned to ash.

Yevleh stepped back. "This isn't over," he said. He turned and ran from the room, his black robe sailing behind him.

Erik examined his wounds, grimacing at his reddened body, his wounded thigh, and his blackened chest. He bent to pick his clothes off the floor and slowly redressed, his body shivering with fatigue. He gazed up at the circle of night sky. Dawn still hadn't come. Turning his back on the Sons' abandoned lightstones and the hapless, dead vaettir, he shuffled out the door, down the hall, and back to his dark sleeping chamber.

44

The rising sun flooded the long and narrow valley with gold. "Thank you, Abba El," Annor whispered.

A ring of mountains surrounded the valley as far as she could see, and not far from the base of her mountain a verdant green hill rose from the valley floor. Three broad streams gushed from the base of the hill. One flowed directly toward her, bright as crystal, before meeting the mountain and vanishing underground.

Just one tree graced the top of that magnificent green hill, an enormous tree with vibrant green leaves that sparkled in the morning light. Annor was captivated by the tree. Just the sight of it filled her with inexpressible joy. She'd found the Shimmertree.

Laughing, she half climbed and half slid down the mountain slope. When she reached the valley floor, she threaded her way through knee-high grasses until she came to the bank of the stream. The water was a delight, chattering to itself as it threaded between its banks. Splashing over rocks, it flung bright sparkling drops in the air like fistfuls of diamonds. At the base of the mountain, a crowd of boulders stood sentinel as the stream ducked under a rocky shelf and vanished underground.

Annor knelt and washed her grimy hands before drinking handful after handful of the crystal water. It tasted pure and sweet, each sip more delicious than her last, and washed away the darkness and worry of her time wandering the tunnels. She bent to wash her face. The water felt glorious on her skin.

The mountains rose around her in a vigilant rocky ring, their tops still capped in snow, their slopes steep and impassable. Trees grew in

ranks on their lower slopes, but tapered off before they reached the
snowy crags that jutted like fists into the deep blue sky.

Annor followed the stream eastward toward the Tree shining on the
green hill. The heavens' blue expanse held the valley protectively in
its arms while a breeze caressed her face and stroked her tangled hair.
Butterflies flitted among the wildflowers scattered in bright dots of red
and blue and yellow in the sea of waving grasses. Bees hummed, and
birds trilled cheerful melodies.

When Annor reached the hill, she found the stream bubbling out
of the ground at its base, while a narrow stone path encircled the hill
just above the gush and spray of water. The Shimmertree crowned the
hill like a gentle giant, beckoning her onward. Its branches spread in
a wide embrace that welcomed all comers, peace and joy radiating
outward in a steady flow that fell on Annor's upturned face like
sunlight on the wildflowers.

Annor started off along the path. Close-cropped grass glistening
with dew coated the hill above her in a swathe of brilliant green.
Golden paving stones glittered under her feet, and when she bent to
run her hand over them, they felt as smooth as glass.

She followed the narrow path until it curved above the bubbling
rush of a southward-flowing stream, and on toward the eastern side
of the hill where a fourth stream came frothing out from underneath
the slope and flowed off into the distance. Just above this stream, the
circling path intersected an even narrower path that arrowed straight
toward the crest of the hill. At last. Annor had ached to ascend the hill
and walk under the sheltering branches of the Shimmertree, but she'd
been reluctant to tread on the lively grass.

She left the singing stream behind to climb the straight and narrow
path. The grass grew thickly on either side, so lush and alive that
Annor felt refreshed just looking at it. Even the air tasted sweet here.
The trials of the past few days felt remote.

The hill was a surprisingly long climb, and her legs were still
sore from all the stairs she'd climbed. Her calves and thighs
complained with each step she took on the golden path, though
the hill rose before Annor as high as ever. She gazed down the
slope, stretching far into the distance before it reached the valley

floor, but the Tree growing on the summit seemed as far away as when she'd started.

Her filthy clothes itched on her dusty skin. She regretted just washing her hands and face and wished she'd stopped to bathe in the stream, even though she had no clean clothes to wear. She hated to be so filthy when she approached the Shimmertree.

Annor had grown quite weary by the time she climbed close enough to the Tree to smell the heady scent of its fruit. It hung from the branches in clusters, brilliantly white in the midst of the shimmering leaves. The scent revived her, and her stomach growled.

She laughed and climbed faster. She was almost there. Almost, but not quite. The Guardian stepped from behind the Tree and reached out to take her right hand in his. Annor took a step forward and stood under the overhanging branches of the Tree. The fruit smelled so marvelous it almost overwhelmed her, like love had been embodied in each and every piece.

"Welcome," the Guardian said, smiling and releasing her hand. "I'm glad you found your way."

"Please," Annor said, "may I taste the fruit?" Her heart ached, longing for it.

"I'm sorry," the Guardian said, "but first you must finish your mortality. The fruit has the gift of eternity. One bite, and you'll be immortal, never to die."

Annor thought about her parents dying and leaving her alone on the island. "Is that such a bad thing, never to die?"

"No, it's a great gift, and after you've lived a worthy, useful life, you may partake freely of the fruit.

"Annor, pluck this leaf of the Tree," he said, bending a branch down within her reach and pointing to one of the leaves. "It'll take you to a place to bathe away the grime from under the mountain. When you're ready to return, the leaf will bring you back to the Tree."

Annor considered the leaf uncertainly, wishing she could pluck one of the fruit growing near it instead. But the Guardian smiled so kindly. She grasped the leaf in her right hand and gave it a quick tug. It came off easily, though it still throbbed with life between her fingers.

The Tree and the Guardian vanished, along with the green hill and the surrounding valley and mountains. Annor stood beside a babbling stream. Wildflowers covered its banks in swathes of blue and yellow.

She set the leaf carefully on the ground, and stripped off her tunic and pants. The stream was just cold enough to be completely revitalizing. Standing in midstream, she scrubbed herself thoroughly. When she was clean, Annor sat in the midst of the wildflowers to dry in the warm sun.

Gloriously refreshed, she hated to dress in her dirty leather clothes. She marveled, though, as she held them up. Her clothes looked new. The Guardian thought of everything.

When she'd dressed, she took one last grateful look at the stream before she picked up the leaf. She turned the leaf over and over, watching it shimmer with light. It felt so alive in her hand, even after she'd plucked it from the Tree.

The leaf pulsed between her fingers, and instantly she stood beside the Guardian smelling the intoxicating scent of the pure white fruit. "Thank you," Annor said. "That was a blessing."

"You must be hungry," the Guardian said, smiling. He made a wide gesture with his right hand and a picnic appeared in the midst of the green grass. "Will you join me?"

"Oh yes, thank you." Annor's mouth watered from the aroma of fresh-baked bread. The smell reminded her of her mother. Grilled fish, yams dripping with honey, artichoke, cheese, apples, blackberries, tender carrots, meat swimming in gravy, and much more dotted the grass. The food was served on beautiful golden dishes that sparkled in the sunlight.

It felt like a moment stolen from heaven to sit under the protective branches of the Shimmertree, inhaling the sweet scent of the fruit with every breath. Annor feasted, trying a little bit of everything. The Guardian chatted pleasantly, explaining the unfamiliar dishes and helping Annor feel welcome. She studied her surroundings while she ate, memorizing the moment so she'd have it to enjoy the rest of her life.

The valley lay spread below them, stretching farther east than she'd realized. The protective mountains formed a u-shape, and a forest grew thickly across the eastern edge of the valley, far in the distance. The huge Tree occupied most of her attention, though. She couldn't eat the enticing white fruit, but the scent fed her soul. The green leaves shimmered and trembled in the breeze, and the branches oozed nectar.

"If you can travel to Abba El's other worlds, as well as travel instantly all over our world, why did my father carve that standing stone with a map to the Shimmertree? You could have brought me here from my island the same way you sent me to that stream and back."

"But then you wouldn't have learned to see through stone, to see inside the horn you found, or even to see in the darkness under the mountain. You also needed to learn not to lose hope when all seems hopeless."

Maybe so, but Annor still wished her journey had been easier. "Do you ever need to walk anywhere?" she asked. "Or have you learned all there is to know?"

The Guardian smiled. "I still have much to learn, and I walk when I have need, but I also walk in time so the Tree is never left unguarded. When I visited you on your island, or the other times we've met, I returned to the Tree just when I left it."

"So you travel into the past as easily as you travel from world to world, just like entering the past or the future through the Horn Gates." Annor sat silent for a moment. "It's all right if I walk into the future, isn't it? My father carved the stone so I'd find my way here, and I guess so I'd learn to see all those things like you said. But he left me the horn as well. Did my father go to the Gates?"

"King Beraqel entrusted Gunnar with the horn, just as he entrusted him with the gauntlets. Your father wanted to give me the horn, but I knew you'd need it. I told him where to leave it for you."

He gave her a thoughtful look. "I must caution you, Annor, that you can't change what is now past. You can't bring your parents back to mortality when they've already stepped into eternity."

"I know. But I enjoyed seeing my father again, just for a little while. That was all right, wasn't it? And I'd like to see my mother again too, sometime."

"In that case, you'll need to restore the Gates of Horn. Yevleh stole both apex horns after you vanished through the Gate, though he left the Gates otherwise intact."

Annor frowned. "I have to go back to their awful temple. I almost got caught last time. Can you send me to the altar room at least? Or maybe you could get the horns. I already did it once."

The Guardian smiled and shook his head. "If I did everything for you, how would you grow?"

"Last time the horn was inside their altar."

"Yes, the altar is one of their abominations. They constructed it from the wood of the Knowing Tree that once grew beside the Shimmertree, here on this hill. Its once sacred wood has been shaped into a false altar, to worship their false god."

"The Knowing Tree from the First Garden?"

"Yes."

Annor's parents had told her the story of how their first parents ate the fruit of the Knowing Tree and brought mortality to the world. She gazed up into the branches of the glorious tree that remained, and shuddered. "That's just wrong. So did Yevleh put both the horns inside the altar this time?"

The Guardian frowned. "No, he set them in the throne room, in the basket that holds the dried fruit of the Knowing Tree. The four-legged serpents guard them there."

Annor swallowed. "The throne room. Great." She remembered how terrible she'd felt just peeking through the chimney vent. "Well, I suppose I might as well get it over with." She stood and fingered her knife strapped on her thigh. "Thank you for the bath and the meal. I feel like a new person."

"I'll send you to the ruins south of the Sons' temple this time." The Guardian reached into the air and retrieved a long narrow bag. "You can use this to hold the apex horns."

The bag was made of thick, white cloth, and had a long strap that fit nicely over one shoulder and around Annor's neck.

"May the blessings of Abba El go with you now and always," the Guardian said.

"Thank you." Annor breathed in a deep lungful of the scent of the white fruit, and gave it one last longing glance. "Can I come back here again, when this is all finished?"

The Guardian smiled. "You are always welcome at the Shimmertree, Annor."

His hands were warm and sure on her head. Annor treasured the moment while it lasted, and then she was alone.

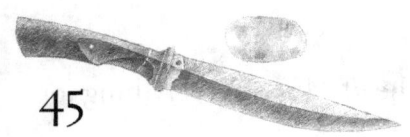

45

Annor crouched outside the throne room's heating grate. The temple chimney was a familiar darkness now, but still repellent. She'd been more focused this time. The temple hadn't oppressed or overwhelmed her, or even slowed her down. Until now.

She could do this. She'd found the Gates, she'd survived torture, and days wandering underground. Taking the horns from the fruit basket would be simple in comparison.

Or it should have been. But Annor hesitated. The crushing power radiating through the grate pounded on her brain, and the fetid odor of the serpents made her nauseous.

She'd seen the Shimmertree, and drunk from a stream of living water. Abba El was more powerful than Heyl El. She knew that. But, Abba El granted peace and endless life while Heyl El strove only to intimidate and dominate. And Annor didn't feel peaceful right now. She felt intimidated. She struggled not to give in and run away.

She found the courage to peek through the grate. The gray room looked just as Annor remembered it, moving walls, dripping stalactite, and all. The apex horns rested in the basket beside the bone throne, just as the Guardian had said. Yes, she could do this. She'd go in there, grab the horns, and be back in the chimney in no time. Then she could take her pounding head and flee, spiriting the horns beyond Yevleh's reach. She grinned. She'd love to see his face when he realized she'd taken them back. Foul, arrogant man.

Erik had warned her of the serpents' venom. No doubt that was what dripped from the stalactite onto the throne. The venom could eat through her skin and poison her blood. She wouldn't get any nearer to the throne than she needed to. And if she kept the four-legged serpents away from her throat, she'd be fine. Just fine. Still, she hesitated.

She closed her eyes and remembered Thaeri's face, the way he'd lit up when he saw her, his hand reaching toward her. Revenge on Yevleh couldn't motivate her to move, but a future of her own choosing could. Annor pushed open the grate cover, swinging it into the room. Still no lock. The Sons must not have figured out how she stole the horn out of their altar. Before she could change her mind, she eased herself through the opening and into the throne room.

The room had six sides and no visible door. If Yevleh checked on the horns, he could come from any direction. But it was all right. She wouldn't be here long enough for anyone to catch her.

The room's gray light had no source. It tricked her eyes and made it hard to judge distances. She took slow, careful steps across the spongy floor toward the dais, her eyes on the endlessly moving serpents. They hissed, but skittered away when her foot hovered above them. She could do this. She ignored her pounding head and the power pushing at her to kneel, to submit, to honor the Prince Heyl El.

One serpent moved out of her path too slowly and Annor stepped on the tip of its tail. It whirled toward her and spat, mouth agape. Serpent saliva dripped down her pant leg, smoking and eating holes through the leather. No one had mentioned they could spit acid. Annor swallowed and stepped more cautiously. The serpents on the ceiling made her the most nervous. They were closest to her throat.

She reached the dais and stepped up onto it. The fruit basket sat on a small table beside the throne, with legs of bone that matched the bone throne. The edge of the table had been intricately carved into the shape of a four-legged serpent with its tail in its mouth.

Annor picked one horn out of the basket and slid it into the waiting bag. The second horn soon followed. She slung the bag across her back and smiled. She'd done it.

Dried fruit of the Knowing Tree half filled the basket, exposed now and strangely desirable. They were about the size of a walnut. The purplish-black fruit beckoned. Annor hesitated. Fruit from the Knowing Tree could be helpful.

Annor's hand hovered over the basket. The Sons shouldn't have any advantage in this battle for the truth, and the fruit of the Knowing Tree was like a secret arsenal. Just one couldn't hurt, and it would be one less the Sons could use in their quest to outwit the forces of Abba El.

A delicate scent caught her nostrils, overriding the bitter scent that permeated the room. Her mouth watered and her hesitation vanished. She picked up one of the round fruits and brought it to her nose, breathing in its heady smell. Dried, it didn't smell as enticing as the white fruit of the Living Tree. But it might have rivaled it when they grew side-by-side in the First Garden, before Heyl El ripped the Knowing Tree out of the ground.

Annor tucked the fruit into her pocket and took another look at the basket. Unless Yevleh counted them, he'd never know one was missing. Maybe she should take one more, just in case.

But before she could reach out her hand, the carved serpent rimming the table edge flickered into life and swarmed into the basket. It hissed, and Annor jumped.

She turned, but before she could step down to the floor, the dais began to spin. Annor lost her balance and sat down hard, narrowly missing the puddled venom surrounding the base of the throne. She grabbed onto one of the table's bone legs while the dais spun faster. It grated and growled as it whirled, like a beast savoring its prey. The fruit bulged in her pocket. Maybe stealing it hadn't been such a good idea.

The dais didn't stop spinning. Annor grew dizzy. If she hadn't been gripping the bone leg, she would have been flung off like the puddled venom beside her. She watched it spray the room and swallowed queasily. The Sons would know she'd been here if she vomited, even if they didn't hear the dais.

The dais slowed and ground to a halt. The dizziness on top of her headache left Annor weak and shivery. The throne room still throbbed with power, commanding her to submit, to bow to the throne of the Prince Heyl El. She shook it off. Light sparkled in front of her eyes, making it hard to see, and a shaft of pain stabbed through her head.

She choked down her nausea and stumbled to her feet. The Sons could enter at any moment and she was in no shape to fight them off. Annor blinked to clear her vision. The chimney vent had vanished.

She struggled to focus on the walls. The flat gray light made the gray walls hard to see. She blinked frantically, swaying on her feet. She needed to escape before her head exploded, and before the Sons came bursting into the room.

Annor circled the dais, searching for the vent. The serpents had mostly ignored her on her way into the room. Now that she wanted to leave, they swarmed up her legs as she stepped between their squirming bodies. She shook off the first few, but they learned to dig their claws through her leather pants and into her leg. She took out her knife and knocked them off with the side of the blade, praying they wouldn't bite or spit acid.

She spotted the open vent around the back side of the throne. Treading across the spongy floor, she swatted serpents off her legs with every footfall. She'd almost made it, just a few more steps to go. But a four-legged serpent dropped from the ceiling and landed on her shoulder.

Annor cried out, but held perfectly still. The serpent dug its claws into her shoulder, and its head slid along the side of her neck. Next it would go for her throat. She teetered on the edge of panic. Her pounding head made it hard to think. Holding her knife at the ready, she reached up to grab the serpent with her free hand.

The serpent spat. The acid seared into Annor's skin and the flesh on the back of her hand sizzled. Desperate, she grabbed the serpent just as its head snaked around to the base of her throat. She tore the beast off her tunic and flung it across the room.

Breathing hard, she slid through the open vent and swung the grate shut. She crouched in the chimney, clutching a protruding brick with her burning hand while she scraped at the back of it with her knife. The gray light slanting through the vent didn't let her see how bad it was.

Annor tucked her knife back in its sheath. The faster she got out of here, the better. The bag of horns still rested safely on her back. She scrambled down the chimney, through the flue channel, and into the pillared chamber.

She crouched in the furnace for a minute to catch her breath and clear her pounding head. The power of the throne room had lost its grip on her. Her hand was blackened and bloody. She coated it with some of her father's salve and hoped for the best. If nothing else, it cooled the burning.

She would run through the night as soon as she climbed out. She couldn't let Yevleh catch her with the apex horns. Annor shivered thinking about the leering look he'd given her between the Gates of Horn and Ivory. He'd enjoy torturing her, but first he'd steal her virtue.

She took a tight grip on the horns, swung open the furnace door, and climbed out. Pushing the door closed, she quietly latched it shut. No reason to let the Sons of Darkness figure out how they'd been robbed. She tiptoed up the steps, readying herself to run.

Lightstones blazed as the waiting Sons pulled them out of their pockets. They filled the space between the two wings of the temple, from one wall to the other. Annor was trapped.

Yevleh stood at the front of the Sons, his braid of office glinting gold in the light. "Going somewhere?"

46

Annor flashed a fake smile. "Good evening, Yevleh. You got some friends to help you out this time. By the way, how's your leg wound?"

Yevleh snarled. "Grab her."

Annor fumbled for her knife, but her aching head and her wounded hand made her too slow. Three guards darted out of the line of black robes and surrounded her. The one behind her took her knife away. He pricked it into the small of her back and whispered in her ear, his breath warm. "Don't think you can run for it this time."

Yevleh stepped toward them and snapped his fingers. "Hand me the bag."

One of the guards pulled the cord over her head and held the bag of horns out to Yevleh, ducking his head.

Yevleh slipped the cord over one shoulder and around his neck, so that the bag slanted across his chest. He clutched the concealed horns with one hand and gestured with the other. "Take her to the altar room."

The line of priests glanced at one another. Anonymous in their hoods and black robes, one ventured to question him. "Heir, shouldn't she be taken to the Citadel?"

Yevleh snorted. "Yes, that went so well last time." He shook his head, eyes grim. "No, I'll question her on the altar, knife in hand, and this time I'll get answers."

The priests stepped aside to let Annor and the three guards pass. The guard behind her walked right on her heels. Her knife lanced her back in rhythm with their steps. A trickle of blood ran down into the waistband of her pants, and for the first time in her life she regretted keeping her knife so sharp.

She looked over her shoulder. "Is that necessary?"

The guard chuckled. "Keep walking."

He jabbed her harder until the blood ran freely. Annor bit her lip and walked on.

They reached the end of the temple wing and turned left toward the entrance. She could hear the river on her right, flowing to freedom. But not for her. Besides, she needed to get the horns back. Somehow. She sighed. Just staying alive would be a stretch.

The temple entrance looked more sinister at night. Red lightstones behind the fangs lit the gaping mouth. The red light bathed the sentries in blood. They stood with weapons drawn, unmoving, until Yevleh gestured for them to open the door.

Annor thought back to that sunny day with Gunilla when they'd come to clean the furnace. Annor could have kept her head down, avoided the fudge party, and spent her days sweeping chimneys and earning a living. She could have kept her one and only friend, and maybe made more. It wouldn't have been the future she longed for, but it would have been better than death. By the dark look in Yevleh's eyes, he would be satisfied with nothing less.

"Take her to the altar room and strap her to the altar."

Annor swallowed. Lucky her. She'd get to see inside the Sons' temple before she died. But she couldn't give up hope yet, or she'd be beaten before Yevleh even got started.

Red lightstones illuminated the long hallway. They shone from the ceiling and the edge of the floor onto walls stacked tightly with skulls. The skulls had no jawbones. Annor imagined bookshelves made out of interlocking jawbones and chuckled to herself.

The guard behind her jabbed her again. "Quit dawdling."

She bit back a comment. It wouldn't help.

Long as the hallway was, it wasn't long enough for Annor's heart to stop pounding. They entered the altar room and the guard pushed her down on the altar. He stood over her with her knife held to her throat, hungrily waiting for her to struggle, while the other two guards made short work of strapping her down face up. The straps were stained black from all the blood they'd absorbed. One of the guards handed Yevleh her sheathed knife, and then he and his fellows left.

Annor glanced at the chimney vent. So close, and so useless. She steadied her breathing. She wouldn't let Yevleh see her fear. She wouldn't. But if he noticed her racing pulse he'd know the terror that beat in her breast. She'd seen what the Sons had done to Bald Erik.

Black-robed priests filed into the altar room, excited, no doubt, to see the show. "Stop," Yevleh said. "I'll take care of this myself. I don't need the energy released by her sacrifice accruing to the lot of you. I'll need it all in the coming days to fulfill the will of the Prince Heyl El."

The priests muttered, but there was a chorus of, "Yes, Heir."

Yevleh shut the door behind the last black robe, and slid an iron bar through the two brackets on either side of the door. He turned to Annor and grinned, his teeth clenched. "Wouldn't want to be interrupted."

He tossed her sheathed knife near the wall and pulled the cord of the bag over his head. He stood the apex horns upright on the floor beside the altar, one at her feet and one at her head. On the wall opposite the chimney vent, Yevleh opened a cupboard built flush into the facade. Metal clinked as Yevleh sorted through the knives inside.

He chuckled to himself. "This one's perfect. Just dull enough."

A wave of sorrow washed over Annor, deep gut-wrenching sorrow, filling her with regret for stupid choices and things left undone. A tear trickled down into her ear.

Yevleh laughed. "It's too soon for tears. Save them until the fun starts."

Anger pushed aside her sorrow. "Were you always this cruel? Is that how Asseldam's mothers raise their little Sons of Darkness?"

Yevleh crossed the room in a bound and held the tip of the blood-stained knife just above her eye. "Sons of the Prince, little wretch," he hissed. He withdrew the knife but bent over her still, his eyes piercing hers. "And no, I was raised on a farm far to the west of Asseldam, but with a deep respect for my Prince Heyl El. I'll teach you some of that respect before you die screaming his name. It'll be a pleasure to send you to meet him." He spat on her cheek and stepped back.

Annor clenched her teeth and didn't flinch. Not at his words, not at the saliva, and not even at his rancid breath and hovering knife. Yevleh had been eating death, living off it, and she was his next meal. Hopelessness spiraled through her heart, but she fought to hide it.

"Now then, little Nor, we didn't get a chance to finish our discussion last time." Yevleh circled the altar, looking her over head to toe, his gaze unhurried but hungry. His eyes paused on the rise of her chest and again on her groin. He licked his lips. Annor clenched her bound and helpless hands.

Yevleh smiled and tapped her blackened hand with his knife blade. "I see you had some problems when you defiled the throne room. After I've taught you some respect, I'll feed your newly hallowed flesh to the serpents. That should cleanse the room for my Prince."

His eyes flicked back to her face and he raised one eyebrow. "When we met between the Gates, I'd hoped to ask you a few questions. But you left so abruptly I didn't get a chance." Yevleh examined the sacrificial knife, holding it up and turning it back and forth. "So I'm going to ask you those questions here, now that we've met again through the grace of the Prince Heyl El. Your answers will be an offering on his altar, to honor his name."

"Ask all you want," Annor said. "I have no answers for you."

Yevleh chuckled. "Maybe not yet, but I can be very persuasive." He cocked his head and eyed her leather tunic. "You have strange taste in clothes, and an even stranger attraction to soot. When the serpents have cleaned your bones, I think it's only fitting I burn them." Using the tip of the knife, he pushed up her tunic, exposing her abdomen. "In the meantime, I'll carve you a picture to help you find a few answers."

Annor swallowed. Did she have to die in fingerwidths? If death were inevitable, she preferred to go in a quick rush. But Yevleh was a cat toying with his prey. This would drag on until he grew bored or too angry to stay a killing blow. She wished she could think of a way to provoke him, but her thoughts churned uselessly. She lay there defenseless with terror clogging her throat and shortening her breaths.

"Now then," Yevleh said, trailing the tip of his knife back and forth across her stomach, "what piece of armor did you touch? I thought at first you might be an armor steward, but you're too foolish for the Puerán to give you such a charge."

When she didn't answer, the knife tip pricked her flesh. "What piece was it, Nor? And where is your little house and your haven of trees?" Slowly, so slowly, Yevleh carved his way across the width of her torso, weaving up and down in a red serpentine line.

Her muscles clenched as the agony of her lacerated flesh shot through her in rhythm with the back and forth motion of the blade.

"Answer me and I'll stop."

The blade wasn't deep enough to kill her, but the blood flowed freely enough. Her skin ripped and shredded under Yevleh's sawing. A whimper escaped her clenched teeth. "Please, Abba El," she thought, "help me bear this by the grace of thy Son."

Yevleh didn't stop until he'd hacked his way across the entire width of her abdomen. "No answer for me?" He dipped his finger in her blood and licked it clean. "Then maybe I should open you to the Prince a little lower." He leered, loosening the tie of her waistband.

Looking up into his hate-filled eyes, Annor cried out, "I rebuke you in the name of Ben El!"

Yevleh chuckled and looked around the empty, six-sided room. "You think some emissary of an impotent god will save you?" He grinned down at her and slowly shook his head. "Sorry, little Nor, but it's just me and you here, and I'm the one with the knife. "Now, where were we?"

47

Bald Erik sat on the dock dreaming in the starlight, his fishing pole cast aside, forgotten. He smiled every time he thought about his confrontation with the Sons in the desecrated altar room. Yevleh, Heir to the Damned, had run as fast as his legs could carry him. Erik chuckled, remembering the priest's black robe flying out of the room.

The Sons had sent a couple of laerlings the next day to drag the dead vaettir out of the altar room. They'd buried him on the southern end of the island. Not a priest in sight. Erik bet it'd be a long time before the Sons of Darkness ventured over to the island again. Good thing he had so little appetite and didn't mind living on fish.

He flexed his hands, remembering the feel of the power he'd brought to bear. Too bad he'd sworn to only wield it according to the will of Abba El. Erik longed to burn the river beast to a crisp.

A wave of anguish thundered through Erik's heart. At first he thought death had come calling, and he welcomed it. But next came a crushing sense of urgency.

And he knew. "Annor's in trouble," he whispered. She'd taunted Heyl El's minions too many times. She must have come too close to the Sons' reaching hands.

Erik lurched to his feet, helpless. He could do nothing for her here on his island. But the urgency gripped him tighter, squeezing his chest. Yevleh had her, High Priest of the Sons of Darkness. High Priest.

Yes, there was something Erik could do. The price would be high, but he would willingly pay it for Annor. His time to serve was past. Hers was just beginning.

He crouched on the dock and pried up one of the splintery boards, nails screeching. Blood spurted from his thigh, but Erik's pain didn't matter. Using the board as a cane, he hobbled off the dock and up the path to the waiting temple.

Hurrying up the steps was as torturous as anything the Sons had done, but Erik didn't slow. Staggering through the hallway to the altar room, the urgency became almost unbearable. "Curse this old body," he muttered. He longed to run, but his legs couldn't move any faster.

The Sons' abandoned lightstones still lit the room as bright as day. The green stone squatted at one end of the torture table, winking in the light. Taunting him. Once it had been a marvel, a gift. But the stone had become monstrous from long years spent absorbing Erik's pain and blood. It fed on his agony and savored his misery.

Still, it had given him such relief. The stone had never healed his original wound, but Erik hadn't given up hope that one day, somehow, it would. He brushed that hope aside now.

Standing to one side of the stone, Erik twisted his body and swung the board with all the strength he had. The board arced around and caught the stone, sending it flying. It bounced on the paved floor with a loud crack and a flash of white light that burned away his vision. He heard it bounce off the wall.

Erik dropped the board and slumped to the floor beside the table, his energy spent and the urgency evaporated. He blinked a few times as his sight returned. Blood gushed from the wound on his inner thigh, soaking his pants and pooling on the floor beneath him. He pressed the wound closed with the little strength he had left, but his effort to staunch the flow was half-hearted at best. Death held no fear for him. Erik's wife and son waited for him there.

His head swam and sweat beaded his forehead, in spite of the cool air streaming through the dome. His hands lost their color and he couldn't catch his breath. Maybe this was the end at last.

Erik eyed the fractured stone. "You didn't think I could do that," he whispered. "Since I couldn't touch you, and needed you so badly." He chuckled. "I should have done it a long time ago. I may have wanted you, but I don't need you."

The green stone grew and shrank and the room spun around him. Erik lost consciousness and fell backward, his head cracking on the floor like a delayed echo of the stone.

48

"Ready?"

Annor glared at Yevleh. She was strapped to the altar like a sacrificial lamb. Helpless. But she wouldn't let Yevleh see fear or hopelessness in her eyes, even though her heart ached with both.

"Waiting eagerly, I see." He smirked and reached to tug down her pants.

The room erupted with a brilliant flash of white light. It seared Annor's eyes, leaving a sparkling afterimage like an exploding fireball.

Yevleh yelped and lost his balance, slumping across her, wide-eyed and shaken. The green amulet strapped to his forehead had cracked, and a trickle of blood dripped down his nose. "What was that? What happened?"

Annor blinked away the afterimage. She didn't know what caused the flash of light, but Yevleh's sprawling weight was an abomination. Her arms and legs had been strapped down, but not her head. She clenched her stomach muscles and drove her forehead into the bridge of Yevleh's nose. Blood spurted, and he sagged across her, unconscious.

She gritted her teeth against the burning in her stomach. The sacrificial knife. Annor's fingers fumbled at Yevleh's waistband, straining against her bonds, searching for the pouch where she thought he'd tucked it.

Her fingers found it, and she grinned. She eased the knife out of the pouch, careful not to fumble it. The knife was sticky with her blood. It was awkward to saw at the strap with her bound hand, and she was afraid she'd cut her wrist.

The strap gave way. Annor grabbed the back of Yevleh's robe and yanked him off her, shoving him to the stone floor. His head bounced and he groaned.

Annor sawed at the rest of the straps, freeing her other hand first, and then her legs. Weak with relief, she slid off the hollow altar and almost lost her pants. She retied them, shuddering. Yevleh's moist, pawing hands would haunt her dreams.

By the grace of Abba El, she'd been granted freedom and a chance to live. "Thank you," she whispered. But now she needed to find a way out of the Sons' beastly temple.

Yevleh moaned, stirring. She needed her father's knife. Not this sticky, evil thing. Yevleh had tossed her sheathed knife near the cupboard, five steps up. Annor swerved past where he lay slumped, his feet near the altar, his head resting two steps higher. She'd feel a lot safer once she had her own knife in her hand, with a blade sharp enough to defend herself.

Yevleh reached out and grabbed her ankle, tripping her and sending her sprawling. She caught herself by her hands, but before she could scramble toward her father's knife, he flung himself on top of her, smashing her flat. Yevleh's hands clawed at her neck, but she tucked her chin and stabbed behind her with the sacrificial knife. He grunted, but the knife barely punctured his robe. So she rolled, catching him off guard and sending him flying.

She struggled to her feet, her father's knife closer now. Yevleh saw it, too, and lunged toward it. Annor growled, diving onto his back and knocking him back to the floor.

Yevleh was stronger than Annor. They wrestled awkwardly on the stepped floor, Yevleh twisting and squirming beneath her until he'd grabbed her knife hand. She smacked her elbow into his broken nose. He cried out and let go. She stabbed him in the thigh, pressing down with her weight while she leveraged herself up and dove toward her father's knife.

She unsheathed it in one smooth moment and whirled to face Yevleh, a knife in each hand. Wobbly, he struggled to his feet. Blood ran from his nose and dripped onto his chest.

Guards must have heard the commotion. They knocked frantically. "Heir! Heir, do you need help?"

Yevleh stood between Annor and the barred door. He risked a glance at it over his shoulder.

"I don't think so," Annor said. She charged him, slashing his right arm when he brought it up to shield his face.

He cried out and clutched his bleeding arm to his chest, the slashed sleeve dangling.

Annor threw the Sons' knife behind her and grabbed a fistful of Yevleh's robe, yanking him toward her and slamming her knee into his groin.

Yevleh shrieked, high and piercing. He bent over, sobbing, while the frantic guards redoubled their pounding. "Heir, open to us. Let us help you."

Annor grabbed Yevleh's head and slammed his temple against the sharp edge of the altar. He crumpled at her feet, blood oozing from a gash near his eye.

She bent over and rested her hands on her thighs, trying to catch her breath. Then she fetched the sheath for her knife and tied it to her leg. Any time now some bright guard would realize he could get into the altar room through the chimney, just like she had. She grabbed the bag the Guardian had given her, shoved the apex horns inside, and flung it over her shoulder.

This time she'd take the king's armored legs as well. She pushed the cut straps aside and wrenched at the top of the hollow altar. But try as she might, it wouldn't open. The Sons had sealed it shut.

Yevleh groaned and shifted beside her, and her heart turned to ice. She remembered what he'd done to her, and what he'd wanted to do. If she left him here, humiliated but unbroken, he'd use all the power of the Sons of Darkness to find her. He'd convene a circle of priests to seek her out. Another ring of hungry faces like that terrifying night on her island.

Unless he were no longer High Priest. But as much as she despised Yevleh, she couldn't kill him.

Annor watched the door shudder under the guards' assault. It made it hard to think.

The Sons wouldn't venerate a cripple as Heir to the Prince. That would imply Heyl El's power had been crippled. Annor dove to the floor and sat on Yevleh's legs. Whipping out her knife, she slashed the backs of his ankles, severing the tendons.

Yevleh shrieked and curled up like a baby, sobbing and whimpering. The golden hairs in his braid glinted in the light, the symbol of his power.

Annor grabbed the tail of Yevleh's braid and sliced it off his head from his neck to his forehead. The golden hairs turned brown as soon as her knife separated them from his scalp. She dropped the severed braid beside him and sheathed her knife.

She needed to get away. The urgency of it thudded in her chest. The guards had found something heavy to hammer against the door, rattling it on its hinges. The iron bar held for now, but the brackets holding it in place had already loosened. Plus Annor kept expecting some soot-covered guard to fling open the grate cover.

The Horn Gates were incomplete without the apex horns. But she'd rebuilt them once, and she would put the soos horns back and complete them again. She'd used the Gates to visit the past and see into the future. She'd passed through them into the dirt tunnels. The Gates existed throughout time and space. Could she use them here?

"Please, Abba El," Annor whispered, "help me make this work." The horns waited, expectant, in the bag across her back. Suddenly she understood. She twisted the bag around to cross her chest and gripped the horns with both hands. "Please," she whispered, "give me a way to escape."

The air shimmered in front of her, arched like a Horn Gate, though she couldn't see the Gate itself. Hope throbbed in her chest.

She longed to step into the protected little valley where the Gates waited, but that didn't feel right. What about Bald Erik's island? A wave of peace swept through her, and his starlit dock appeared in the gap of shimmering air.

Annor stepped forward, eyes alight. Leaving Yevleh blubbering on the floor behind her, she emerged into the gray light of a new day.

49

Dawn broke just as Annor stepped onto Bald Erik's dock. A rich orange color crested the temple mount, fading gradually as the sun ascended. She smiled. She'd survived an endless night, and it was a glorious new day.

She crouched to wash the blood off her hands, and cleaned her knife. One of the dock's weathered boards had gone missing. Maybe the Sons had used it on Erik.

Suddenly anxious, Annor hurried up the path to the temple. Her abdomen stung, and blood oozed from the serpentine wound. It hadn't hurt while she wrestled with Yevleh, but it did now.

She took the temple steps two at a time while the bag with the apex horns bumped along on her back. She might be worrying about nothing. Erik was probably asleep, unhurt. But she couldn't shake her anxious feeling.

Annor gasped and stopped short when she entered the desecrated altar room. It was flooded with light, and Erik lay beside the table, soaked in blood. She ran to him and dropped to her knees.

"Erik, Erik," she said, stroking his pale, clammy cheeks. He didn't stir, but she could see the rise and fall of his chest. "Oh, Erik, what have they done to you?"

The back of his head was sticky with blood, but most of the blood came from the wound on his inner thigh. The wound that never healed. She'd seen it bleed so many times, but the blood had always vanished. Not this time.

That's when she noticed the board beside him, and the shattered green stone lying near the base of the curved wall. The image of Yevleh's cracked amulet flashed into Annor's mind and she understood. "Oh, Erik, thank you." A tear coursed down her cheek. "But look what it cost you."

She wiped her eyes on her dirty sleeve and scanned the empty room. She needed to stop the bleeding.

"Annor?" His voice was a thin thread. His eyelids fluttered, but didn't open.

"Yes, it's me." She took his clammy hand and stroked his pale fingers. "I'll go look for something to use as a bandage."

Erik grimaced. "Don't bother," he whispered. "It probably looks bad, but it won't kill me."

"You're lying in a pool of your own blood. What makes you think it won't kill you?"

He snorted, and his eyes flicked open. He blinked a few times before he found Annor's face. "It won't kill me because I can't die. At least, not yet."

"But the blood … you broke the stone."

Erik smiled. "I did." He shifted his head uncomfortably. "High time."

"But my father died when his wound went septicó"

Erik flicked his hand and cut her off. "You're not listening. The wound won't kill me."

"But the stone can't heal you anymore."

"The stone isn't what holds me to life. It'll take time, but I'll recover." He gave her a wry smile. "While I wait for that to happen, could you wash the blood out of my pants? They're the only pair I have."

Annor tried not to jar him, but Erik grimaced while she eased the pants down his legs. She caught her breath when she saw the wound. It was a deep red slash, opening his thigh down to the bone. "Is that a knife wound?"

"Sword," Erik said.

"It's so deep."

"Wounds that kill you generally are."

"Kill?" Annor's mouth dropped open. "You died?"

"Yes, but power transmitted through the stone brought me back. It amplified Abba El's power even in the hands of the Sons. Though it never healed my death wound. And then the power of the stone became corrupted."

Erik reached up and felt the back of his head. He grimaced. "Oops."

Annor smiled and stroked his pale forehead. "Next time lie down before you fall down."

"Hmph. You'd think you'd have a little sympathy for an old man."

"I'll help you to your bedding and let you rest while I wash out your pants."

"I am tired, but I'd rather sit in the sun."

"Let's take you out to the temple steps then, and I can bring out some of your bedding and make you comfortable."

"Thank you, Annor." He squeezed her hand.

Getting him out to the steps was harder than she'd expected. Once she had him on his feet, he swayed dizzily. He tried not to put any weight on his injured leg, but he strained it enough for blood to trickle down and drip along the hallway.

The temple steps were still in shadow, but Annor eyed the blood dribbling down Erik's leg and stopped on the landing. "This is as far as we go. You'll just have to wait for the sun to rise over the temple."

"That's fine. I'm good at waiting."

Annor settled him at the top of the steps and frowned at his gaping wound. "Maybe that gash won't kill you, but can we bandage it so I don't have to look at it? Besides, you'll get your pants all bloody again."

Erik looked down at his thigh and snorted. "You're right. It's not very pretty. There are some empty sacks in the room with my bedding. We can tear one up for a bandage."

Annor grabbed a sack and sat on the temple steps while she tore it into strips. Erik helped her wrap his leg, crisscrossing the bandage the way her father had taught her.

When they'd finished, Erik smiled. "Happy now?"

Annor hugged him. "You saved my life, you know. I'd lost all hope, and then Yevleh's amulet cracked and gave me a chance."

Erik held her tight. "I'm glad."

"All right, you relax here while I slave over your pants. And I'd better put the board back for you. I wouldn't want you tripping over the gap in the dock." She frowned. "You don't think the Sons will come to your island today, do you?"

Erik snorted. "Don't worry. They won't."

Annor hesitated at the entrance to the domed room. A puddle of Erik's blood stained the floor, and the cracked green stone still lay where he'd hurtled it. She knew the room had been sacred to Abba El, but it made her shudder. Too much evil had happened here. At least she'd never have to walk in this room again.

She grabbed the board, careful of splinters, and carried it down to the river. It only took a moment to pound it back into place with a rock. It still astonished her that Erik had willingly done what he could to help her, in spite of the cost.

She soaked his pants in the river and fished for their breakfast. While the fish fried, she washed out as much of the blood as she could. Her abdomen stung from bending over the river. She needed to clean out that wound if she didn't want to die like her father. Jaw locked, back arched, convulsing with pain.

Annor grabbed an old pot that lay beside the fire ring and filled it with water. When the water boiled, she lay back and poured the hot water over her abdomen. The wound hurt as badly as when Yevleh had carved it. Tears stung her eyes, and it was all she could do not to drop the pot.

Yevleh had been in too much of a hurry, or too stupid, to check her pockets. Annor retrieved her father's ointment and patted the fruit lump in her other pocket. She'd been captured, but with Erik's help she'd escaped. And now she had a chance to find Thaeri.

She carried the fish, a fresh pot of water, and the dripping pants back up to where Bald Erik waited in front of the temple door. He'd dropped off to sleep. Annor laid his pants out to dry on the steps and sat beside him, tearing off a bit of fish and chewing it thoughtfully.

She would put the apex horns back, and then nothing should stop her from walking through the Horn Gates to Thaeri's time. But the Gates would only be safe until another Son of Darkness came wandering through the portal. She needed to destroy that portal. Without it, the Sons would never find the Gates again.

"Are you planning to save me any of that?"

"What?" Annor met Erik's eyes, then looked guiltily at the half-eaten fish. "Sorry."

Erik chuckled. "That's fine. I'm not that hungry."

"Eat the rest anyway. You need your strength." She winced when she reached over to hand him the fish.

"You're hurt," Erik said. "That's not my blood all over your tunic. And what happened to the back of your hand?"

"A four-legged serpent spit acid on it, but it's doing better already." Annor fingered her stained tunic. "This is mostly from Yevleh's broken nose. He gave me a little present across my abdomen, but it's not as bad as all the blood might make you think." She lifted her tunic and showed him the wound.

Erik frowned.

"It'll be fine," she said. "It's tiny compared to yours. Besides, I cut Yevleh across the back of his ankles. He'll be hobbling the rest of his life."

Erik snorted. "Sounds like you two were busy. But you don't want to wear that mark of Heyl El the rest of your life." He held his right palm over the serpentine slash and closed his eyes. His forehead wrinkled with effort, but a pure white light shone from his palm and radiated through her flesh.

The white fire engulfed her abdomen, warm and comforting. Annor closed her eyes while it lasted. It felt wonderful. Peaceful and energizing at the same time. It reminded her of the feeling the Guardian gave her, and in her mind she was back on his green hilltop. All that was missing was the smell of the white fruit.

When it ended, Annor smiled and opened her eyes. Her abdomen was unmarked, better than healed. She rubbed it with her fingers and marveled. Erik had slumped back on his bedding, sweat beading his upper lip and forehead.

"Are you all right?" she asked. "Maybe you shouldn't have done that."

A faint smile crossed Erik's face. "Just trying to earn a little sympathy."

Annor chuckled. "Thank you, Erik. Again." She stroked his palm. "How did you do that? Are you a Puerán?"

"I believe as they believe, and I act as they would act, but I had other stewardships in my time. I'll leave you the wound on your hand. Wear it, and the scar that follows, as a mark of honor for what you've achieved."

Annor studied his bandaged thigh and frowned. "I guess you can't heal your own wound."

Erik shook his head. "No."

"I don't understand, with the stone cracked, how you're so sure you won't die."

Erik shrugged. "I haven't completed my life's mission yet, whatever it might be."

Annor gazed across the river at Asseldam. The sun had climbed to midday, bathing them in warmth and gilding the city. They were too far away to see the fudge addicts lying in the gutters, or to smell the reek of the leat. The foulness of the Black Citadel lay concealed behind crisp, straight walls, like a symbol for all that Asseldam pretended to be and wasn't. Annor sighed.

"What's wrong?"

"I wanted it to be so simple, to stop being lonely and return to my parents' city. But it wasn't simple for them, so I don't know why I thought it'd be simple for me. Why does life have to be so hard?"

She considered Erik, lying wounded and weary on his bedding. "I'm sorry. I know your life's been harder than mine could ever be. But why does it work like that, Erik? You're a good man. You can wield the power of Abba El. Why have you needed to endure so much? It doesn't make sense."

Erik shrugged. "If this life were the end of me, it wouldn't make sense. But death is just a new birth into eternity."

"I know, but still."

"Still. Yes." He sat quietly for a minute, fingering the fish bones, then tossed them over the side of the landing to the courtyard below. "Annor, your father was a soldier. Did he say much about his training?"

"A bit."

"How well could he wield a sword the first time he tried?"

Annor snorted. "Not well at all. He trained for years to have the muscles and skill to swing a sword well enough to serve his king." She remembered watching, wide eyed, while her father whirled and slashed at invisible opponents, trying to hold onto the skill he'd worked so hard to obtain.

Erik grimaced and shifted his wounded leg on the bedding. "So knowing how to swing a sword wasn't enough. He built his strength, and practiced."

"Yes."

"Eternal life with Abba El waits beyond the door of death. Can you fathom how glorious that will be, Annor? We might suffer in life, but we're also building our strength. We're training to become who we'll need to be in the life beyond. Mortality is an eye blink in eternity. When we're living that eternity, it'll make sense. Even if right now we can't comprehend how.

"Abba El sees the end from the beginning, Annor. Trust him. The path he gives you might seem rocky and steep, but following it will bring you more joy than you could ever find on your own."

Like a life with Thaeri. Annor smiled. "I think it's time for me to go find some of that joy. But what about you? Next time the Sons come they'll find the broken stone."

Bald Erik chuckled. "Their last visit didn't go quite like they'd planned. It'll be a while before they come back. In the meantime, I'm going to write my history. I'll fish, sit in the sun, and remember the past. The perfect life for an old man."

Erik deserved peace and quiet. Annor hoped he found it.

She stood and slid the apex horns out of their bag.

50

Annor gripped the horns with both hands and willed herself to see a way through the Horn Gate to the valley where the four Gates stood. The air shimmered before her, and as she focused, the valley appeared.

"Come with me," she said to Bald Erik. "The river beast can't stop you. You can write your history somewhere else. Some when else."

Erik gazed through the Gate at the paved square, the flourishing green grass, and the encircling cliffs beyond. Annor could see he longed to leave his dusty island with its desecrated temple, but he smiled sadly and shook his head. "That path isn't for me."

"Are you sure?" She hated to leave him behind, battered and alone.

"Here is where and when I belong, at least for now. You'll come visit an old man now and then?"

Annor gave him a long hug. "Of course I will."

She stepped into the Gate, her eyes on Erik. He smiled, but a tear trickled down his cheek. It matched the tears on her own cheeks.

And then she was in the valley, the dusty island gone as if it'd never been. The Horn Gates were empty, broken without the apex horns, and Erik had been left behind. She'd go back to see him, though, and she'd bring him delicious things to eat, and new clothes, and a warm blanket for winter.

The valley looked just as Annor remembered it. She turned in a circle on the square, absorbing the peace and the beauty. Then she stood on tiptoe to slide the apex horns back into place, one in each Horn Gate. Power blossomed between the Gates and the air brightened around her.

She stroked the horns on the side of the Gate. The Gates' power thrilled through her, like one pure note made of joy.

But the portal drew her eye, white and menacing. Yevleh might never come back after what she'd done to him. But some other Son of Darkness was bound to brave the tunnels to exploit the valley.

Annor sat cross-legged on the square and stared at the portal. Maybe she could bring down the side of the cliff above it to cover the portal's exit. She toyed with the idea for a while, but she had nothing to start a rockfall with, except her knife and her bare hands.

She could walk through one of the Horn Gates to grab a tool. But where, and when? Without a destination in mind, the Gates would be useless. She might end up stranded somewhere like the dirt tunnels. She shuddered.

The lump in her pocket caught her eye. The piece of fruit from the throne room. Annor fished it out of her pocket and turned it in her hands. It looked no different from when she'd first grabbed it, even after all she'd been through. She held something as old as Creation in her hand. Incredible.

Annor inhaled the fruit's deep scent. Without the stink of the throne room around her, the smell captivated her. It reminded her of the smell of fudge, but cleaner. More like the enticing taste of the chocolate pudding the Guardian had given her long months ago. The fruit smelled like chocolate, only better. Richer. Darker. More intense. Luscious.

Annor salivated and her stomach rumbled. Maybe she was being presumptuous, thinking it was alright for her to eat the fruit. She was nobody. The Knowing Tree had been a gift from Abba El. The fruit had taught their first parents to discern truth from error. It had opened the path to mortality and joy.

But the fruit might help her find a way to break the portal and open a path to her future.

And it smelled so amazingly good.

Annor took a little nibble. The dried fruit mingled with her saliva and became a sweet confection in her mouth. She rolled it around on her tongue, not wanting to swallow, but to relish it as long as she could. Energy surged through her and her mind expanded. The fruit tasted so delicious, so satisfying. And she wanted more.

She swallowed and took another nibble, as delicious as the first. Warmth spread through her torso and into her limbs. One nibble more, and then another nibble. She savored every morsel until, too soon, she'd eaten it all. Annor sniffed her empty hands where the scent of the fruit still lingered. She ached for more. She should have taken more of the fruit when she'd had the chance.

But then the aftertaste hit, as bitter as the fruit had been sweet. She gagged and tears sprang to her eyes. She needed water, bread. Anything to alleviate the bitterness. She shuddered and coughed, scrubbing her tongue along her teeth until only a hint of bitterness lingered.

One piece of fruit from the Knowing Tree was enough. As delicious as it had been at first, Annor never wanted to eat another. She wiped her streaming eyes with her sleeve and studied the portal. And she knew.

Even if she had a proper tool, it wouldn't be enough to bury the exit in rubble. The Sons would just shift the rock out of the way, a piece at a time, until they'd cleared a way through. Annor needed to destroy the portal, not hide it, and she could only do that by bringing down the tunnel at its entrance.

She pictured the cave beast waiting for her to step through the portal, angry and one-eyed. Even if it weren't lying in wait, Annor still didn't have a tool. Yet she knew without any doubt that she needed to travel back through the portal.

If she could see a few hours into her future, maybe she'd know where to find a tool so she could bring down the tunnel. She stood before the Ivory Gate that mirrored her face. Annor looked a mess. Her leather tunic was coated with a stiff layer of Yevleh's blood. No wonder Erik had been concerned. Besides the blood, she had a glaze of soot from crawling through the Sons' furnace and chimney. So much for the bath she'd had after finding the Shimmertree.

She lifted her tunic and marveled again at her unmarked abdomen. She'd almost forgotten about the gash the guard had carved in her back, while he prodded her with her own knife. She walked over to the other Ivory Gate and examined the wound just above her blood-soaked waistband. It wasn't too bad. She smeared her father's ointment over the gash, then stepped back to the first Ivory Gate.

Behind the reflection of her face, she saw another, and another, and so on. Her future. Annor focused on the first reflection. It grew larger until it stretched to fill the rectangular surface.

The cave beast worried her more than anything else. She could survive crossing through the white emptiness of the portal again. But if the beast lay in wait, she couldn't destroy the portal while fighting for her life.

Annor formed the image of the cave beast in her mind, and it appeared before her on the crystal Gate. It lay near the tunnel entrance, gazing out into daylight. The knot loosened in her stomach.

Two guards stood on the ledge outside the tunnel, watchful of the city, but wary of the beast. Annor chuckled. "Thank you, Yevleh," she said. With guards to entertain the beast, it didn't bother to patrol the tunnels or watch over the portal entrance.

Now all she needed was a tool. Had the people who'd widened the tunnels left any tools behind? The image in the Ivory Gate spun and shifted. A sheet of whiteness filled the crystal. The portal. Annor licked her lips. The flat, white surface looked more ominous in the darkness of the tunnel than it did on the cliff face behind her. Here, the light of the valley muted its malice.

The image in the crystal drew back, away from the portal's entrance, until Annor saw where a tunnel branched off to one side of the whiteness. The cave beast must have blocked her view of it when she'd been there before. The image in the Gate turned down the side tunnel, and not ten steps from the portal a long-forgotten pick leaned against the tunnel's wall. Perfect.

Annor trudged across the grass and stood in front of the portal's exit. She tried, but she couldn't bring herself to step into the light. She turned to look at the valley instead, and fingered her knife in its sheath. She'd be back. She'd destroy the portal, and then she'd be back. The valley would be safe from the Sons of Darkness, and Annor would have nothing more to do with them and their foul devotions.

She turned and plunged into the portal before she could have second thoughts. The empty whiteness surrounded her, pressed against her. She held her hands up in front of her face and pushed back. She put her weight into it, digging in her toes and shoving as hard as she could against… nothing. But the white nothingness was solid, resisting, holding her back.

Had it been like this for Yevleh? Or did the portal know she planned to destroy it? Annor pushed, struggled, and strained until the nothingness gave way before her, tearing away with a shriek. She stood once more in the black tunnel.

She shivered. She'd had all she could stomach of tunnels and being buried in the dark. But the side tunnel was right there, on her left.

The light of the portal didn't penetrate far. Her body blocked too much of the narrow passage. She dug into the bottom of her pocket for her lightstone. Before she pulled it out, though, she blinked in confusion.

A lightstone approached her, held high in a man's hand. She could see his dusty features, his torn and dirty clothes, and her heart stood still. One of the Sons. She pressed back against the wall and gripped her knife. She'd jump him before he even knew what was happening.

But as he stepped closer, she recognized the face under a week's growth of beard. He was older than the night they'd met on the beach. "Thaeri?"

He didn't hear her. He walked past, brushing through her in the narrow space and vanishing as the white light of the portal shone through his image. A waking not-dream. Thaeri hadn't been in her time.

Annor shook off the scare he'd given her. The sooner she finished this, the sooner she'd find out what Thaeri had been up to. She brought out her lightstone and walked forward half a dozen paces until she found the pick.

She carried it back to the portal and gave it an experimental swing against the tunnel wall. The blade bit into the limestone and a small chunk flew off. She wished she'd thought to focus on the second reflection. The Ivory Gate could have shown her how she was going to bring down the tunnel and destroy the portal. Too late now.

Annor took a close look at the walls on either side of the portal. They were rough, but solid. It'd take a lot of work to do much to the walls, and widening the tunnel wouldn't destroy the portal anyway.

She craned back her head and examined the ceiling. It looked much like the walls, except for one crack. The crack ran straight out from the portal entrance half a bodylength, before curving to one side and dwindling to nothing. With her back to the portal, Annor hefted the pick above her head and tapped it inside the crack. Chips and dust rained down on her upturned face. She coughed and wiped the granules out of her eyes.

She wiggled the tip of the pick into the crack as far as she could, ducking the pebbles and loosened debris. When she had the blade good and wedged, she took a deep breath and glanced at the portal behind her. She could do this.

Heaving on the pick handle, Annor strained against the ceiling and the mountain of limestone above her. She struggled, wrenching the pick handle with all her strength against the vast load of rock until her arms ached with effort. Dust pelted her. She jerked on the pick, rocking the handle with the full weight of her body. And surprisingly, something gave. She heard a shattering snap and the ceiling started to crumble.

Annor dropped the pick and dove into the portal.

Rock rumbled at her heels, sprayed her legs, and thudded against her back. A wave of dust filled the passage, reaching for her, choking her, as she fled into the nothingness.

She tore through layers of whiteness, shredding it around her, hoping, praying to burst into the valley. But the whiteness was endless. Another layer ripped, then another. Annor coughed and shoved her way through. She could feel the portal collapsing around her, eroding, so that the nothingness shivered and shook before her eyes.

And then she'd beaten the emptiness and blue sky greeted her as she stumbled, hacking and spent, onto the grass. She scrambled away from the portal's exit as rubble followed her into the valley. The white portal flickered and ruptured. The entire opening filled with rubble and the portal vanished in one last glimmer of white. Annor coughed the dust out of her lungs. She had done it.

Laughing, she fell back on the grass and reveled in the light of the valley. The encircling cliffs held her safe.

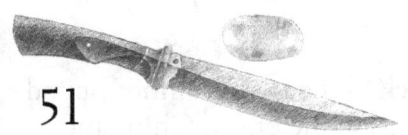

51

"Congratulations."

Annor jumped, then sat up. The Guardian's eyes twinkled. His robes and countenance shone with pure white light that shimmered against the cliff behind him.

She leapt to her feet. "I did it! I can't believe I did it." Joy swept through her, and tears filled her eyes. The presence of the Guardian always gave her a feeling of peace, even when she didn't want to hear what he said. But this feeling went beyond that to utter happiness.

But then a niggle of worry crept in. "I'm done, right? I mean, I walked the entire path my father carved in the standing stone. And more."

The Guardian took her hand and smiled. "You've done well, and walked the path set before you to the best of your ability. Abba El couldn't ask for more. Well done, Annor, daughter of Gunnar and Dagny."

She grinned. "Thank you. I can't believe how happy I feel right now." She laughed, took a step back, and twirled under the blue sky. When she turned back to the Guardian, she saw he'd set a feast out on the grass. "Chocolate pudding!"

The Guardian laughed. "Join me and celebrate your first victory over the powers of darkness."

The pudding tasted as glorious as she remembered. Not as enticing as the fruit of the Knowing Tree, but she could enjoy it without fearing the bitter aftertaste. Annor feasted on sweetbread, strange fruit dripping with juice, and drank sparkling nectar from a crystal cup. She savored the meal and the company of the Guardian. His presence was a feast in itself.

Her mind boggled at the contrast between how she felt at that moment, and how she'd felt strapped to the hollow altar with Yevleh hovering over her. That had been Heyl. This was a tiny glimpse of heaven.

Full from the delectable meal, Annor sat back on the grass and looked over at the Guardian. "I'm sorry," she said.

The Guardian chuckled. "You were a little greedy with the chocolate pudding. I barely got a taste."

Annor blushed. "You know that's not what I meant." She looked down at her hands. "I'm sorry I was stubborn and tried to avoid the hard path. I wanted to feel this joy without having to endure the terrors and struggle through the wearisome spots."

The Guardian waved away the remains of the feast and rose to his feet. "Past mistakes are forgotten. You were willing to change when you saw the need, and the desires of your heart are true." He held out his hand. "Come with me, Annor."

She stood and took his hand. "Where?"

"You've walked the path and become a seer, so I have a gift waiting for you."

The Guardian gestured, and one of the Horn Gates shimmered into life. A stone altar stood just past the gateposts, and thick trees grew outside a surrounding circle of stones.

Annor smiled. "My island."

"Yes. It's time to take you home."

She looked around the little valley. "But I can come back whenever I want to, right?"

"Of course. The Gates of Horn and Ivory are your stewardship now. You restored them. You understand their purpose."

Annor had thought her joy was full before, but when she stepped through the Gate and touched the altar her father had built with his own hands, her joy threatened to overwhelm her. Light filled her, so that she thought she must be shining as brightly as the Guardian.

"Kneel beside your father's altar, Annor," he said.

She dropped to her knees. With his index finger, the Guardian traced a golden spiral of light on top of the altar stone. Annor bent and briefly touched her forehead to the center of the glowing spiral. "Please accept the offering of my life in the service of Abba El," she said. Her eyes met the Guardian's and sparked, as if the spiral had entered her forehead and passed through her soul.

"I accept your life in the name of his Son, Ben El." The Guardian's voice was benevolent and resonant. He set his warm hands on her head. "And by his will, I give you a new name to mark your role as his servant and friend. From henceforth, when you serve him you will be known as El-Annor. You were called, and because of your willing heart, you have been chosen."

His words filled her. She stood, a little breathless. "El-Annor." The name felt strange on her tongue.

The Guardian smiled. "You are both the girl Annor, and the seer El-Annor." He turned in a slow circle, holding out his arms. Power radiated from his fingertips, blazing through the encircling trees, and beyond, in a wave of light. "This island is protected now," he said, "as securely as the Shimmertree. No one can step foot on its shores, or invade its sanctity, unless you welcome them here." He smiled. "I wish you joy in your life, and in His service, until our paths cross again."

And with his hand lifted in farewell, the Guardian vanished.

Annor felt marvelous. With a start, she realized her hand and the knife wound on her back had healed just as miraculously as the wound on her abdomen. Though, she had a scar on the back of her hand as a reminder, just as Erik had said. Her clothes were as clean and new as the day they'd been made. Energy rippled through her. She'd been reborn.

She laughed and sped down the familiar path to the shore. Annor turned to look at her island. Her island. It shimmered faintly in the sun, protected forevermore from the wiles of the Sons of Darkness. She laughed again and ran to where her cottage waited beneath the trees.

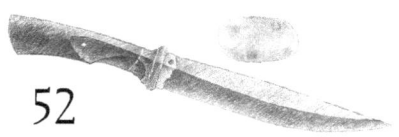

52

Annor caressed the latch on her cottage door. The joy of homecoming was only marred by knowing her parents didn't wait on the other side. Still, she was home. The ache of their passing had faded from overwhelming grief to a wistful yearning. And if she ever missed them too much, she could ask the Gates to show her moments from the past.

She smiled. Not only had she left behind the loneliness of her island, but the limits of space and time as well.

"El-Annor," she said. She was a seer now. So strange. She didn't fully know what that meant yet, but it sounded exciting.

She opened the door and stepped into the cottage. Her mother would have been scandalized by the layer of dust that had crept onto all the surfaces. "Sorry, Mama," she whispered. She'd clean it later. And after Annor had scrubbed the cottage top to bottom, she'd ask the Ivory Gate to show her mother living in Betavar, serving the queen. Annor smiled.

She ran her fingers along the bookshelf and stroked the spine of each well-beloved book. Her father's sword hung above the mantel, the sheath dusty in her hands when she took it from the wall. She drew the sword and examined the blade. She'd oil it when she cleaned the cottage.

Something was missing. But then Annor remembered the chest buried under the floor. She'd done a good job hiding it. The dusty floorboards gave no hint of what lay hidden beneath them.

She chuckled. Thanks to the Guardian, she didn't need to worry any longer about the king's gauntlets being snatched by the Sons of Darkness. She could dig out the chest and restore it to its proper place. But not now. Annor could return to the island and her cottage whenever she wanted.

What a strange, exhilarating thought. The power had limits of course. She could visit the past, but not change it. She could travel the world and the future, but only within the bounds of Abba El's desires. Still, her options seemed limitless. And whenever she needed to return and find the peace and assurance her island gave her, she could. As long as she had this place, she'd never be bereft of her parents and the life they'd shared. Her past was her foundation.

And now she was ready to find her future. It was time. She concentrated and reached for the Gates in her thoughts. They stood whole and powerful, thanks to the path she'd walked. She'd learned to see as a seer sees, to use the Gates of Horn and Ivory and act in the name of Ben El. She'd changed so much from the girl weeping beside the river.

Annor focused, and the outline of a Horn Gate formed before her between the table and her bed. The air shimmered beneath the arch, waiting.

"Thaeri," Annor said. "Where are you? When are you?"

She reached her mind through the Gate and found the shore where they'd met beside the fire in her not-dream. She crouched and leaned through the Gate. When she probed the ashes in the fire ring, she found a hint of warmth.

She turned the view in the Gate toward the sea. Somewhere out there was an island. And Thaeri. Annor sent the Gate skimming across the surface of the water and laughed when a wave splashed her through the opening. "Faster," she whispered.
This must be what it felt like to fly. She sped across the sea, the breeze ruffling her hair, searching the edge of the horizon until a dark blot appeared. The shape grew larger until it became a steep, rocky island rearing out of the sea.

A boat lay beached on the black shore. It could only be Thaeri's, but Annor saw no sign of him nearby. He must be somewhere on the slope. She sent the Gate toward the hill, the black ground falling away beneath her as her view flew skyward.

And then she saw him, a small figure scaling the side of the black slope, nearing the summit. She sent the Gate soaring to the top of the slope where smoke rose in a thin column. A fire? Thaeri must be meeting someone.

No, not a fire. Not exactly. Annor took a step back from the edge of the Gate. A crater of molten rock bubbled below her, with a small ledge running around the rim next to a terrifying drop. The hot air smelled like rotten eggs. She'd heard stories about volcanoes, but her imagination couldn't compete with the reality. A strange place to search for a seerstone.

Annor took one last look at her cottage behind her, then stepped from wooden floorboards to black rock. The cottage vanished. The air blasted hot and dry from the bowels of the volcano. A wandering breeze caressed the back of her neck, and for the first time she didn't regret her butchered hair.

Annor wiped her damp hands nervously on her clean skins. He'd be surprised to find her waiting here. But he'd be happy, too. Wouldn't he? She caught her breath and swallowed when she heard his shoes rasp against the rock. He was close now.

Thaeri's head crested the top of the slope, his honey-colored hair damp from his exertions. Her heart thudded in her chest. She couldn't stop the smile that spread across her face. "Thaeri."

He looked up from his handholds and his mouth dropped open. "Annor!" He scrambled up and joined her on the ledge. "You're here." He smiled. "I just saw you last night. I thought it'd be ages before I saw you again. Another dream?"

Annor smiled shyly. "No, not a dream. I'm here this time."

Thaeri's eyes widened. "You're here," he said, marveling. "You're real."

She reached out and took his warm, dusty hand in her own. "See? I'm not vanishing back into the past."

Thaeri laughed and grabbed her, sweeping her up into a big hug, her chin on his shoulder, his arms holding her tight. "I can't believe it," he said. "I've waited years for this."

He released her, wonder and joy shining so brightly in his eyes that Annor couldn't breathe. Hesitant, Thaeri leaned toward her, his face filling her world. Their breath mingled, and then his lips met hers. Gently. Sweetly.

Thaeri stepped back and took her hand, his fingers sliding between hers. His smile lit up his face, and for a moment Annor could see nothing but his eyes gazing into hers.

"Would you like to help me find a seerstone?" he said.

Annor laughed. "I'd love to."

ABOUT THE AUTHOR

Robyn was born in the Rocky Mountains, but grew up in southern California. She received the top academic scholarship from Brigham Young University and attended BYU before serving an 18-month mission in Sweden for the Church of Jesus Christ of Latter-day Saints.

After her mission, Robyn graduated magna cum laude from San Diego State University with a bachelor's degree in English and a minor in Business. She married shortly thereafter and gave birth to two sons and a daughter before returning to SDSU and earning a master's degree in English. She currently lives with her husband in Riverton, Utah.

Robyn has wanted to be a writer since second grade. She dreamed up the Shimmertree while writing her master's thesis comparing the world creations of Narnia, Middle-earth, and Genesis.

www.ingramcontent.com/pod-product-compliance
Lightning Source LLC
Chambersburg PA
CBHW060916180626
46817CB00004B/1287